Brittany,

Thank you for continuing
the journey!

Best,

ORDER
OF THE
SEERS

THE RED ORDER
BOOK II

CERECE RENNIE MURPHY

J Murphy

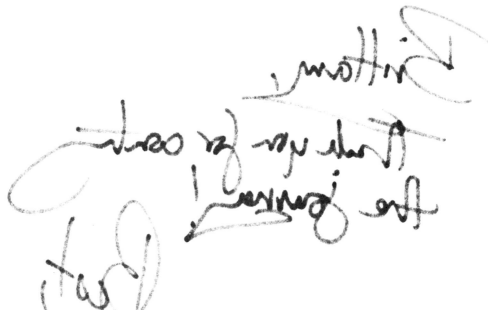

Published by LionSky Publishing

Copyright © 2013 by Gerece Rennie Murphy

Cover design by Kea Taylor for Imagine Photography

Interior design by Jessica Tilles for TWA Solutions

Printed in the United States of America

ISBN 13: 978-0-9856210-2-5

Library of Congress Control Number: 2013907043

This book is dedicated to the people who have waited for it the longest—the fans that helped refine Order of the Seers into something truly worth sharing. Shawn McGerr, Lori McMullin, Sarah Clarke, Jessica Bryan, J.D. Wolf, and so many I know only by pseudonym—without you, I would never have had the courage to give this story the chance it deserved.
Thank you for your patience. I hope this is worthy of you.

Other Titles by Cerece Rennie Murphy

Order of the Seers — Book I

Order of the Seers: The Red Order — Book II

Order of the Seers: The Last Seer — Book III (Coming Soon!)

Acknowledgements

There are sooo many people to thank! First, let me start with my family—Mom, the kids and my amazing husband, Sekou Murphy—you are the center of my world and my greatest purpose. Thank you for showing me what love is.

Some writers can get by with one editor. I am blessed beyond measure to have two. Jessica Faulkner, we did it again! We both know you didn't have to do this, but I'm grateful you did. Thank you for making sure my words make sense. Stephanie Carnes, thank you for the enthusiasm that you bring to editing my work.

Trice Hickman (for your fearless example), My brother Al (for lending me your glasses when I can't see where I'm going), Kenya McGuire Johnson, Ella Curry (for promoting me even when I don't know it!), Kea Taylor (for making me and my book covers look good), Shawn McGerr, Kamishia Lee, Monica Washington, Samiha Dauk, Jessica Tilles, Bettina Lanyi, Lori McMullin, Michael Daugherty (for your friendship AND your honesty), Ebony Ross, Sharon Lucas, Carla Galloway, Michelle McMichael and "The Order" Street Team, Vee Edwards and all The Vibettes, Bill Baker, Aton Edwards, Charles Pelto, Kareem Murphy and DeWayne Davis, Deatri King-Bey, Lynn Emery, and my Reading in Black FB family for keeping me on the straight and narrow. Seth Godin (for coaching those you've never met), Sarenity Milton and Shonqila Thomas for watching our littlest love so I could write. Constellation and Cricket Bookstore, for the encouragement and support. And finally, to everyone who picked up *Order of the Seers* and read it. Thank you. ☺

Order of the Seers
Glossary of Terms

Seer: A person who can see the future and may have other supernatural abilities.

The Lost Seers: Used to refer to the four Seers who first escaped from the Guild (Marcus, Alessandra, Kaido, and Lucia.) Later, the term was used to describe any Seer who eluded capture and stood against the Guild.

United World Organization (UWO): An international governing body comprised of heads of state from around the world. The UWO replaced the U.N.

The Guild: A clandestine organization financed by the UWO to coordinate the global initiative to capture and exploit Seers for the exclusive use of their powers by the UWO. The public believes that the Guild is responsible for trying to rehabilitate Seers who have been removed from society due to their violent and unstable nature.

Purification Center: Training facilities run by the Guild for the purpose of breaking down and assimilating captured Seers into the Guild structure.

Quorum: A group of Seers brought together to envision the future. Within the Guild, a Quorum is made up of 7 members.

Prime: The thought-based language used by Seers during Quorum to communicate and share visions.

Luridium: The drug developed and used exclusively by the Guild to control Seers while facilitating accurate monitoring and access to a Seer's visioning capabilities.

ORDER OF THE SEERS

THE RED ORDER

BOOK II

Chapter 1: The Defeated

The fact that Crane Le Dieu had barely escaped with his life intact less than ten hours ago did nothing to humble his demeanor as he stormed out of the steel-glass elevator, as bold and arrogant as always.

"You!" Crane shouted, pointing his finger at the middle-aged Asian woman who sat at the far side of the room. "Did you hear what happened? How could you let this happen?"

As he cut across the sea of cluttered work stations that made up the office level of the Guild's lead research facility in Geneva, Dr. Ming Jhu seemed all but oblivious to Crane's approach. In contrast to the crackling tension in the room, Ming looked utterly detached as she took a long draw from her cigarette and stared at the email message on her laptop. As head of Research and Development, it was bad form for her to just be sitting there, so indifferent to her superior while the other scientists around her froze in terror at Crane's presence. But she'd been like this for at least an hour. Even with the Guild's lockdown protocol, which had them sequestered in their offices at 11 o'clock at night, Crane bursting into their facility yelling demands at her was nothing new. What felt refreshing was that for the first time, Ming didn't give a damn.

It would have been nice, she thought, to have had this objectivity twenty years ago, before she had bartered her life away while most of her colleagues were being killed. In the early days of the International Science Team's research on Seers, Eli Tanner, Gerard Morrow, Willem

Knight, Neva Patel, Hasaam Al Attar, and the other lead scientists had been such good mentors to her that she had considered them family, or so she thought, before she chose self-preservation and advancement over them. By the time the Guild had asked for her allegiance, she knew Willem Knight and Gerard Morrow were dead because of their refusal to cooperate with the Guild's new agenda to catalog and harness new Seers against their will.

Back then, she was just another eager, twenty-nine year old junior researcher, but she had shown tremendous promise, and the Guild made their interest in her known as soon as it was clear that most of the Seer Project's lead scientists would need to be replaced. With the gift of hindsight and twenty-three years of experience behind her, Ming could almost laugh now at the fact that she had been naïve enough to be more flattered than frightened when Crane came to her apartment to recruit her. It was only later that she learned how much blind ambition and stupidity had in common.

But Ming's desire for advancement wasn't the only thing that kept her with the Guild. She had also just met Thea Case and was only starting to learn what it meant to find the one person you would do anything for. In the years that followed, Thea made most of the despicable things Ming had done bearable, if not quite worth it. The irony of what Ming now knew made the rims of her weary eyes burn with the need to cry, but she refused to do that here. Instead, she squinted at her computer screen while flicking the ash from her unfiltered Dunhill on the floor before taking another long deep drag. *And it's all for nothing now. It's all for nothing,* she thought as she exhaled and read the email in front of her for the 47th time.

M — Got your message and saw the news about the lockdown. Wish I could have told you this in person, but since I don't know when you'll be home, I think it's better to get this out now. Just came from Dr. William's office. I've gone into stage four of my cancer. There's nothing left to do. I think it's time to start letting go.

Love,

Thea

"Do you hear me talking to you? Are you suddenly deaf? I know you've heard what happened in Chicago. Andreas and I were lucky to escape with our lives!" Though Crane was now standing directly behind Ming, his voice had not descended one octave from when he began screaming at her from across the room.

"Pity," he heard Ming say softly.

"Excuse me?" Crane sneered. He wasn't sure which part of what he said made her respond so inappropriately, but the insinuation of indifference only made him angrier.

He reached for the back of her chair and spun her around with such force she would have made a complete 360-degree turn if she hadn't jammed the left 3" heel of her boot into his foot.

When she finally looked up to meet his gaze, she noted that he looked more surprised than in pain, as if he really thought that she had, for a moment, gone deaf.

Stupid fuck, she thought as she flicked her ash in his direction before taking another drag. Though she had heard about the events in Chicago, she had received the news shortly before Thea's email and as a result, it fell into the same category as Crane's presence—nothing she cared about anymore. The calmness she felt now was in sharp contrast to her demeanor two hours ago when she'd first received Thea's email. Immediately after reading it, Ming had rushed out of the building to call her, seeking what little privacy she could attain within the Guild's heavily guarded three city-block perimeter.

"I'm coming home now," was the first thing out of Ming's mouth when Thea answered her cell phone.

"M, you can't," Thea replied as gently as she could.

"They can't stop me. Not this time," Ming said, as the tears began to fall.

"Yes, they can, M. The news said that the terrorists are targeting Guild facilities. It's not safe, and anyway, I'm not even home. It's ok. I'm ok with it," Thea paused for a moment to make sure her voice was steady before she added, "Everything dies, M. Everything dies."

"I don't care," Ming sobbed. If she wasn't so stricken with grief, she would have been shocked to find herself crying in the middle of the street. Public displays of emotion were not her thing. "I need to see you. We don't have time. We don't have any more time."

"Shhh. Don't cry, baby. Don't cry. I love you, ok? That will never change."

Ming let the sound of Thea's voice calm her, as it always did. "I want to see you," Ming said, after her voice was back under control.

"I know, but you know how I am, I need some time to wrap my head around this. I just need a minute, ok? When you come home, we'll talk and figure it out."

Ming nodded her head even though Thea could not see her acquiesce. This was her Thea, always calm and quietly optimistic — even in death.

"Ok, but I'll try to slip away as soon as I can." Ming said softly. "I love you."

"As I love you, M. Be safe and don't worry, okay? When you come home, I'll make your favorite, chicken and dumplings."

Ming thought about protesting. Thea had been too weak to cook anything for months and she didn't want her to strain herself, but

Ming also knew that cooking made Thea happy, and her happiness had always been more important than anything else.

"Ok, just take it easy. You still have to be careful..."

"I will. I promise, M. Now, let me go. I'll talk to you soon."

After Thea hung up, Ming walked straight to the shoeshine stand on the first floor of her building and bought a pack of Dunhills. *Everything dies*, she thought, as she lit up her first cigarette in 15 years.

● ◦ ·· ◦ ●

No one, including Crane, moved a muscle as she exhaled her smoke in disgust and finally responded to his question.

"I said, what a pity you escaped with your life."

Watching the shock flash-freeze Crane's entire expression was the best present she'd received all year. Ming settled back in her chair to enjoy it, letting a satisfied smirk spread across her full, heart-shaped face.

Recovering slowly from Ming's brazenness, Crane could not help but smile as he saw the hate Ming had always tried to hide from him on full display. While he preferred fear, hate from those he considered to be truly powerless was also something he enjoyed, and his mood lightened at the thought of watching Ming attempt to spar with him. Clearing his throat, Crane rearranged his amusement into a stern expression.

"You failed," he began. "You should have known about their true potential. It was your job."

"Oooh," Ming responded, as her eyes went wide with mock curiosity, "*Now* you want to know about potential. That's funny. I don't even know what you're talking about. We don't *do* science here," she explained calmly with a wave of her hand around the room. "We only do what you tell us. So what can I say? I guess we're all just as limited as your imagination."

Crane hadn't expected her to cut to the chase so quickly, to turn the tables and blame him for what happened. His enjoyment was gone as quickly as it came and Ming knew it. She arched her brow in anticipation of his response.

"What the hell has gotten into you? You know better than to test me." Crane bent down toward her slightly and lowered his voice to a hiss before adding, "I will have her ki-"

"Yeah, see, that's the thing," she interrupted. "I hear you. I really do."

Ming turned from him and put out her cigarette on the edge of her desk while keeping her heel firmly dug into what she believed was his big toe. *Why isn't this hurting him*, she wondered in passing as she turned back to Crane with a new cigarette dangling from her lips and a matchbook in her hand.

"Except, you're a little late—which is unusual for you, I'll admit," she began while looking down to light her cigarette. "This just hasn't been your week."

The corners of Crane's eyes trembled with the effort it took for him to refrain from reaching out and strangling her where she sat. Though she was focused on lighting up her new-old habit, Ming didn't miss the twitching of his hands as he waited for her to finish. It made her proud to see him so out of control. It had been a long time since she'd had this much power over anything.

Nodding her understanding of his restraint, she continued. "You see, Thea *is* dying. I got the email two hours ago," she paused to fully exhale before adding, "So there literally is no one left for you to kill except me, and as you can see, I'm suddenly feeling up for a fight, so... how should I put this? Fuck off."

Crane responded with a loud and mirthless laugh. Ming fought to keep her back straight as the ice-cold sound made its way down her spine. *There is nothing more he can take from me,* she reminded herself as she continued to smoke her cigarette with a slightly less than steady hand.

When his laughter finally died down, Crane returned his gaze to Ming and smiled at her, almost lovingly. "Ming," he cooed, "You're always so articulate. It's one of the things I like about you."

And in less time than it took for Ming to pull the cigarette she had just inhaled from her lips, Crane was over her like the pitch black cover of night as he grabbed the hand that held her cigarette. Though he was not a particularly large man, Ming was shocked that he still managed to block out all the light from the overhead flood lamps and ceiling-to-wall reflective windows that were meant to inspire greatness from the scientists that worked there. But Ming couldn't see any of her colleagues as they stood by passively, couldn't see anything beyond the charcoal of his herringbone suit as he pushed her chair against the edge of her desk while his face, smooth and pallid, hovered close enough for her to smell the 100 year-old scotch he'd consumed an hour ago.

"And I do like you, Ming, but not enough to keep you alive if you're not willing to cooperate," he said softly. The dulcet tones of his voice contrasted sharply with his vise grip on her left wrist and hand. Ming turned slightly toward her twisted fingers to see her cigarette drop red ash on the backside of his hand. He didn't flinch.

Even through the pain in her hand, her inquisitive mind could not shut down. *Something is wrong here,* she thought. Her heel was still buried in the fine leather of his shoe and the flesh of his big toe and he had yet to react to it.

By the way he shifted the bones in her hand, she knew he wanted her to scream. But as frightened as she was, she knew she was stronger than the breaking of her wrist. Though her courage had waned, her resolve held firm. Not trusting her voice to remain steady, Ming did the only thing she could as she forced her gaze upwards to meet Crane's and exhaled the smoke she'd been holding in her lungs into his face.

If she could have predicted what would happen next, she would have tried to hold her breath forever. But by the time Crane leaned in closer, it was too late. She watched in growing horror as Crane's eyes fluttered closed just before he leaned into the smoke she'd exhaled, and breathed in as if savoring a lover's caress. The intimacy of the gesture made her stomach spasm with revulsion. When Crane opened his eyes to meet hers, he was pleased to find the fear he'd been waiting for. He finally had her attention.

"I love the taste of something burning," he whispered, just before Andreas Menten interrupted them.

"Crane, step back, NOW! What are you doing?" Andreas demanded.

Though Crane kept his proximity, he did drop Ming's wrist, causing her cigarette to fall to the floor. Crane held Ming's terrified gaze as he answered Andreas' question.

"Dr. Jhu has refused to cooperate in our efforts to determine how we were so outmatched in Chicago. Isn't that right, Ming? Do I understand that you wish to test our resolve in this matter?"

The importance of her next words made each syllable quiver in her throat, as if they were afraid of their own power to condemn her. When she first heard Crane coming toward her, her only goal was defiance, but now she wondered how she could not have seen how swiftly the consequences of her actions would come. With Crane's intentions for her so clearly visible in the cruelty of his gaze, Ming doubted that she would even be allowed to go home. *Will I see Thea again? What will they tell her about my disappearance,* she wondered with a clarity and calm that surprised her. *She'll know,* Ming reassured herself. *No matter what story they tell her, she'll know I finally stood up to them.* Even with fear twisting in her gut, she knew Thea would be proud of her, of the choice she was about to make, no matter what it cost them.

"No. I won't be a part of this anymore," Ming finally answered, still holding Crane's gaze.

With a broad smile slowly spreading across his face, Crane did not try to hide his exhilaration at Ming's response. *You have no idea all the ways I will make you regret those words*, he thought earnestly before pushing away from her and turning his gaze from Ming to Andreas.

"As you can see, Andreas, she's obviously hiding something and I was just telling her of my intentions to get the answers we need from her," Crane pronounced.

Andreas could sense where things were headed from the minute he stepped out of the elevator. Normally, the office level of the research facility was buzzing with scientists entering, rechecking, and setting up data charts for the constant testing that went on there. So when Andreas' entry onto the floor was met with complete silence, he knew something was off. With two dozen scientists on the floor, each person seemed frozen in place with every head turned and facing what had become the center of attention—Crane hunched over Ming's body in a stance clearly designed to intimidate and subdue.

Andreas understood that Crane's accusation was meant to set off a specific chain of events—immediate imprisonment, followed by Crane's personal petition to conduct the interrogation. When Crane received the inevitable green light to proceed, he would have his opening to do what he wanted with her. *So single-minded*, Andreas thought with exasperation. Having just mapped out a plan for internal damage control from the incident in Chicago, Andreas suddenly had another use for Ming's unexpected insubordination.

"Yes, we'd all like an explanation for Dr. Jhu's change of heart," Andreas began as he closed the distance between himself and Crane, "but I believe we have a more pressing matter. Someone needs to be *held accountable* for the mistakes that have clearly been made in our efforts to advance Seer potential. In light of our recent failures, I think Dr. Jhu's lack of cooperation seems oddly timed and suspicious. Don't you?"

Crane caught up quickly to Andreas' train of thought. Though it wouldn't give him the personal satisfaction of seeing Ming bleed to death in front of him, she would serve a larger purpose that was almost as important as his own gratification.

"Yes, Andreas, I think you're right. It is very suspicious that her refusal should come at a time when we need answers the most. Perhaps she has been withholding information that could have saved the Guild from the terrible loss of life we saw today." Crane sighed heavily with feigned concern as he took his place beside Andreas.

"We can only hope she hasn't somehow been conspiring with the lost Seers to undermine the Guild," Andreas added, looking around the room to the other scientists. "If she was, it is hard to imagine that she would have been acting alone."

"This is such bullshit!" Ming shouted as she realized that she was being framed for what happened in Chicago.

"Is it?" Andreas asked calmly before motioning to his assistant Christof to call security.

"You're just trying to save your own asses because you're the ones who fucked up. I've been trying to tell you for years that we should be *helping* the Seers not controlling them!" Ming barely finished her sentence before she was hoisted up out of her chair by two large men in grey fatigues.

"Let's not make this uglier than it has to be. We'll make a public statement of your pending investigation within the hour," Andreas said to the small crowd of scientists who watched as Ming was whisked away to the Guild's private prison facility.

Andreas and Crane exchanged brief glances as they waited for the security guards to leave the floor. When Ming's screams could no longer be heard, they turned their attention to the group before them. Crane nodded for Andreas to continue with his plan to divert attention away from their own culpability.

"The investigation that I mentioned will naturally involve all of you, as you were Dr. Jhu's closest colleagues. While I can't imagine that she was working alone in her efforts to sabotage our mission, I sincerely hope for each of your sakes that that is somehow the case." Andreas summoned his most sincere affect before continuing. "If any of you have information that you think would be helpful to our inquiry, it would serve you well to mention it now. There may not be another opportunity for leniency."

The murmurs that erupted in the room after Andreas' last words were deeply encouraging to him. As he assessed their innocent, worried faces, Andreas marveled at how some of the smartest minds in the world could be so easily led to deception. Though Andreas didn't know Ming half as well as anybody else in the room, he was almost sure she had nothing to do with the events that took place in Chicago. She had always been too aware and too afraid of the Guild's absolute power to try anything like that. Her colleagues, he mused, should have known this, but the mere suggestion that she could have been involved was enough to make them question each other. That's why Andreas called for security. He knew that all you needed was a discrediting scene to make people begin to question things, and nothing looked worse than being escorted out of your office by security. *You may know every minute facet of the human brain,* he thought with superiority, *but I know politics, and politics trumps facts any day.*

"Of course," Crane chimed in before the group could work itself into a frenzy, "we are also looking for ideas and people to help us rebuild what has obviously been a flawed endeavor on our part. You all heard what happened today in Chicago. Our need to defend the global peace and order that our work creates has never been greater. We need your allegiance, now more than ever."

Crane and Andreas stood in the center of the group for several moments in silence before Ming's third and most junior assistant, Dr. Mark Cleary, wiped his sweaty brow and spoke up.

"Umm, I'm sure Ming would have told you this... I mean, if she hasn't already, so I guess it's no big deal, but she was working on a different version of the Luridium, one with fewer side effects." As soon as Mark became aware of Crane's singular attention on him, he began to hurriedly stammer his way through the rest of his explanation, regretting that he gave in to the need to speak up in the first place. "I mean... this was about a year ago, just as a side project. It might not mean anything, I mean it was never tested on Seers... but I think, I mean, it might be a start."

"What is your name?" Crane asked quietly as he assessed the young man before him. He looked no older than Ming was when he first approached her.

"Umm, Mark Cleary, sir. Dr. Mark Cleary."

"Dr. Cleary, did you assist her in the development of this new drug? Do you have information on the process—enough information to replicate it?"

Every eye was on Mark as he prepared to answer Crane. Some of his colleagues looked relieved while others looked wary and frightened.

But whether it was for him or for themselves, at twenty-nine, he wasn't old enough to know or understand. He answered Crane's question honestly and sealed his fate.

"Yes, sir. I did assist Dr. Jhu in the development of the new drug, and I have all my notes."

CHAPTER 2: THE HONEYMOON IS OVER

Alessandra didn't know what was more upsetting—news coverage of the Guild's manhunt to find them or the sight of her husband morphing from a carefree tourist to his old severe self as he checked and rechecked the windows in their two-story flat. She let out a long sigh, hugging her knees closer to her chest before finally deciding to let them hang over the edge of the bed.

"That won't help, you know," Alessandra said softly as she gestured toward the window latches. "I still can't see anything. Our future gets more obscure the longer we stay here."

"Neither will that," Liam replied, pointing towards the TV before heading back downstairs to recheck the backdoor. "You should stop watching that stuff. They don't know anything about us."

The sudden return to real life from their three-month extended honeymoon had been jarring. With the exception of a brief visit by Lilli and Joel after Marcus' burial, Liam and Alessandra had spent their time together in blissful isolation. Their lazy days were spent on bike rides and picnics—just learning and enjoying each other. They hadn't even turned on the TV until three days ago, when Lilli called to tell them what Liam already knew: that they had lingered too long in San Gimignano.

'They have your general vicinity, though Katia was able to block them from getting your exact location. You have a couple days, but you need to leave soon,' Lilli had warned.

They were packed within an hour of Lilli's call, with a private plane chartered to take them to London, but inclement weather had kept them grounded for the better part of two days, leaving them stuck and anxious in a small duplex in Florence.

"It's just hard..." Alessandra said absently as she stared at the screen. "We're terrorists in the world's eyes. We've gone from being pariahs to terrorists in less than four months."

"Not everyone believes that, Alessandra." Liam said as he stopped short of his destination to turn around and stand to the side of where she was seated at the foot of their bed. By the way the images from the TV took up all the light in her eyes, he could tell she had barely heard him.

The truth was he didn't know what to say to comfort either of them. From the tension and stress that hung in the air, it was hard to believe that less than a week ago they had been chasing each other through the vineyard that was just behind the villa they had rented for the summer, drunk on wine and laughing without a care in the world. Those carefree feelings were nowhere to be found as Liam watched Alessandra's grip on the comforter tighten as the news of the Guild's smear campaign against them droned on.

"Hey, look at me," Liam began, as he grabbed the remote and turned off the TV. With only the light from the street lamps streaming in, he knelt down directly in front of her and gathered her hands in her lap. "Look at me."

Alessandra closed her eyes to rein in the panic that was beginning to take over her mind. *You knew this would happen. We couldn't stay hidden forever,* she tried to reason.

"Alessandra, come on. Look at me," Liam asked again. But she wasn't ready to see the fear in her own eyes mirrored back at her, so instead she leaned forward until her forehead rested on top of his.

"I'm scared," she whispered. "I don't want this again. I'm not ready to lose who we are now to all of this."

Her hands were rigid with the effort it took to keep them from shaking, but he still felt the tremor. In response, he gripped her hands tighter until he could feel the tension in her grip ease, just a little.

"Baby, it's just us. Look at me, please."

He could see the outline of her shoulders fall and relax the minute their eyes met, just as he felt the tight coil of tension release in his own back.

"I don't know what's going to happen, but I know we're going to be okay—not because I can see it, but because I believe it," he said, inching closer to her before he continued. "I need you to believe it too, Alessandra, because that's the only way we're going to make it through whatever comes next. We have to believe it. Do you understand?"

"Yes," she sighed as she took a deep breath and wondered why she ever doubted that he would know the words to say to calm her down. "I believe it."

They were allowed only a few moments of their renewed peace before they heard the snap from the latch on the living room window as it broke off and fell onto the parquet wood floor. Besides the twitching in Alessandra's finger when they both registered the sound, neither of them moved an inch as they heard three sets of feet hit the floor below them.

Should we try to run, Alessandra wondered as her eyes darted from Liam's to their bedroom window and back again. Liam shook his head at the implication in her gaze before rising slowly off the floor and pulling his gun from the backside of his jeans. The meaning of his actions was as clear to Alessandra as if he had spoken them. *We will face this now,* she thought. With one hand, Alessandra grabbed her small satchel which held their passports and cash and slung it around her neck and shoulder quickly before rising to her feet. Liam squeezed her hand once more before letting it fall to her side. He motioned for her to get behind him as he began to inch his way towards their bedroom door.

Aside from the initial sound of their intruders, nothing could be heard from the living room. Liam guessed that they were listening for any indication of their location, just as he and Alessandra were. Though the building in which their duplex was situated was over five centuries old, the owners' renovations had been meticulous, down to the sturdy marble tile that Liam and Alessandra silently crept across towards the cavernous servant's staircase that led directly to the kitchen.

Behind Liam, Alessandra worked hard to calm herself enough to access her sight. When her breath finally became even and deep, she immediately caught an image of one of their assailant's feet hitting the bottom step of the molded staircase just as they reached the edge of the top landing. Alessandra grabbed Liam's shoulder to get his attention. When he was turned towards her, she held up one finger before pointing it in the direction of the staircase.

Nodding his head in understanding, Liam returned his gun to his jeans. If there was only one of them on the stairs, it would be safer to take him out as quietly as possible, Liam reasoned. His plan was to try to make it down the staircase unnoticed, giving them as many options as possible for maneuvering and escape.

They descended the steps slowly until they were hidden from view behind the curve of the stairs. They caught their first assailant easily as he rounded the corner to find Alessandra and Liam waiting for him. Before the hulking man could recover from his surprise at their appearance, Liam used the leverage of his high ground position to grab him by the wrist in a lock position that immediately made him unable to fire the gun that was in his hand. Using the same momentum, Liam folded the assailant's body into his own, so that his back was pressed firmly into Liam's chest as Liam held him in a tight choke-hold position. Before the man could scream for help, Liam used his free hand to grip the man's jaw. With a powerful jerk of his jaw and neck in opposite directions, the assailant's body went limp in Liam's arms.

The altercation happened so fast Alessandra didn't even realize the man was dead until she saw Liam struggle to keep him upright as his lifeless body threatened to slip down the steps. But it only took a moment for Alessandra to catch up and begin helping Liam drag his body up to the top landing before they took his gun and headed back down the stairs. Once in the kitchen, they could hear the ascent of another pair of feet on the main staircase to their bedroom.

This is it, Liam thought as he replaced the assailant's gun with his own and motioned for Alessandra to get behind him.

"Shit. Anderson is down. They're not up here," the second man shouted from upstairs. As they both listened to his rapid descent down the back stairs, Liam wished for the millionth time that Alessandra would agree to carry a gun. Even though he had taught her some self-defense maneuvers, she refused to pick up any type of weapon. 'I know what these things can do,' she'd said once as she gently pushed away the gun that Liam offered her.

But now they were about to be cornered as the man coming downstairs blocked their path to the second floor while whomever was on the first floor would soon discover their location.

Liam silently counted the bullets in his gun and the 9 mm standard issue he'd taken off the 1st assailant while looking for a place to take cover in the small kitchen. *The center island should buy us some time,* he thought, as he inched closer to the kitchen's main entrance. With less than five feet to go before they were out of the kitchen, Liam heard the moment the second man's feet went from molded plaster to terra cotta tile.

Liam fired immediately, driving the 2nd man back into the stairwell while he and Alessandra took cover, just before the assailant began firing back.

"Henley, I'm trapped!" he yelled. "Get over here, man, they're in the kitchen!"

"Yeah, I got 'em," Liam and Alessandra heard from a cool and confident voice that hovered just above them. "Nice and slow, guys. Hands up."

As Liam and Alessandra looked above them, they were met with another 9mm that was held by a man whose large smirk stretched across his angular face.

"Call Jackson and come on out, Dean. They know we've got 'em," Henley continued.

Liam slowly pulled Alessandra and himself to a standing position so he could assess both of the men before him. He'd seen their type before—rugged, dirty, and slightly high from the thrill of the chase. Taking in their demeanor, he knew that these men weren't from the Guild. *Contract killers*, he surmised quickly as he raised his hands in surrender, keeping his gun high enough that someone would have to reach over the counter to get it, which was exactly his plan.

"All right, hot shot, put the gun down easy," Henley said, as he looked Alessandra over. "Don't make this harder than it has to be."

When Liam didn't move, Henley let out a snort, before explaining. "Look, if you weren't worth more to me alive, I'd have no problems killing you, so give me the fucking g—"

Henley was about two inches shorter than Liam at a full grown 6'2", so when he leaned over to swipe the gun from Liam's hand, he was left a little off center, which was all Liam needed. Liam grabbed Henley's hand by the wrist and brought his entire arm down against the granite island countertop—hard. Next, Liam brought the butt of his own gun down sharply onto the delicate ulna of Henley's forearm, shattering it on impact.

Henley screamed out in pain before crumpling to the floor. Liam barely had time to kick the gun out of Henley's reach before shifting his attention back to Alessandra. But by that time, Dean had already emerged from the stairwell to grab Alessandra. With Alessandra's body facing forward and held against Dean's chest like a human shield, Liam couldn't get a clean shot of the man who was now pointing a gun at him.

"Put your gun down, or I'll kill her."

Liam took a deep breath as he kept his eyes on Alessandra and tried to think clearly through the rage of having anyone put his wife in danger. As she held his gaze, he was proud to see that she looked strangely calm. By the way Dean was holding Alessandra, Liam could tell that Dean didn't have a lot of experience fighting women. *Your grip needs to be even more precise*, Liam thought as he watched all the subtle hints in Alessandra's movements that let him know she was preparing to break Dean's hold. *Women have a way of wiggling out of things*, Liam thought as he remembered the faint sparring scar under his left nipple that he'd earned from a female black belt who taught him this lesson the hard way.

Liam kept the relief from his eyes as he placed his gun on the counter and stepped to the side, just out of Dean's direct line of fire. As soon as he shifted his position, Alessandra understood that Liam knew exactly what she had planned. Now all she needed to do was wait for Dean to make the mistake of assuming that because they were both unarmed, they were not dangerous. The moment Alessandra felt Dean's muscles relax, she made her move. She groaned loudly, as if she was in pain, before bending down to let the weight of her body fall forward into Dean's arms around her waist. When she felt his torso extend with hers to compensate for the shift in their center of gravity, Alessandra raised up swiftly, swinging her head back and connecting squarely with Dean's face. His grip on her opened immediately as his hands flew up to catch the blood rushing from his broken nose. Once out of his grip, Alessandra swung around and grabbed him by the right side of his torso so that he would not be able to use his gun as she kneed him in the groin three times. By the time she released his shirt, he was breathless as he fell to the ground, gasping for air.

Liam couldn't hide his smile as he stooped down and took the gun from Dean's hands without the slightest resistance. While Alessandra had been teaching Dean a valuable lesson in underestimating women, Liam made sure Henley was unarmed and incapacitated.

"Nice," Liam said proudly to a slightly stunned Alessandra before knocking Dean out with a blow to the temple. "Come on, we need to go."

Alessandra could only nod her head as she took one last look at the man who had become her victim before grabbing Liam's hand.

They made it as far as the foyer before three more men burst through the front door. No one moved an inch as they faced each other down—three gun barrels to Liam's two and Alessandra at his side, ready to strike.

The bald man directly facing Liam spoke first. "You're outnumbered. Unless you want to die, I suggest you put down your gun."

"That's what the other three thought, too," Liam sneered in response, as he tried to find a distraction that would allow him to even the score. "Now they're in pieces," he lied.

Liam used the man's momentary glance toward the kitchen to shift the balance in their favor.

"Get down!" he shouted at Alessandra as he used his right hand to grab Jackson's wrist and swing him around, so that when Jackson fired reflexively, he ended up killing one of his partners. But before Liam could swing him around again to take aim at the third man who was now trying to grab Alessandra, the right side of Liam's face was hit hard by the blunt force of Jackson's smooth head. Both men fell back then, losing their guns on impact with the floor as Liam lost his footing. With both hands now available, Liam used his position underneath them to maintain his chokehold around the man's neck.

"Get out of here," Liam yelled to Alessandra as he struggled. But Alessandra had no plans to leave without everything she came with as she evaded the 3rd man's desperate attempts to catch her alive. As she ran through the living room toward the kitchen where Henley and Dean's bodies lay unconscious on the floor, Alessandra threw everything she could in her path to slow his progress. She was in the kitchen when she heard Liam cry out in pain. Without a thought, she ran toward the foyer. Her vision was immediate as she saw the knife that pierced through his skin and sliced clean and vertical through the muscle in his upper thigh. A half a second before she reached him, she could see the tip of the blade reach and scrape his bone.

The look of pain on Liam's face as he gritted his teeth in agony while refusing to relinquish his grip on Jackson's neck was something she knew she would never forget. Alessandra felt the very air around her come to a standstill as she sensed the current of her visioning energy bubble up and through her body in a rush. She could feel it in the tips of her hands and feet like never before as she let go of her fear completely to make room for the one thing she was suddenly sure she could do: save him.

"Stop." Alessandra said as she turned to her attacker and held up her hand. She could feel the power of her energy creating a form and a mass that would do her will—anything she thought or said. The man chasing her halted abruptly as if frozen upright and in place. Her senses where suddenly infinitely acute and attuned to everything in her environment so that she could hear the rushing of blood from Liam's wound and the absence of sound as her assailant's lungs and heart refused to pump.

Don't kill him, she heard Lilli say in her thoughts. *Help Liam.*

Understanding that he was not the one who she most needed to subdue, Alessandra took another moment to order the man who had been pursuing her to be still, then turned before she could see his lungs expand with air as his body fell paralyzed to the ground. Facing Liam, Alessandra focused on Jackson's blind attempts to inflict further harm on her husband as the hand that held his 5" hunting knife stabbed wildly at the ground, trying to reconnect with Liam's leg.

You will not hurt him again. Before she'd completed the thought, the fingers around Jackson's knife handle were crushed beyond what could ever be repaired. The scream that escaped his throat could be heard three apartment buildings down.

"Get off him!" she hissed. Jackson's body was immediately pulled from Liam's grasp and hurled out the door, landing on the hood of the black SUV that he had driven to their home by the sheer force of Alessandra's determination to have this man as far away from Liam as possible.

Alessandra could hear Liam's heart beat too fast as he struggled to manage the terrible pain in his leg. But even his wound could not distract him from what he'd just witnessed.

Lifting himself gingerly to his elbows, his eyes tracked Alessandra as she crossed the room and knelt down beside him.

"What was that?" he huffed in amazement through quick shallow breathes.

"Shhh. I don't know. Lie still. I think I can heal this."

As soon as she said the words, Liam could feel his pain subside as a strange twisting-tingling sensation began emanating from the wound just before Alessandra placed her hands at each side of the opening.

"What are you doing?" Liam asked breathlessly as he felt the deep gash on his leg begin to close. Where her hand touched his leg, he could feel energy, like adrenaline, coursing into him like he'd felt only once before, with Lilli.

"Giving you my energy, my ability to heal," she finally answered. She released her hands and wiped away the blood from the top of his thigh to reveal the sun-kissed color it had been this morning, without a scar to even reference the events of the last half hour.

"How… how did you know? When did you learn to do that?"

"I don't know," Alessandra replied with tears of relief in her eyes. "I heard you scream and I just… reacted."

Despite her relief, the cool night air flowing in through the open door reminded them of just how exposed they were in their current location—to the Guild and the local police.

"Thank you," Liam said, cupping her face in his hands as he wiped the tears from her cheeks. "But..."

"I know," Alessandra said as she leaned in for a kiss before rising from the floor with Liam. "We need to get on that plane. Now."

CHAPTER 3: RESTORATION

T here's no point in even trying to hide it," Joel teased as he watched Lilli attempt to contain the smile that stretched across her pink cheeks. Though the rain had stopped at least an hour before, the late afternoon wind was like shards of ice across their faces as they weaved through the congestion and scaffolding along the sidewalks leading to Aldgate East Station. It was the closest stop to their home in the East End of London. From there they would catch a train to Paddington Rail then transfer to the Express train that would take them to Heathrow International Airport, where Liam and Alessandra would be waiting for them.

Lilli's smile only stretched wider as they hurried down the train station's cracked-tile staircase toward the underground tunnel. *I can't help it. I haven't seen him in two months*, Lilli said silently.

I know. I can feel how happy you are. It's making me giddy, Joel answered her as he swiped their Oyster fare cards and began flailing his arms around playfully.

Lilli laughed out loud then, drawing questioning stares from the people who stood next to them on the dimly lit platform. Joel drew her into his lean frame and kissed the crown of the thick green hoodie that covered her head.

See. Now they think you're completely mental, he teased.

You, too. 'Cause you're with me, she thought proudly as she hugged him tighter.

With the exception of their brief visit with Liam and Alessandra in Italy, Joel and Lilli had spent most of their time since the confrontation in Chicago alone. Shortly after burying Marcus in Tanzania, they had begun using their thought-sharing capabilities more regularly. By the time they reached Italy, the connection between them was so strong they had stopped communicating aloud entirely, unless they were in Liam and Alessandra's presence. Their intentional isolation, combined with their unique ability, fostered a trust and understanding of one another that would have taken a normal couple decades to nurture. Through their thoughts, they were able to experience each other's unfiltered emotions and intentions in an immediate and powerful way. Even now, despite being fully settled into their life in London, it was hard to come out of their own cocoon and remember to act normally in public.

Lilli hummed contently as she wrapped her arms around his waist. From behind, they looked like lop-sided twins with their worn leather jackets over hoodies, faded black denim and matching black Doc Martens.

Although they easily could have afforded a private car to take them to Heathrow, Joel and Lilli tried to keep their lives as normal as possible, given who they were. Despite the constant loop of misinformation and composite sketches of their faces that were featured on the news, the renderings were inaccurate enough to afford them a fair amount of anonymity. Behind their shades and hoodies, they were easily mistaken for just two more members of the East End's dodgy crowd.

In addition to preserving their privacy, their understated appearance was a necessary part of concealing the work that Joel, Neva, and Hasaam had started in an abandoned warehouse over ten years ago, when the East End was mostly a forgotten part of town. Joel had grown up in the area when it was predominantly home to London's poor, working class, and immigrant residents. In selecting the location, he knew that the poverty that surrounded them would provide the kind of public avoidance and lack of police attention necessary to conduct their operation discretely. In those days, they could run their facility with little protest from the neighbors. But the recent wave of gentrification that had begun to transform the community also brought more attention, as investors sought to buy up nuisance properties and drive out "undesirable" elements from the emerging hotspot. Unfortunately for the more affluent neighbors and investors, the warehouse owner, Xavier Renoit, would never think of selling the property against Joel's wishes. Joel had helped Xavier save the most important thing in his life, and in return for this favor, Xavier was more than willing to grant Joel anything he wanted.

When the pressure to sell became political, and the city authorities threatened to condemn the building without so much as a site visit, Xavier used his considerable resources as one of the wealthiest men in Europe to buy eleven more highly-sought after properties in the East End. He subsequently threatened to maintain them all as nuisance properties if the authorities didn't back off.

No one suspected that the decrepit warehouse that was tucked away in an alley off Brick Lane was anything more than a neglected tenement. But inside the crumbling edifice, the first two floors housed a state-of-the-art facility where Neva and Hasaam continued their research, and Joel ran his entire operation to find, offer sanctuary, and train Seers all over the world. The third floor consisted of a group of rooms equipped with medical beds and monitoring equipment. At the top of the building was a large open loft were Joel and Lilli now lived.

It took Joel and Lilli just under 45 minutes to get from their flat to Heathrow. But once they arrived at the airport, they didn't follow the crowd to the security checkpoints. Instead, they exited the terminal heading towards the main airport entrance to wait for an escort that would take them to one of the runways reserved for private plane arrivals. Though this was Lilli's first time circumventing airport security and international law on someone else's behalf, Joel had done it many, many times.

"How long do we have to wait for him?" Lilli asked as she wiggled her legs back and forth to ward off the cold.

"I'm sure he's here already. He's just watching us to make sure that we haven't been followed. When he's sure, he'll come. It shouldn't be long."

"Right," Lilli replied. She knew better than to try to look around for the stranger that Joel referred to only as "the escort." Joel had already explained that the people he worked with were professional smugglers of any number of illegal, high-value items. It was the escort's job to remain unseen. Unless she used her sight to find him, he wouldn't be anywhere that a novice like herself would guess. She had checked with Maura just that morning to make sure their escort was someone they could trust, but even Maura's calm reassurance hadn't completely settled her. In arranging for Liam and Alessandra's escape from Italy, Joel had explained to her how the process worked, but she was still anxious. What had happened in Italy turned out to be more dangerous than she had foreseen, and she couldn't wait to have Liam closer to her where she could make sure he was safe.

Don't worry. They'll be with us soon, Joel promised as he pulled her closer to him.

As Lilli breathed out slowly to calm her nerves, she suddenly noticed a full-size black sedan with tinted windows appear out of nowhere to pull up along the curb beside them. Joel opened the backseat door immediately for her to get inside. As soon as she entered the vehicle, she was surprised, first by the light cream leather and wood grain interior that seemed almost cheery given the gloomy atmosphere outside, and second by the unassuming, spectacled man sitting in the driver's seat. He turned around with a wide grin and wished her a "G'day" in an enthusiastic Australian accent.

"You must be the missus. Good to meet you. Mr. Renoit sends his regards."

"Ah, thank you," Lilli stammered as she traced the underside of the tattoo on her left ring finger with her thumb. Before Joel was fully settled in his seat, the car pulled off.

"And you, mate," the man began while checking his rearview. Lilli could only see the creases at the corners of his eyes as he smiled and added, "You look good. Marriage agrees with you, I see."

"Yeah, she's the bee's knees," Joel replied as he squeezed Lilli's hand before he leaned forward in his seat and cuffed the man in the shoulder. "And you, duffer? Where've you been? The last bloke wasn't nearly as nice—a bit smarmy, actually."

The man's rolling laughter filled the car and laid the last of Lilli's nerves to rest. Hearing Joel settle into his full-on cockney banter relaxed her even more. Since they had arrived in London, Lilli had been trying to study the accents around her so that she could mimic and incorporate them into her disguise.

"Yeah, well. What can I say, every once in a while, you try to give a bloke a shot, you know? But in the end, what do the Americans say?" the man asked as he glanced back at Lilli. "If you want something done right, you've gotta do it ya self, yeah?"

Their collective laughter died down as the car began to slow. Approaching the gate to the private landing strip, Joel sat back in his seat as their driver pulled out a manila envelope from his inside jacket pocket that was too full with Euros to close. Lilli was happy to note that while Joel's face was serious, he was not tense. The change in his demeanor was no more than him returning his full attention to the business at hand.

But Lilli smiled as she saw the vision of her brother walking down the stairs from the private plane onto the tarmac, with his leg perfectly functional and unharmed. She had felt the pain as he did when he was stabbed. She didn't have to, but she chose to. She wanted to be with him in any way that she could until Alessandra could get to him.

After they had passed the gate without incident, Lilli's hand flew to the door handle. Joel knew he would be lucky if Lilli waited until the car had come to a full stop before she opened the door and started running towards her brother. They had paid a lot of money to reserve the runway exclusively for the entire evening. But even with that provision, all the flight staff still had to be thoroughly checked or hired privately to ensure that their location would not be leaked to the Guild or the press. Before Chicago, Joel had never needed to take that level of precaution to transport a Seer, but now there was no escaping it. It was the only way they could travel securely.

As soon as the escort began flashing his high beams in the sequence he had discussed with the pilot to confirm their identity, the plane door began to fold down. Three seconds later, Lilli's door was open.

"Just let her go," Joel said as their escort slammed on the brakes and Lilli bolted out of the car. "They haven't been apart for this long since their mother died." Joel knew his wife wasn't at all athletic, but you couldn't tell in that moment. She was all high knees and clear purpose as she crossed the tarmac to where the steps were just touching down on the ground. Liam was at the door immediately and met Lilli's grin with a matching smile of his own.

"Hey, little sister," he said as he walked down a few steps before extending his arm back into the plane to reach for Alessandra.

The emotion was so thick in her throat she could only laugh as a tear she hadn't meant to shed escaped from the corner of her eye. Lilli made herself stay where she was for the full eight seconds that it took for Liam and Alessandra to descend the staircase, but the minute Liam's feet touched the pavement, she crashed into him.

"Hey..." She finally answered as Liam held her close.

"I missed you, too," Liam whispered into her hair.

While Liam and Lilli continued their embrace, Alessandra and Joel greeted each other with hugs and quiet amusement.

"He's been grinning like a--" Alessandra began.

"--her, too. All day," Joel responded with a laugh.

"Hey, we're right here, don't talk about us!" Lilli teased as she released her brother and drew Alessandra in for a hug. Lilli and Alessandra were both a bit surprised to look up from each other to find Liam and Joel locked in a similar embrace.

"It's good, man. We're glad you're back, safe and sound," Joel offered as they pulled away from each other.

"I can see that," Liam said as he looked at Joel earnestly. "She's happy. I can tell. Thank you."

Joel's grin was proud and broad as he patted Liam on the back. "Come on. Let's get out of here. We've got a lot to tell you."

Eli left for London as soon as the Seers they had rescued from Chicago were able to travel. To say that he had been anxious to see his former colleagues and understand the progress they had made in understanding the Seer phenomenon was a gross understatement. In truth, he hadn't looked forward to anything that much since Liam and Lilli arrived at the commune more than two years before. In the three and a half months that he had spent getting reacquainted with Neva and Hasaam and working with their newest researcher Ngozi Fade', he had learned more about Seers than he had discovered in the eight years he had studied them with the International Science Team.

Being there to witness and assist in the breakthrough that had taken them over five years had been the highlight of his career as a scientist. He couldn't wait to share the potential of their new discovery with all the commune members who they had called together.

For this reason, he was the first to greet Liam and Alessandra as they walked through the door of their research facility. The dark circles under his eyes as he slid open the steel front door before Lilli could even get her key out did nothing to diminish the anticipation in his eyes.

"Hey... hey everyone, welcome," he said excitedly as he stood aside to let them in.

"Eli," Liam called as he leaned in to pat his shoulders. "I don't think I've ever seen you this excited. I'm sure this isn't all for me."

"Don't mind him," Neva called in her husky voice as she walked into the main area from the back room carrying an empty IV bag and two vials of blood. "He's been like this for a week. I should check his adrenaline levels." She placed the tray carefully on her desk before heading toward the front door to greet the newcomers.

"Hello, my name is Neva Patel. It is a pleasure to finally meet you both. I've heard so many good things."

"Likewise," Alessandra replied as she smiled warmly and extended her hands. Just as they had finished with their introductions, Hasaam and Ngozi hurried through the front door as they tried to shield their dinner packages from the torrential downpour that had just erupted.

"Good, I see everyone is here. We'd planned to take you out for dinner, but when we saw the weather change, we thought it might be more comfortable to have dinner here," Hasaam said in a rush. After hanging up their coats, Ngozi and Hasaam quickly crossed the room to greet their guests.

"I hope you like Lebanese," Ngozi offered as she led them to the small break room that had been laid out with simple china in preparation for Alessandra and Liam's arrival. "The shop around the corner really is the best in London."

"Sounds perfect," Liam replied as he patted his stomach. "I'm starving."

Despite the late night flight from Italy to London and the harrowing escape Liam and Alessandra had endured just hours before, the group stayed up all night talking. They shared news they had each gathered from Hanna about the others in the commune and laughed at funny stories from their time apart, but mostly they talked about the progress Neva, Hasaam, Ngozi, and Eli had made in their research and the surprising new developments in Alessandra's abilities.

"Lilli told us what happened," Eli began, "but we haven't seen this ability in any of the other Seers yet. Do you know what triggered it?" he asked Alessandra excitedly as he leaned his body further into the table. Even though it had been months since she was subjected to one of Eli's tests face-to-face, she marveled at how his thirst for knowledge and understanding never waned.

"No, not really. I just knew somehow that I could do it. I wanted to do it, so I did."

"So it was more about your intention than any feeling or change in your body?" Ngozi asked.

"Yes, I guess you could say that. It was like my thoughts were shaping the energy around me into whatever I wanted or needed in that moment. I don't know if that even makes any sense."

"No, it does," Lilli jumped in. "I mean, it does for us." Lilli looked toward Joel as he nodded his head in agreement.

"Can you do the same thing?" Alessandra asked Joel.

"I don't think so. If I could have, many things would have been different." Joel's voice trailed off as he thought of his father and what might have happened if he had been able to save him.

Understanding the cause for Joel's shift in mood, Alessandra's mouth fell open as she stared at Joel in shock. "Do you think I could have saved Marcus?" she whispered. With their quick escape from Italy still weighing on her mind, she had not had time to consider the possibilities of what she had done.

"No," Hasaam said gently. "I don't think so. You probably didn't have this ability then, or at least you didn't know you had it. From the information we have gathered, Seer abilities are progressive. They evolve and grow. From what Eli has told me, you are still fairly new in discovering your abilities. When we met Joel, his gifts were nowhere near what they are now. You can't blame yourself."

"Alessandra," Joel began, looking at her intently, "I know you love my father as I do, but I never saw another future for him."

Grateful for Joel's words, Alessandra was eager to shift the conversation away from her and back to the purpose of their coming together.

"So tell us what else you've discovered, why we've all been brought here together."

There was a brief silence among the scientists at the table before they rested their eyes on Eli, who looked like he was about ready to burst.

"Why don't you go ahead, Eli?" Neva said with a chuckle.

"We've found a way to activate the Seer ability in people like us, people who have shown no paranormal ability before now," Eli blurted out excitedly.

"We're still in the testing phase," Neva cautioned, "but we believe we've identified the RNA strands and the proteins necessary to ignite the Seer ability in dormants."

"Dormants? What do you mean?" Alessandra asked Neva, but before she could respond, Eli chimed back in.

"That's what we're calling people like me and Liam — non-Seers."

Still a bit confused, Alessandra asked, "But how will you activate them? I thought you either had the genetic marker or you didn't."

"Yes, that's what we thought at first, but we were wrong. I was wrong. It's what Joel was trying to explain to us back in Chicago. The genetic marker that we thought was unique to Seers was really just RNA that everyone possesses. The only difference is that in Seers, this genetic material is synthesized and activated in a way that expands your physiological and cognitive capabilities beyond the normal range of human functioning.

"Twenty years ago, when I was studying Seers, the technology had not advanced enough for us to identify this marker for what it was. Back then, we were calling it "junk DNA" because it didn't seem to serve any particular purpose. And it doesn't — not in dormants. But in Seers, we now know that this so-called "genetic marker" comes from a class of catalytic RNA strands or ribozymes arranged in a unique pattern that looks and functions almost like an extra chromosome, like in Down's syndrome. This is the marker we discovered, and the Guild uses it to identify Seers. Unlike me, Neva and Hasaam were able to continue this work with the technology and resources necessary to fully understand what we discovered all those years ago."

"Ok..." Liam said slowly as he tried to recall the small amount of genetics he'd learned from high school biology. "So what patterns are these? If dormants have the genetic material to do what Alessandra and Lilli can do already, why aren't we activated?"

Leaning forward, Eli inhaled, ready to answer Liam's question before he caught himself. Even though the discovery he was about to share felt like the culmination of all his previous work, the truth was he had not made the connections that led their team to that moment. Sitting back in his chair, he turned to Neva and Hasaam, summoning the restraint he needed to let them explain the work that was rightfully theirs to claim.

With Eli's non-stop banter, Hasaam had not expected to have the chance to speak for at least another hour, so he was caught completely off-guard with a mouthful of kibbeh and hummus when Eli finally turned to him and nodded for him to take over the discussion. Unprepared, Hasaam turned to Neva and Ngozi to fill in, but Neva insisted. "No, Hasaam, we'll wait. I think this may be your only chance to speak," she teased. After hastily swallowing his food, Hasaam took a large gulp of water before answering Liam's question.

"Yes, Liam. You're right. That was a big question for us for a while before Ngozi here helped us see the problem differently. Once we identified the necessary ribozymes, we couldn't figure out how to make them react the way they do in Seers naturally, or how to make the necessary elements bond together. Ngozi had an idea that hadn't occurred to us before.

"Seers have a number of physiological anomalies — greater numbers of capillaries and alveoli in the lungs, stronger immune systems and healing capabilities, and increased sustained brain activity are just a few examples of this. Ngozi hypothesized that while Seers share almost all genetic and physiological traits with dormants, they might actually descend from a different lineage of the "homo" genus – a lineage that may have been more effective at synthesizing external elements and using them to power their abilities.

"For example, a Seer's higher capacity for oxygen intake and consumption allows their brain to operate at a more accelerated rate then mine. It also allows you to metabolize and transform the energy from that oxygen at a higher yield throughout your body than I can. Ngozi wondered whether or not the missing element that allows Seer RNA to synthesize the necessary proteins was linked to this oxygen supply, or rather the elements within oxygen. Some element that you can process that we can't. We started looking at elements in our environment, both prehistoric and current, that could possibly act as catalysts. At the same time, we ran a more extensive analysis of Joel's and the other Seers' blood, looking for any uncommon elements.

"To our surprise, we found higher levels of xenon in all the Seers we tested. Although xenon was abundant in the atmosphere during the Ordovician period due to the prolific volcanic activity, its presence now in our air composition is almost negligible. It is so rare that we don't even test for it in the bloodstream under any normal circumstances. It's not present in dormant blood in any significant quantity. The elevated levels found in Seer blood suggest that, like oxygen, they are able to harness and synthesize higher quantities of this element in the atmosphere. We believe that this element, combined with another element called xithus that was also present in abundance during the Ordovician period, is the key to activating the RNA sequence in dormants."

"Wow… how did you even make that connection?" Liam asked Ngozi in amazement.

"My dissertation was on how atmospheric changes during the Ordovician period created the conditions for amphibious life forms," she shrugged before continuing. "But what we're hoping to do now still doesn't answer the biggest questions. If my theory is correct, we still don't know where this new lineage of man came from or why it disappeared and, most importantly, why it has come back in the form of the Seers.

"The fact that all of us have this genetic raw material makes me wonder if what we're really talking about here is evolution or regression."

"What do you mean?" Liam asked.

"What I mean is, if we are successful in activating this ability in dormants, will we be pushing the limits of human potential forward or will we simply be restoring an ability that we used to have but lost somehow?"

"We were very lucky to find her," Neva added.

"How did you find her?" Alessandra asked.

Ngozi looked over to Joel to see if he would clarify, but instead he raised his hand in deference to her. Ngozi narrowed her eyes playfully at Joel before answering. "We were in primary school together, Joel and I, rescued from the same terrible orphanage in Tanzania and brought here. Being odd and smart… children aren't always kind. Even though I was three grades ahead of him, he looked out for me," Ngozi said with a smile. "When he started having visions of his father, Joel dropped out half way through secondary school, but he told me to finish, that we would see each other again. I'd just been offered a fellowship at the Museum of Natural History in Washington, DC when he found me again and told me what he was doing. I came right away, of course."

"I've never heard of this xithus… How do you even find it?" Liam asked.

"It's very hard to find in large quantities, but we've been able to work with a number of geologists to identify likely sites where deposits may have formed. The process of extracting and processing the xithus and xenon together is another challenge, as it is extremely labor intensive and costly, but thanks to Joel's resources, our expeditions have been very successful. Our initial lab trials have been exciting. We finally have enough data and xithus to begin the first human trails."

No one spoke as they waited patiently for Liam and Alessandra to absorb all the information they had been given. But as the seconds stretched on, Eli couldn't contain himself any longer.

"We're calling it 'The Restoration Project'," he said excitedly. "If we're successful, it could mean that we may be ushering in an entirely new phase in human evolution." As the full implications of his words began to show on Liam and Alessandra's faces, Eli settled back into his chair with a huge grin that was in sharp contrast to the more cautious expressions of his colleagues.

"Now I'd say that's cause for a reunion!"

CHAPTER 4: REUNION

"Oh my God... this isn't even fair," Tess said, as she mopped up the last of the thick brown sauce in her bowl with spongy bread.

"Nothing should taste this good," Rachel agreed.

"I want to lick the bowl. I think I'm going to lick the bowl," Eric declared, half-expecting someone to stop him, but no one could look up from their own bowls to pay him any mind.

"Do what you have to do, man," Joel said gravely. "She can't make any more until tomorrow. It's the beef. The butcher doesn't open until 8 a.m."

With new understanding of the utter hopelessness of the situation, Eric brought the bowl to his face.

"I'll make more tomorrow. You come back tomorrow," Anya Patashka promised from the kitchen door with a chuckle. The delighted restaurant owner looked on with pride as the group of foreigners who rented her entire restaurant for the evening devoured the last of the goulash she had made. She never imagined that they would have three helpings each.

"Thank you so much, Mrs. Patashka," Lilli said sleepily as she emerged from the bathroom with the top button of her jeans unfastened. "We wish we could." Lilli gave the portly woman a big hug before making her way back to her table.

As Lilli eased down into her seat, she noticed that most of the commune members had assumed an awkward reclining position in their straight back chairs with their bottoms situated closer to the edge of the seat to give their bellies more room to expand.

"I think I ate too much…" Maura murmured in surprise as she watched her stomach strain against the waistband of her skirt, which, of course, made everyone else burst out in laughter.

"You think?" Liam teased before he was punched in both arms by Alessandra to his right and Maura to his left.

"You are much happier than the last time I saw you," Maura laughed as she rested her hand over her belly. "I like this side of you."

"Thanks." Liam smiled quietly before raising the glass of red wine he had barely touched.

"I think we need to make a toast — to the goulash," he said in a reverent tone.

"To the goulash," They replied in unison as they raised their glasses, together again in Prague.

The effort to get them all to Patashka's Bistro safely had taken weeks of planning and days of commercial flights and private charters. Although it had been less than six months since they had all been together, the differences in the demeanor of each member of their group was easy to see. With the exception of Katia, who was still struggling with her own self-doubt and guilt over Marcus' death, most members seemed refreshed and renewed from their time apart, even though they were happy to be back together.

With her unique insight into the character of anyone she met, Maura was tasked with finding a location where all 27 commune members and Seers could meet safely. The discussion they needed to have during their first reunion required time and absolute privacy, but she also wanted it to be a proper homecoming of sorts where they could be comfortable and enjoy the rare opportunity to be together. As soon as Maura walked through the heavy wooden doors of Mrs. Patashka's small restaurant, she knew that she had found the right place. Maura had only seen the beautiful color of pale turquoise light that emanated from Mrs. Patashka's torso in one other person—her grandmother in Cape Verde. The shock of seeing something so dearly missed in another human being brought tears to Maura's eyes as she watched Mrs. Patashka take in her long dreadlocks, dark-skin, and features with a child-like curiosity that matched her open heart. The five thousand euros Mrs. Patashka received in exchange for exclusive use of her restaurant from 6 p.m. to 2 a.m., her vow of silence, and the provision of a simple buffet-style meal didn't hurt either. That kind of money was more than she would make in three full months at the height of tourist season.

When the laughter from Liam's toast died down, the mood in the room shifted almost immediately as people sensed that it was now time to attend to the reason they had risked so much to gather there. Maura rose from her chair quietly and walked to the kitchen to retrieve the restaurant keys from Mrs. Patashka.

"I promise we will make sure the restaurant is secured before we leave. Are you sure you don't want us to clean up?" Maura asked calmly as Mrs. Patashka placed the keys to the restaurant in Maura's hands without hesitation.

"No, child. Just put your dishes in the sink. I will come back... after you leave, of course." Although Mrs. Patashka had agreed to leave them in her restaurant alone, the questions about why they needed this and what they would be discussing were at the tip of her tongue. Maura could see their presence in the pulsating color of her light. But Maura knew she would not ask them aloud.

"Thank you." It was the only answer Maura offered before Mrs. Patashka swallowed her curiosity, grabbed her coat, and left them to their meeting. As soon as Maura locked the door behind her, Eli rose from his chair.

"All right, guys, as much fun as this has been, you know we have a lot to discuss tonight. For safety reasons, this is probably the only meeting we can afford to have with all of us together for a while. Lilli, Tess, Hasaam, Ngozi, and I will be leaving for London as soon as this meeting is over with whoever decides to come with us. The rest of you will fall into the roles you choose to participate in. But before I go into the why of this meeting, I think maybe Joel and Lilli should give you guys a little context as to where we are with the Guild."

"Thanks, Eli," Joel said from his chair. Even though he did not stand, every eye was drawn to him.

"In the months since Chicago, Katia, Jared, and I have been working with an expanded group of Seers to build up our capacity to block the Guild's efforts to find us. We've had some close calls," Joel added, glancing briefly towards Liam. "But for the most part, we've been successful. I can say with some certainty that we are safe here tonight.

"But something has shifted. Because of what the Guild witnessed in Chicago, what they know we are capable of, they have begun experimenting with a new group of Seers to understand how they can minimize the effects of the Luridium while maximizing the potential of the Seers in their possession. They understand now that the Luridium that they have relied upon to control their Seers also suppresses their gift. They are hoping that this new group of Seers will be able to match our abilities while still remaining loyal to the Guild. This new group of Seers is called The Red Order."

"Can they do that?" Marshall asked with alarm. "I thought they needed the Luridium to keep their Seers in line."

"Yes, that is how they used the Luridium in the past, but they have developed a new formula that they're calling L-2B. It seems to have fewer physical and mental side effects, and even though that means that the Seers are more aware and able to decide their own level of participation within the Red Order, the Guild wants the potential that they witnessed in us badly enough to risk some level of autonomy. From what we can tell, they are using a combination of the L-2B compound, lies, and money to ensure The Red Order's cooperation."

"But they can't do it, right? They can't match you?" Jean asked anxiously. The room was silent as they waited for Joel to wash away their fear with his words.

"It's unclear," Joel said honestly. "In the last few weeks, we have sensed them in the Collective…" Taking in the confusion in the room, Joel realized he needed to clarify his meaning. "It's what we're calling our visioning now, because ever since Chicago our connection to each other has expanded beyond our sight and the Quorum. We can… sense each other's consciousness, sometimes speaking directly into each other's minds, even over long distances.

"Anyway, a couple weeks ago, we began sensing these new Seers in the Collective. We can't tell if they are aware of us, but the fact that they can even reach this level — which has never happened with any of the Seers still connected with the Guild's Quorums — must mean that they are at least more capable than any other Guild Seer we've come across."

"So what does this mean for us?" Marshall asked warily.

"It means things just got harder. We have our work cut out for us, but we still have a job to do," Joel answered.

"And what job is that?" Jean asked.

"That depends on you," Lilli interjected. "At this point, you have three options. The first is that you don't have to be involved in this at all. As you see by tonight's showing, not everyone from Iowa chose to be here. As each of you already knows from the insane precautions it took to get here, the Guild is in overdrive, trying to find us. If any of us were caught now, we'd be tried for treason and most likely put to death. So..."

"No offense, Lilli," Eric began as he cut Lilli off, "but that's been true since I first met you guys and your brother over there put a gun to my head." Eric took a moment to shoot a friendly smirk Liam's way before continuing. "So as far as I'm concerned, you can skip this part. We all know what we're up against. That's why we're here, so we can face it together."

"Okay," Lilli conceded. "I just wanted you to know that no one would hold it against you if you chose to leave. The others who aren't here wish us the best, but they had to make their own choice." When Lilli saw Tess roll her eyes impatiently, she decided to press on.

"The other option is to be a part of the first human trials to reactivate each of you as a Seer." As Lilli anticipated, there was a long moment of stunned silence before Hanna spoke up.

" 'Reactivate' us? What does that mean? Was I ever activated?"

"Possibly. At least some branch of our ancestors may have been," Eli began. "It seems that the genetic potential to be a Seer has been lying dormant in all of us, and we think we've figured out a way to activate that ability. When we return--"

"So it's true, what you said in Chicago?" Marshall interrupted, directing his question to Joel, who stared back at him cautiously. Joel could see the burgeoning excitement and desire for new power growing in Marshall's eyes.

"Yes, it's true. Eli was there to witness it when Hasaam and the others made the breakthrough. But, I warn you and everyone here to think carefully before you agree to the trials. We are not sure what other abilities you may discover beyond greater insight into the future. Despite what you may think, Marshall, a Seer's power is not how you imagine it to feel. In many ways, it's more of a burden. You can't change the future you see. You must be willing to surrender to it and realize that your only true insight is in understanding your role within it. The awareness changes you. What you want, how you see the world — everything."

Marshall's intended protests fell silent as he let the implications of Joel's words sink in. Outside of Rachel's insistence that they "had to come", the main reason he had wanted to come to Prague was for the chance to become like the man who had rescued them from a suicide mission in Chicago — Joel. He'd forgotten all about how that same man wept helplessly as he watched his own father die in his arms, unable to save him from a future he had seen coming for years.

"Well, I'm in," Kyle called out, breaking the pensive silence in the room. "Don't knock it 'til you try it, right?"

"Me, too. I just want to know exactly how this is gonna work," Hanna agreed.

After a lengthy discussion on the mechanics and science behind the trials, 19 of 21 of the commune members who came to Prague agreed to participate. Rachel and Liam were the only ones who declined.

"Can I decide later?" Rachel had asked timidly as she fidgeted with her hands. "I don't think I'm ready for this yet."

"Of course," Lilli assured her. "There's no rush. Just let us know."

When all but one had declared their intentions, Eli looked at Liam expectantly to find him completely distracted and engrossed in a private conversation with Alessandra. "Liam?" he called, slightly confused. Eli had assumed that given Liam's leadership qualities and his strong connection with Lilli, he would naturally want to be involved.

"Hmm?" Liam began, genuinely surprised to be addressed during the discussion he had all but tuned out of the moment it began.

"Aren't you going to be a part of the trials?" Eli asked. "I'd assumed…"

"No," Liam said simply, never taking his eyes from Alessandra. "I plan to be the last ordinary human standing." Eli was about to try to persuade him otherwise, but he was curtailed by Lilli's hand on his shoulder.

"He's sure, Eli. Don't worry."

"So what do you plan to do with yourself, 'ordinary man', while the rest of us are getting super-sized?" Vincent teased.

"Me? Oh, I'm going with Option 3," Liam said, suddenly alert and engaged. "I'll be at the front lines of this fight while you're in a lab getting needles stuck in your ass."

"Wait a minute, what's Option 3?" Vincent asked, suddenly unsure if he had made the right choice.

Joel couldn't stop grinning at Liam's sense of humor as he tried to answer Vincent.

"Option 3 is basically the continuation of what we started in Chicago. We can't just let the Guild paint the story of who we are and what is going on here with their lies. We have to get *our* message out—the truth out about Seers and what our ability could mean for everyone. Your participation in the trials will help us understand the extent to which this ability can be reintroduced, but you guys are just the first phase. Once we're sure this works, we plan to offer the treatment to anyone who wants it. The Guild still doesn't know about our plan, but when we go public, which we're about to do, then the fighting will really start, because it will cut off the Guild's entire source of power—its control over all Seers. That's why stopping us is so important to them, but that's also why we have to succeed."

"So how are you going to do that? What's your plan?" Vincent asked.

"Well, we're going to split up. Lilli and Tess will be heading back to London with Eli, Hasaam, and Ngozi to work on administering the treatments. Since Lilli and Tess have the ability to project thoughts into the minds of non-Seers, we think they will be able to help each of you reconnect with the part of your brain that understands and communicates in Prime.

"In the meantime, with Hanna and Kyle's help in setting up media interviews, Liam, Alessandra, and I are going to try to get the word out about what's really going on, while Katia and Jared take the remaining Seers and head up our monitoring and blocking efforts. When we leave here, Liam, Alessandra, and I are headed to Germany for an interview with Nadia Spencer of World News Today."

"Please tell me you don't mean the reporter who followed the French Prime Minister into the bathroom to get a statement on his alleged affair?" Rachel blurted out in disbelief.

"Yeah, I thought the same thing," Liam chimed in.

The visual of being caught on camera at a urinal made Joel shudder and Lilli snort with amusement.

"Look, I don't like her methods either, but I'm not planning on going to the loo while she's around. Besides, she approached us through one of Hanna's email accounts," Joel explained a little sheepishly as he rubbed the back of his neck. "Look, the bottom line is that she hosts one of the most watched news programs in the world. I don't think it's an opportunity we can refuse."

"Exactly," Rachel responded, "she'll do anything for a story. How can we trust that she won't give away your location to the Guild, just to film the slaughter?"

"We don't trust her," Liam answered firmly. "I thought the same thing, Rachel, but even though I don't like it, Joel is right. This is a perfect opportunity to get our story out. So we've put in some conditions that will work to our advantage. She won't know the location of the interview until we take her there. We control time and transportation to and from. You know what Alessandra can do and Maura, of course, is on standby. It's not foolproof, but it will give us a chance…"

"She's not a bad person," Maura added confidently. "She's just ambitious. She knows we are taking a big risk to meet with her. She's more interested in getting an exclusive on our side of the story than turning us in."

"So can I postpone my participation in the trials?" Vincent asked Eli.

"Why?" Eli asked curiously.

"Because I think they're gonna need my help with Option 3."

The realization that Crane had been waiting for this moment for most of his long life came slowly, born of the shock and necessity that can only come from having your very existence threatened. In all the years he had enjoyed absolute power, it had never occurred to him that what he needed or even longed for was a real fight, a true adversary to challenge and dominate. As much as he hated Marcus for outsmarting them, he now saw the ironic blessing of it. He had not realized how tedious his supremacy had become until it was called into question. He found himself now fully engaged and awake for the first time in eons.

As he stepped before the Guild's Council, he felt vigor and anticipation course through him like never before.

"Ladies and Gentleman of the Guild, I know we suffered a crushing defeat in Chicago, but it is my sincere belief that we can not only recover from this setback, but that we can regain control over the Seers and stop Marcus' son... this Joel, from following through with his plans to destroy us.

"With your permission, I would like to use the painful lessons we have learned from these Lost Seers to create a new caliber of Seer that is capable of all the things we witnessed six months ago. They will be set-apart from our current stock in that they will join our cause of their own free will, thereby eliminating the need for the high doses of Luridium that diminish the realization of their potential. This new generation of Seers would be known to us as The Red Order."

The looks around the room as Crane finished his speech were everything he expected — surprise muted by the reticent skepticism that he knew was ever-present in less imaginative minds.

"Can this be done?" Yusef asked. Even though the man was old and frail, Crane was encouraged by the flicker of excitement he saw in his otherwise subdued posture. "How can we be sure of their loyalty without the Luridium to control them?"

"My dear friend," Crane began with a satisfied smile, "It has already begun."

In response to the wary grumbling that erupted among the 12 members of the Guild's Council, Crane continued in his most placating tone. "Council, while my admission may unsettle some of you, allow me the opportunity to explain myself and the magnitude of the threat that faces us. We have lost more than half of the Seers who were to be gathered this year alone. We can only assume that they have fallen under the influence of this Joel and his band of renegades. Our entire operation is now under attack as a result of their accusations and lies.

"In this desperate hour, I took the liberty of leading our response in a way that would enable us to strike as soon as possible, without the administrative delays that would have cost us more of what we cannot afford to lose. I think the progress we have made warrants your indulgence."

"And what progress is that?" the Council Chair asked doubtfully. "It is well known that our indulgence of your ideas may be what has brought us to this crisis."

Rather than respond to the chairman, Crane turned towards Miguel and nodded for him to open the Council doors.

Miguel did what he was told, though he did not enjoy being relegated to Crane's errand boy. Even before the defeat in Chicago, his exclusion from the inner workings of the Guild had been sudden and almost complete, though he still had only his own suspicions as to why. As Miguel opened the Council chamber doors, two people he had met only once before marched in and past him without so much as a glance in his direction.

"May I introduce Nina and Michael Grey, two of our most talented Seers."

The Chairman became completely erect in his chair as he took in their resemblance. "They are related… by blood. How did you find them?" he asked in awe as he leaned his portly body forward to get a better look at the pair of young adults standing confidently before him.

"Carefully," Crane responded possessively, as he watched the Council take in Michael and Nina's almost normal appearance.

"Don't be coy!" the Chairman snapped. "Our patience with you is limited."

"They were separated at birth through adoption. That is why their relationship to each other was not immediately discovered when they were tested. We were fortunate that they both lived in the same state and we met in time to save them."

The Chairman's eyes narrowed only slightly as he listened, otherwise keeping his reaction to Crane's lie to himself. In fact, the entire Council was quiet as they observed the brother and sister before them, wondering how much Michael and Nina understood about the Guild and their role in its plans. Rather than hear Crane lie again, the Chairman decided to address Michael and Nina directly.

"Do you remember how you came to us?" the Chairman asked, trying to infuse his voice with as much warmth as he could muster.

"No," Michael spoke first. "My memory is still hazy. I can remember the smell of gasoline and my mother screaming, but I can't see the men who killed my parents. Crane told us later that it was Joel. That they wanted us because we were special and we could become more powerful than them because we are related."

The Council members and even Miguel could not help but admire the way Crane had twisted the truth of their circumstances to his advantage. Having been the man directly responsible for Michael and Nina's presence here and their parents' deaths, Miguel was grateful for at least some insight into why he needed to remain out of sight, lest they recall the truth about how they came to be with the Guild.

"And you, Nina?" the Chairman asked. "What do you recall?"

"Mostly the same things Michael said," Nina offered in a pillow-soft voice. "But I wasn't as close to my parents as Michael was. I think they knew about me and it scared them. After the car accident, I just remember waking up to see Crane looking over me, with… this look on his face. He said he was happy I survived." The Chairman knew from Crane's exploits that the girl standing before him was too young to understand anything about the "look" on Crane's face and was grateful when other council members returned his thoughts to the business at hand.

"I thought Marcus was the only one, the only case of two Seers in the same family," another council member asked in disbelief.

"Yes, it is rare, but we believe there is at least one other case. It appears that Lilith Knight's mother, Jill, was also a Seer. We believe that this information was hidden from us by their father, Willem Knight, who was among the first scientists to discover the marker."

"Does the genetic link make them more powerful?" the Chairman asked.

"See for yourself," Crane responded as he stepped aside and motioned for Nina and Michael to demonstrate what they were capable of.

Chapter 5: The Interview

Lilli could still feel the strength of his heartbeat vibrating down through her knees from when she had kissed Joel goodbye almost 24 hours ago. The memory lingered on as she held the phone close to her ear and heard him tell her what she already knew, that they had arrived in Berlin safely. But she still wasn't used to the absence of his scent in the air she breathed. Though their mental connection was as strong as ever, it was unsettling to not have him physically near.

"I know you're worrying, but you don't need to. Nothing is going to happen to us." he insisted. "We have to face them sometime." It was the truth, but it wasn't what Lilli wanted to hear. Alessandra had already warned them that the interview with Nadia Spencer would not last the full 2 hours it was supposed to. From their visioning they could see pieces of how the Guild was involved, but even with all the Collective's efforts they could not see the full plan. They were being blocked by a force that grew more powerful every day.

"We're walking into a trap," she whispered.

"It's not a trap if we know about it," Joel tried again. Before Lilli could respond, Liam took the phone from Joel.

"Lilli, don't worry. We know about the second camera man. It'll be alright. I'll bring him back to you in one piece. Ok?"

"I love you" was all she could say in response to her brother as uncertainty churned in her stomach. "You have to go. I'll stay connected," she added with resolve. In her mind, Lilli watched Joel and Alessandra load up the car they had driven to Berlin, while an impatient Vincent stood waiting near the pair of black sport bikes that he and Joel would take to the Adlershof business park where the interview would be held.

"Do you want to talk with Joel again?" Liam offered as he re-counted the clips in his backpack.

"No. He just used the phone for you. I'll see you soon."

Still getting used to the connection she and Joel shared, Liam could only shake his head as he mumbled "You bet" before disconnecting the call and running to their car.

Liam had been an admirer of Berlin's Oberbaum Bridge ever since his mother got him his first building set and a picture book of the world's most famous bridges. Though he'd spent many a night as a boy trying to recreate its beauty with Legos and broken castle pieces, the structure's architectural merits were the farthest thing from his mind as he stepped from the rain-misted street onto the mostly-dry pavement of the bridge. Looking around at the sparsely populated setting, Liam confirmed what he'd determined yesterday when he had come to scope out the area. *This is a good place to kill someone, if you have to,* he thought as he glanced out at the water below. There was only one path of escape for either party and Liam hoped this mutual disadvantage would make Nadia Spencer and her crew weigh the potential consequences of their actions carefully before making any moves. In terms of survival, Liam figured the odds were as even as they could get, which was why he chose the bridge as the location for their meeting.

The two stocky men who walked slightly behind Nadia looked deceptively innocent as Liam and Alessandra approached them from the other side of the bridge. For most of their excursions, whether they were rescuing a Seer or gathering new resources for the Restoration project, a 1:1 Seer to non-Seer security team ratio was sufficient. But given the lack of clarity in their overall vision of how this day would unfold, Joel had wanted to make an exception to that rule for the meet-up with Nadia. Liam insisted that since this part of their visioning had been fairly clear, they needed to stick to the plan.

Standing beside Liam with a known Guild spy walking towards them, Alessandra could taste the adrenaline pooling in her mouth. She knew she was supposed to wait until they were closer together, but she just couldn't fathom letting someone who meant them so much harm get any closer.

"That's far enough," Alessandra declared, making sure her voice carried over the wind and the fifteen-foot distance that separated them. To her right, she could see Liam nod in agreement before he spoke.

"You — in the blue coat — start running."

Three pairs of feet halted in mid-step. Nadia's mouth fell open in a mixture of surprise, annoyance and a sudden certainty of danger. Though she hated to show it, she was clearly unprepared for the impromptu start of the interview she had been working to arrange for months. Nadia was used to being the one to catch people off-guard and didn't appreciate the element of surprise when it was turned against her.

"Wait!" Nadia called out as she tried to diffuse the situation, raising her hands to hip level in the most discreetly defensive manner she could manage. Nadia had only heard disjointed, second-hand accounts of what happened to the Guild's Purification Center in Chicago, but she understood enough to know that the distance between them was not nearly enough to protect her.

Handle this, Nadia, She told herself. *Just start talking. You can handle this.*

"We did everything you asked," she continued. "No one has followed us. My producer doesn't even know where I am and you have no idea how difficult *that* was to pull off. I... I don't understand. I just want to talk. I thought you guys wanted to tell your story."

What kind of people ambush a reporter in the middle of a bridge in broad...? Nadia's thoughts trailed off as she looked around, noticing for the first time the rapidly darkening clouds around them as rain began to come down in full force. Her throat went dry as she realized that she could count the number of people in her view on both hands with four fingers to spare. She couldn't remember now if she had passed anyone else on her way to the spot where she now stood.

And no one knows where I am, she thought as Nadia felt her stomach clench with fear. *This is perfect,* she thought. *They planned this perfectly.* Picking the less hostile of the two gazes before her, Nadia tried to match Alessandra's stare in a valiant effort to mask her panic. But before she could think up a way to gain the upper hand, Alessandra spoke.

"The man in the blue coat—he has 24 seconds before he gets shot in the head on this bridge. His intention was to shoot at least one of us already, but he suspects the cold isn't the real reason why my husband has his right hand in his jacket pocket. His plan after that was to kill each of you."

Nadia noticed two things then. The first was the slight smile on Liam's lips as he stared down the man she knew as Chuck, her brand new camera man from New Jersey. The second was the way Chuck rocked back on his heels, preparing to run. Her mind went blank with realization for only a second before she stammered out the only thing she could think.

"He's my camera man…" she offered feebly as she watched Chuck drop 40 lbs of camera equipment on the ground and take off down the bridge without uttering a single word.

"I…" For the first time in her life, Nadia was speechless. Chuck had come highly recommended from Ed, a trusted friend and her main cameraman for four years. When Ed had called in sick two days ago, he had recommended Chuck right away. She never even questioned it, but now, watching Chuck fade into the crowd, she wondered if Ed was even sick… or alive. Looking back at Alessandra and Liam, Nadia could only imagine how guilty and careless she must have looked for her association with this man who left her and her remaining cameraman, Ben, alone to face the consequences of his actions.

"We know you didn't have anything to do with him," Liam said to Ben, who was beginning to perspire and shake with fear. "He was sent by the Guild once your company found out about our interview. Pull yourself together. We need to move."

Nadia was still in a daze as she watched Liam grab Chuck's camera equipment and throw it over the bridge. She thought she heard Liam say the word "tracking," but she couldn't be sure.

Grateful that Liam made no move to throw her over the bridge with the camera equipment, Nadia added "I only told my producer."

But Liam's terse request for their phones finally snapped Nadia out of her daze, as she realized that she would be completely isolated from the world with no way of accessing help if she needed it. She barely noticed that she had been walking across the bridge until Liam stopped and looked at her expectantly.

When did Ben hand over his phone? She wondered as she saw his antiquated analog resting in Liam's large hand.

"But how…?"

"Now," was all he needed to say for her to finally understand that she had no choice.

She and Ben walked in silence to the black sedan with tinted windows that Liam and Alessandra led them to. But in the back of her mind, Nadia knew that if she was ever going to get the interview that she had apparently risked her life to get, she needed to begin regaining control of the situation. The black satin hood that Liam handed to her and Ben when they got into the back seat was not a good start.

"Are you serious? I'm sure you don't like being thought of as terrorists, but your methods make it hard to distinguish between..."

The look on Alessandra's face as she whirled around from the front passenger seat to face Nadia made her shut up and take the hood.

As she placed it over her head, wondering where this would lead, Nadia couldn't resist asking a question before she felt the car pull off.

"Why didn't you kill the other cameraman?"

There was a long pause before she heard Liam's voice.

"Because there's no point. They already have our location on the bridge. The tracker was in his camera bag. Leaving it there just buys us time. Your cameraman was only the first phase of their plan. We just need to get this interview over with before they find us—because they will find us."

"Is your need for publicity so great that you would risk your life for this interview?"

It was Nadia's first question and her attempt to regain control of the situation she had found herself in the minute she stepped on to the Oberbaum bridge to meet the infamous and elusive Joel Akida. Sitting in a warehouse, she meant to cause some disturbance in the calm, unwavering confidence that was too mature for the smoothness of his face. *He can't be more than 22, maybe 23 years old*, she'd surmised upon their meeting as she took the warm hand he offered her. Though she had him by at least 5 years, she didn't like the way his gaze made her feel like she'd suddenly regressed to the stature of a small child who knew nothing of the world around her. There was no malice or even condescension in his gaze as he met her stare, nothing to justify the faint feeling of defeat that nagged her, as if he knew things she would never know and could never hope to understand.

Nadia tried her best to keep the unease of all this from her face. She'd had too many surprises already today. Though she had done her research and combed over every piece of data she could find on this renegade band of Seers and their allies, her file was barely two folders deep. Between the Seers' ability to evade and the Guild's refusal to turn over any of their records on the first group of Seers who escaped, their rehabilitation efforts with the Seers still in their custody, or their current knowledge of the remaining fugitives, she had little background information. But she wasn't used to being the oldest person in the room with the least amount of control, so she did what she could, what she did best: to try to regain the upper hand.

And there was a moment, in the brief pause after her question and before Joel began to lean forward in his chair, when she thought she had won, but then he smiled the kindest, most indulgent smile she'd ever seen.

"I could say the same of you, Ms. Spencer. You've risked at least as much as I have to come here. But, no, it's not your attention I'm hoping for. It's your ability to tell our story that I am after. Your ability to tell the truth once you see it."

Nadia's saliva was suddenly thick in her throat as she swallowed. "And what truth is that?" she asked.

"That we are not what the Guild says. The Seers are nothing to be afraid of. We have been born with these abilities to serve this world, our world — to help lead all of us into a deeper understanding of our potential."

"Yes," Nadia answered coolly, "I've watched your tapes on YouTube. You're quite the sensation with over 10 million views. You claim that anyone is capable of doing what you can do. So what's stopping us, me, from seeing the future right now?"

"It takes training and an awakening of both your mind and your body on a genetic level, but — and this is why I wanted to talk with you — we believe that we have discovered a way to restore this genetic potential that has been dormant. We are testing it on our first group of volunteers right now. When we're successful, we can help anyone that wants to possess this ability."

Nadia almost dropped her mini-recorder. She couldn't believe what he was admitting — on camera. When she received the first response to her email indicating that he was willing to do the interview, she was thrilled but skeptical. She assumed he'd only wanted to use her for an "I'm not the bad guy" piece. But this was a real exclusive — breaking news from a never-before interviewed fugitive. Her ambition made her almost giddy as she leaned in carefully and tried to control the victorious smirk on her face. "You're testing this treatment... on humans? Right now?" she asked.

"Yes. As I said, we believe we can restore-" Joel began before Nadia interrupted him.

"You know, that's illegal. You're admitting to unsanctioned testing on humans with untested or verified treatments. You could go to jail for that." But just when she thought she'd cornered him, Joel's smile returned as he chuckled a little and leaned back in his chair.

"Me being alive and talking with you is illegal. I don't usually worry about what's illegal anymore."

"Is that because you think you're above the law? You're above what's right and wrong?" Nadia responded pointedly.

Nadia was pleased to see Joel seemed to take her question more seriously as he straightened up in his chair and met her gaze again. "In the world we live in, what's right and what's wrong is not the same as what is legal and illegal. It is legal to hold a human being indefinitely without their permission or consent because they have an extraordinary ability. Does that seem right to you, even though it is legal?

"The Guild claims that people like you are a danger to society. That if we break the quarantine- if released, Seers will…"

"Yeah, the quarantine," Joel began, shaking his head. It was the latest buzzword the Guild was using to describe the enslavement of every Seer in their possession. "In the last 20 years, have you ever heard of a crime committed by a Seer?"

"No, not until you," Nadia admitted, "but that just suggests the quarantine is working."

"Yes, but if I can wreak havoc as they say I have, why wouldn't other Seers, before they are captured, do the same if we are all inherently evil, as the Guild claims?" Nadia didn't have an answer for that, but she was determined not to lose her momentum.

"I think you're evading the question," she began in an attempt to redirect their discussion back to him. "Do you believe you are above the law?"

"I want… I seek to do what is right. It helps that I have the benefit and certainty of knowing that what I am doing is what I am meant to do, whether it is legal or not."

"And you believe God is telling you these things, showing you what you see? That you are tapped into some sort of Divine order, is that right?"

"Yes," Joel answered plainly.

"Well, I go to church almost every Sunday and I can't see the future. Am I going to the wrong church or something?"

Joel leaned in toward her again with a gravity of expression she had not seen in the 45 minutes since they met.

"It doesn't matter where you spend your Sundays. God *is* not what you say God is or even what you believe. God *is*. Don't confuse your perception with truth. What I'm connected to is not a religion. I'm talking about a connection to a source that unifies all living things—every single thing that exists. It is an ultimate truth, an infinite understanding."

"And how do we all find this enlightenment you're referring to? What makes you so special?"

"The only thing that makes us special is that we are the first. As I've said, anyone can do what we can do. We are working to unlock that potential right now."

"And then what? We'll become a race of people who can see the future."

"It would seem that we once were," Joel said distractedly as he looked towards Alessandra.

"What does that mean?" Nadia insisted as Joel rose slowly from his chair.

"How long do we have?" Liam asked.

"They are very close," Alessandra answered, shaking her head in an effort to see more clearly. "I can see them, but they are blocking me. I can't see the precise time. Ten minutes, maybe less."

Nodding his head, Joel reached out and hoisted Nadia up by the arm, lifting her completely from her chair. "I'm sorry, you need to go," was all he said before taking the recorder from her hand and bending down to gather her purse.

"What's happening? I'm not finished..." she began, but even as she talked Joel was securing her bag on her shoulder and helping the camera man repack his bags.

"This is not over," Nadia declared as she watched those around her prepare to leave. "I have *pages* of questions left for you to answer and we paid good money to come out here and get this interview, so if you think that I'm leaving here because you're paranoid, you've got another thing coming! I want the truth!" She was about to pull out her recorder again when Joel strode up to her and pushed her hand back in the bag.

"Don't drop this. You're going to need it," he said in a low voice. His voice was calm, but his eyes were nervous as they darted from her face to the front door of the small warehouse that surrounded them. Even though she was aware she should heed the wordless warning on his face, she had to ask, insist, one last time. "But I need to know," she said, with all the determination she could muster.

Joel looked at her for a long moment before nodding his head and speaking to her.

"If you seek the truth honestly, it will find you."

Nadia was about to ask him what the hell that meant when her train of thought was interrupted by the strange screeching sound of metal as it twisted and folded. In the next instant, she felt herself being forced to the ground. Bracing herself against the cold concrete floor, she looked up just in time to see the metal brackets that held the large steel door they had walked through peel back and fall away. For a second, the door seemed to levitate before it turned on its side, in mid-air, and launched in Joel's direction. Understanding immediately why she was pushed to the ground, Nadia followed the path of the projectile towards its intended target, who still stood beside her—exactly where she had last seen him. His body and attention were still pivoted towards her as she looked at him in panic — panic that she did not see reflected back in Joel's eyes. Before she could get out the scream that was bubbling up in her throat, hoping to tell him to "Run!" or "Get out of the way!" or any other direction that should have been obvious to someone so clearly under attack, it was too late. In her peripheral vision, she saw the sheet of metal about to collide with his body. As Joel finally turned towards it, so did she — just in time to see it rip in two as if sheared by a saw. Joel didn't blink as the sparks flew up from the metal being cut in half by an invisible point of intersection which appeared to be just inches away from Joel's steadily beating heart.

Nadia flinched as Joel discarded one of the newly unsoldered pieces of metal, without ever touching it, less than a foot from where she lay. Turning to her side, she could see the edges of the softened metal burn as it smoldered and smoked beside her. But she didn't have time to consider the impossibility of all that she had just witnessed. The sound of rapid footsteps drew her attention once more to the front entrance as five people dressed in red robes entered the warehouse.

CHAPTER 6: PLAYING WITH POWER

Even though it was their first true meeting, Joel already knew the five Seers standing before him well. He had watched Michael and Nina for almost a year before the Guild found them and he had been monitoring their progress closely ever since. As the most recent members of the Red Order, Pytor Ushakov and Aaron Mueller were the most tentative about their gifts and their involvement within the Guild despite their rapidly growing powers.

Of the five, these four had been recruited to The Red Order under the guise of protection from Joel and "his kind." Given what each of them had been told, it made sense to Joel that they would see their primary mission as standing against the man they believed sought to destroy them for his own gain. Only Tyrol Hammond, the fifth member of their group, had volunteered to join the Red Order out of his own desire for wealth and power.

By the stunned looks on their faces, Joel knew they were genuinely surprised by his effortless deflection of their assault. But the small victory gave him no pleasure. Almost everything they had been told about him was false. From Maura, Joel could see that Michael was the most upset as he believed that Joel was personally responsible for his beloved parents' death.

Look at how they hate us, Joel thought with a sadness he had not expected. *Look at what they think we've done.* Though he knew going into this the lies the Guild had told to secure their allegiance, facing the fury in their eyes made the depth of the Guild's deception and the sad irony of two groups of Seers pitted against each other more real.

Even with the sharp smell of static electricity gathering in the room, he still had to try.

"We are not your enemies," Joel began before Michael cut him off with the abrupt extension of his hand outward as he focused the electricity around them into a lightning spike that he then hurled toward Joel and those behind him.

Joel's left forearm came up reflexively, creating a protective shield out and around him to shelter the others from the blast. Alessandra was at his side in an instant.

"Get them out of here!" Joel whispered urgently to Alessandra as she watched the lightning streaks spread around the invisible shield Joel sustained. She hesitated for a moment, trying to see beyond the opaque in her mind. When no new vision emerged, she turned back to Liam. "Finish packing. I'm going to help Joel until you're ready."

Looking up at the lightning storm Joel held back, Liam understood that any weapons he possessed would be useless in this fight. "Be careful," he said solemnly before reaching down and pulling a limp and awestruck Nadia to her feet.

"Can you hold them?" Vincent asked as he and Ben backed away from the confrontation, faces alight with thunder.

"Yes. We'll be fine," Joel replied before he heard Michael's voice.

"More!" Michael shouted to his group as they raised their hands in unison. "Nina, help me!"

"I'm trying," Nina answered, already struggling to extend her power and help her brother. "He's stronger than we thought."

Alessandra raised her hand, prepared to deflect the surge of energy coming towards them, and help Joel maintain his shield, but a moment after feeling the initial increase in power, it was clear Joel could handle it by himself.

Why isn't this more... difficult? There's only two of us, she wondered to Joel in silent confusion as she watched the obvious strain the others were under to maintain their assault.

I don't know. Maybe it's the Luridium? It must still limit them. This isn't even close to what they are capable of, but they don't know it. They don't know how it works and there is no one to teach them, Joel replied.

Behind them, Liam hurried to finish packing up all of Nadia and Ben's equipment. He zipped up the last duffle bag just as the sparks from the electricity began burning holes in the corrugated roof. "We're ready," Liam announced tersely as clumps of hot metal fell from the roof and slid down the sides of Joel's shield. "What's the plan?"

"Joel can handle this until we get everyone out of the building," Alessandra answered, nodding to Joel for confirmation. When he nodded back, she continued, "But we should move now."

"I got no problems with that," Vincent said as the entire warehouse began to buckle and shake.

When Alessandra lowered her hand and turned to join Liam, she could hear Michael yell out again in frustration.

"We need to do something! We can't let them get away!" he shouted in a panic. But even as Michael tried to sound resolute, his body shook with a level of exhaustion he'd never experienced before. Watching Joel's undaunted stance through the sweat that poured into his eyes, it was clear to him that the Guild's training had not prepared them for what they were up against.

To the left of Michael, Tyrol was incensed. He had joined the Guild for one reason and one reason only, to become a god. And with the Guild's training, that is exactly what Crane told him he would become. He'd undergone months of discipline and training to learn how to extend his sight beyond anything he ever imagined possible. Coming to Berlin, he felt invincible. To find himself and the other members of the Red Order bested by only one man was beyond his comprehension. But even worse than being out-matched was the ease with which Joel held them back with a look on his face that was too close to pity for Tyrol to tolerate.

"Push harder! We have to push," he roared. "Don't let him win!"

And in a last-ditch effort to somehow prevail, the members of the Red Order pushed their own shield outward so that it touched Joel's—establishing an immediate fissure and an opening from one shield to the other. Even in his exhaustion, Tyrol cracked a smile.

Though the fracture in Joel's shield made no sound, Alessandra could feel the tear in the frantic pounding of Joel's heart as it echoed through the Collective and into her. Alessandra gasped as she looked up towards the ceiling to see more cracks begin to divide and separate the shield around them.

"Joel!" Alessandra shouted as she began to run towards him.

Though he did not turn around, Joel could feel Alessandra's approach. Not understanding what was happening or why, he did the only thing he could to protect what was most important. "Liam, stop her!" he shouted as he began to struggle to pull back his shield from theirs as they disintegrated together. "You have to go NOW! I can't -I don't know if I can stop this!"

"What's happening?" Liam shouted as he let go of Nadia just in time to catch Alessandra around the waist and hold her back.

"I don't know! I don't know!" Joel yelled back just before he heard Alessandra's scream.

"No! No!" It was all she could manage as her vision of what Tyrol had planned came sharply into view.

The movement was slight and seemingly insignificant in the chaos and rubble that surrounded them. Tyrol extended his right hand as if holding a paper cup and squeezed his fingers together tightly.

Ben fell to the ground instantly, so overwhelmed with pain that the only sign of his agony was the blood vessel bursting through the white of his left eye. Understanding what she saw and had tried to prevent, Liam eased his grip, allowing Alessandra to run to Ben's side. Looking up to see the lightening streaks around them subside, it only took Liam a second to catch up with the new reality of their situation. *We're not going anywhere now*, Liam thought as he pulled his gun from the back of his jeans and ran to help Alessandra move Ben and take cover.

As if the dull sound of Ben's body hitting the floor had woken her from a long stupor, Nadia was suddenly reanimated as she stood at Liam's side, staring in wide-eyed horror at the newly concave shape of Ben's chest. "What happened to him? What's happening?!" she screamed as she was lifted over Vincent's shoulder. "Put me down! What's happening?"

"Lady!" Vincent began as he dumped her unceremoniously on the ground behind a stack of metal barrels. "If you don't stop screaming in my ear, I swear to God, you're going to be the first woman I've ever hit in my life. It's going to hell and we're trying to save your life, so please do me a favor and shut the hell up!"

Ever since Joel had pushed her to the ground, Nadia felt like she was in a daze, unable to believe or comprehend the things happening around her. But Vincent's words cleared any confusion from her mind. She was immediately sobered by the knowledge that she might not make it out of *whatever* was happening alive. Not wanting to distract Vincent from his efforts with an argument, Nadia decided to do exactly what he said—for now. Instead, she peeked out from behind Vincent's back enough to see Liam and Alessandra dragging Ben by the collar of his jacket behind a large set of rusted metal crates at the opposite side of the room. Ben made no sound as they moved him. If not for the sporadic convulsing of his chest, there would have been no sign that he was still alive.

● • ·· • ●

With each millimeter Joel tried to pull back from the Red Order, he could feel himself drawing nearer, his mind becoming one with theirs. He wasn't sure how much he would be able to block them from within the forced Quorum their shields were creating and he couldn't—wouldn't—risk exposing the others.

Alessandra, what's happening? Joel asked as his mind ached for clarity. *I'm trying so hard to hold on, I can barely see.*

His heart, lungs, ribs, intestines, everything. They're all torn, broken. I'm going to try to heal him. He can't die. His daughters won't survive without him.

Unwilling to take his focus away from maintaining his shield as long as he could, Joel could only catch glimpses of the vision Alessandra was trying to share, but it was enough. *Yes, I see it, too. Do what you have to, but I need to disconnect. I am being drawn into them and I can't risk us, our plans…*

I feel it, too, Katia said from within the Collective. *But we can help. You don't have to do this alone. I'm ready. Jared and I will block from here.* Flashes of Marcus falling to his death in Chicago threatened to cloud her mind, but she fought it back as best she could.

Katia, Joel began, feeling her fear, her guilt. *I know you're thinking of my father, but this doesn't feel like dying. The strain I feel is because I'm resisting this pull. I don't know. This is something different. I need you to block not just them; I need you to block me, too.*

The implications of what Joel was asking her to do were not lost on anyone. Joel's superiority in visioning and blocking were well-known within the Collective. Only Katia and Jared could match him, but no one had ever tried to block him out.

I won't fight it, Joel tried to reassure her. *I know you can do this.*

Don't let them down. There's no time for doubt, Katia reminded herself. *Do now what you couldn't do then.* She didn't respond until she was sure she could focus, sure she could do what Joel asked. *I will*, Katia responded stoically. *I'm stronger now. I won't fail. We will protect the Collective from here.*

Joel, I'll go with you. Lilli interjected. *I'll hide myself from them like you did with me,* referring to the first time Joel had ever contacted her during their Quorum in Iowa.

From the conviction in her heart, Joel knew Lilli would not be dissuaded, and truthfully he had no mental energy to spare to convince her otherwise. The space between him and the Red Order was moments from complete disintegration, drawing them inexplicably together. But as hard as he tried, he could not understand why, against his will, all his energy was being drawn inward, towards this connection with the Red Order. He'd never fought another Seer this way. He'd never had to.

"Hang in there, man. Just… try, ok? Hang in there." Liam couldn't bring himself to say it was going to be alright. From the hollowed out look of Ben's chest, he had serious doubts that it would be. But it was all Liam could think to say as he tilted Ben's head gently to drain some of the blood pooling in his mouth. He was buying time—waiting for Alessandra to finish communicating with Joel, his sister, and the others in their Collective. And hoping they had better news for this man than imminent death. As he spoke to Ben in confident, reassuring tones, he watched Alessandra move her hands over Ben's torso with a light touch that seemed even gentler given how tightly her eyes were shut and the deep grimace that contorted her lovely features. When she finally opened her eyes a moment later, revealing a steady, determined gaze, Liam understood not only what she had done, but what she was planning to do.

"Can you do it?" Liam whispered as he felt the fading thread of Ben's pulse.

"Yes," she replied, more out of hope than certainty. "But you need to move back."

She placed her right hand three inches above Ben's heart, which caused his body to jolt upward as if inexplicably drawn to her hand. He remained suspended in that position for several moments before he finally collapsed onto the ground. Just as before, there was barely any sign that Ben was conscious until tears slipped from the corners of his eyes and his lips began to make the shape of words with no sound. The silence allowed Liam to detect the start of a strange noise—like small pebbles being turned in a jar—emanating from inside Ben's body as Alessandra spread her hands across Ben's rib cage. Slowly, Liam realized that he was listening to the sound of bones being gathered and assembled. The noise he heard became louder, culminating in a few muted cracking sounds, before the top four ribs on each side of Ben's torso snapped back into place.

The three witnesses to this miracle of healing shared a quiet moment of disbelief before it was shattered by Ben's voice screaming out in pure agony. The sound echoed off the walls and vibrated through Liam's entire body, making him shudder uncontrollably. But when he looked to Alessandra, her posture remained rigid as she hovered over Ben. There was no sign that she had even heard Ben's cries, except for the fact that her hands were now trembling and sweat was beginning to gather on her forehead despite the chill in the room.

"Hey — you ok?" Liam asked, but she didn't answer. She was so deep into her meditation that to Liam she seemed completely disconnected from her surroundings. His instincts drew him closer as he wrapped his arm around her waist to keep her steady.

We don't even know how this works, he thought as he watched her reassemble the rest of Ben's ribcage. With the clearing of bone and blood from his lungs, Ben used his unrestricted access to air to start begging.

"Please, please, please…" he whimpered.

By the time both lungs were re-inflated, Alessandra was drenched in sweat and gasping for her own breath. Her skin under Liam's touch began to feel cold.

"Alessandra, stop! Stop this now. You can't do anymore," Liam spoke roughly into her ear. When she didn't respond, he tried to physically drag her away, but her body was like lead, rooted in place by her own will. She had made her decision.

"Don't do this, baby. You can't do this!" he said, leaning his body into hers, hoping to reach her, to pull her back. Her skin was turning sallow and grey before his very eyes. When she didn't respond, he knew her mind had gone to a place he couldn't reach or follow.

Lilli, stop her. Don't let her do this. Please, Liam begged, trying in desperation to use the connection that Lilli said she had with him — to sense his consciousness, to read his thoughts.

He didn't have to wait for a response. When he heard Lilli's voice, it was as if she was standing right over his shoulder.

We won't let her die, Liam. Just be with her, she hears you. She just can't talk. She can't break the connection. We're trying to give her our energy.

Enough for him to become stable, so he can make it to a hospital. Right now, he's still too damaged, Lilli explained quickly. *Trust her, Liam.*

And he tried, but when she began wheezing it was hard to believe that he wasn't going to lose her. But she couldn't speak or reassure him of what he hoped to hell she knew for sure, that she would survive this. He didn't know that a continent away in a warehouse in London, half the Collective members were on their knees, just to give Alessandra the strength to continue. So he held her tighter — sharing his warmth as he fought his own fears and listened to the sounds… of bits of bone rolling, cracking and snapping into place, of Ben begging, yelling, whimpering in unimaginable pain, and of Alessandra's slowing heartbeat as she risked her life to guard the future of two little girls by saving their father — a man she'd just met.

The slow shuffling sound of Ben's body as he rolled himself tentatively from his back to his side was new and loud in Liam's eardrums, causing his head to snap up from where it had been pressed against the side of Alessandra's head. In complete shock, Liam watched as Ben extended his shaking limbs to the floor and managed to kneel for a few seconds before lowering his head back down to the ground.

Almost immediately, Alessandra fell back into Liam's arms. With her eyes closed and her breath shallow, she said nothing as Liam stared into her face for only a moment before crushing her body to his.

Liam cradled her limp body in his arms for what felt like an eternity. He knew she was alive, but in what state or for how long, he had no idea. Despite the vise of his hold, she made no effort to resist him or seek more room to breathe. As the seconds ticked on, Liam could feel the panic he had been trying to keep at bay burst forth from the pit of his stomach. The first of his tears were about to fall just as Alessandra's fingers found the strength to grip the front of his shirt and hold on tight.

Above the sound of his own heart beating out relief, Liam could just hear Ben's voice as he whispered, "Thank you. Thank you for saving my life."

Joel could feel it the moment his connection with the Collective was severed. Katia was blocking him and though his mind felt strangely void, he'd never been so grateful for her strength. Lilli, on the other hand, was ever-present. He only hoped the others could not sense her.

Without the filter of their shields, Joel was immediately bombarded with the chaos of their thoughts as they began yelling at him and each other.

You tricked us!

How- how did he do that? He's in our Quorum!

I can't block him. I can't.

What the fuck?! What the fuck?!

He's unprotected, Tyrol thought smugly as he stepped towards Joel with unrestrained malice.

So are you, Lilli whispered back. The distraction of her watery image appearing before Tyrol was all Joel needed to land the kind of punch that would effectively eject Tyrol from the Quorum. With his mind unconscious and his body no longer within the protective shield that surrounded the newly formed Quorum, Tyrol lay vulnerable and open to the very real threat that Vincent now posed.

Stunned that one of their own could be taken out so quickly, Michael immediately prepared to strike.

Stop! Joel said, holding out his slightly swollen hand. It had been awhile since he'd been in a fist fight—not since he'd had to pound his way through bully after bully in secondary school—but the burn in his knuckles was still familiar. And though he was sure he could handle himself with Michael, it was not his goal. So he tried to reason with

Michael again. *You can hear my mind. You know I did not come here to harm him or any of you. Use your gift. Calm yourself and hear me.*

In Quorum, truth could be obscured, but not denied. Carefully, Joel opened up the parts of his mind that were not blocked by Katia and Jared and waited for the others to accept what they already knew.

Realizing that they were on equal footing with Joel for the first time since they arrived, Nina decided to use the opportunity to get some answers to her questions. *Who was the girl who appeared? How did she do that?* Nina asked tentatively.

Her name is Lilith. She is my wife and is one of the Seers you've been trying to hunt. We're not what you think and despite what you've been told, I didn't kill your parents, Joel answered, looking from Nina to Michael.

Though the truth of Joel's words was undeniable, it did not soothe the bitterness Michael carried over the loss of his family and the realization that he had been lied to about exactly who was to blame. But Nina cared less about resolving the past than she did about finding out why they had been lied to in the first place.

Why are you stronger than we are? She continued. *How did you learn to shield yourself from all of us like that? We were told that we were more powerful. That was the reason why you're after us.*

I'm not sure. My power was discovered and learned freely. You are still captive. Your gift is still being manipulated –

We're not captives, Michael seethed, still angry and unwilling to let go. "We came to the Guild to escape you! They're helping us do what you can't!"

"Do you honestly believe that… even now?" Joel answered aloud.

"Crane told us that you would lie," Michael spat. "That you would do anything to use us."

"Why should we trust you?" Pytor asked with weary eyes.

"I don't need to convince you," Joel said softly. "While there are things I can hide from you, that I *am* hiding from you, Quorum is not a place where lies can be told. You know this. Beyond that, you will have to find your own truth. After this, you will have an opportunity."

Pausing for a moment to hear Lilli's warning, he added, "But I believe Alessandra has repaired the damage done by your "team member," as you think of him, and it's time to go before the real enemies come."

She healed him? Aaron thought in surprise.

Joel didn't answer. He didn't need to.

Can you do that? Nina asked.

No, Joel replied. *Our gifts are all different.*

Могу ли это сделать? *Can I do that?* Pytor wondered in Russian, remembering his childhood dream of becoming a doctor.

I don't know, Joel replied honestly. *I hope you get the chance to answer that question for yourself.* Before they could continue, the static from Nina's radio interrupted their conversation.

"Is the area secure?" a clipped male voice grumbled from the walkie-talkie hanging at her belt. The four remaining members of the Red Order had no answer as they looked at Joel while listening to a directive that no longer seemed applicable.

"I repeat — is the area secure? Do you have the Seers?"

Nina took a moment to take in her surroundings. Outside of the peaceful cocoon of their Quorum, she could see Nadia helping Ben ease to his feet while Liam hoisted Alessandra up into his arms as he made his way to a black sedan that was parked just outside the open back door. He paused at the threshold until Vincent appeared in the doorway from outside.

"All clear," she heard him say with a smirk.

"You sure?" Liam asked, bringing Alessandra's resting body a little closer to his chest.

"I was as quiet as a mouse. Guys with guns I can handle." Vincent's smile broadened as he thought about the dead bodies he deposited behind the recycling dumpster. In truth, he was just happy to get back in the action.

With a nod of Liam's head, Nina watched as he and Alessandra disappeared from her sight, followed by Nadia and Ben, who leaned heavily on Nadia as he mounted the back of a motorcycle.

"Hold up," Vincent shouted over his shoulder to Ben before Nina watched him jog back into the warehouse. "Forgot one."

To her far left, Nina watched as Tyrol emerged from unconsciousness just in time to be greeted by the barrel of a riffle. The look of disappointment on Vincent's face was unmistakable as he glanced over to Joel just before pulling the trigger and found him shaking his head in disapproval. In a daze, Tyrol reached out for Vincent, but he wasn't quick enough. In two swift motions, Vincent broke his nose and bashed the side of Tyrol's head in with the butt of his rifle, knocking him unconscious for the second time. Nina found she didn't really care. She'd never liked Tyrol that much anyway. Afterward, Vincent simply turned his back on The Red Order and walked away.

He didn't even glance back, she noted wistfully as she realized the truth. *With Joel here, we're no threat to him.* The feeling of powerlessness was sobering. Turning back to Joel, the exchange between them was silent but understood. There would be no alliance, but the fighting was over between them—for today. The truce would extend for as long as it took for Joel and the others to leave.

As their Quorum ended, Joel bid them a silent goodbye before turning toward the back door. Nina took her time lifting the receiver from its holster. She hesitated a moment longer before answering. "Yes, the area is secure, but we don't have the Seers. They are gone." She didn't know what to expect next. None of them did, but the sound of shouting and gunfire still took them by surprise as 3 men rushed through the door behind them and began firing at Joel while the others drove off. Pytor, Aaron, Nina, and Michael watched in silence as the Guild's gunman fired their weapons uselessly at Joel's shield, which stood as strong as ever against their assault. Amidst the futile expense of ammunition, Nina was surprised to see a large man in weathered clothing emerge from behind them. Although she did not know him, she recognized his face as one of the two men she had seen at her first and only Guild Council presentation. Given that she had not seen him before or since, and had not heard a vehicle pull up against the gravel road to announce his coming, she had no idea how or why he was now in Berlin.

"This is useless," the man stated in a thick accent Nina could not place. "Keep him occupied. I will pursue the others myself."

Nina stood in place for a while longer, watching the valiant efforts of the Guild's security detail go completely to waste before she turned and walked out into the rain. Without the same certainly of mission and purpose that she'd possessed when she first entered the warehouse, Nina felt bare, with only questions and suspicions taking the place of all the facts she thought she knew. Nina stared absently at the two large SUVs in which they had arrived for a long time before she noted the lack of tread marks to the left or right of their vehicles. With a heavy sigh, she thought again about the people she had just let escape, the people that she'd thought of as enemies a mere hour ago, and allowed herself one last question before she let her eyes close in exhaustion— how did the large man she had just seen plan to pursue two different vehicles going in opposite directions on foot?

Chapter 7: Person, Place, or Thing

Watching Vincent take a sharp turn as he accelerated out of sight, Nadia couldn't keep from worrying. The only friend she had in this godforsaken situation was speeding away from her. She watched helplessly as Ben weighed down the back of Vincent's motorcycle, holding on for dear life—a life he had just gotten back.

Nadia had thought it was a bad idea from the beginning. She wanted Ben to ride with her, but Vincent had insisted that they needed to split up.

"I'm taking him to the hospital and *you* need to be on the move. They didn't just come here for the Seers, they came here for this tape," he insisted. As if to prove his point, Vincent banged his hand once on the side of the hard case that held their camera equipment before carefully placing it in the trunk of Liam's sedan. Their conversation was interrupted by the sound of Ben throwing up blood and bile over the side of the bike he was trying to mount. Vincent prided himself on being a man who could handle almost anything, but the smell of vomit wasn't one of them. Watching Ben double over for the second time, Vincent tried not to let his squeamishness show.

"Hey! I can't have you throwing up on me while I'm ridin'. I'm serious. You gotta hold that shit down 'til we get to the hospital."

"This isn't going to work," Nadia tried. "He can't even…"

"I'm fine," Ben said, holding his left side gingerly. "I can make it. I must have swallowed a lot of blood before, but I can make it. I swear."

Before she could say another word, Liam emerged from the passenger seat, where he had just finished buckling in a very weak Alessandra. Slamming the trunk closed from behind Vincent, his jaw was tight as he looked Nadia in the eye and said in a tone that left no room for discussion, "Get in the car. We're leaving now."

As soon as they pulled off, a heavy rain began to fall, effectively erasing Ben's outline from her line of sight.

"Which hospital will they take him to?" Nadia asked quietly, not expecting anyone to answer.

"Maura is... we're checking now," Liam explained. "We'll text Vincent the hospital once we're sure which one is safe."

"Reading text messages while riding a speeding motorcycle in the rain... that's smart," Nadia scoffed.

Liam opened his mouth to respond before shutting it abruptly. What he wanted to say would have shamed his mother from the grave, and what he wanted to do just wasn't possible while driving 120 miles an hour. Sensing his rage, Alessandra put her hand on Liam's leg and swallowed the faint taste of blood in her mouth before addressing Nadia.

"He'll make it," she said softly. "His injuries are healed, but his body is still bruised from the impact. He just needs time and rest."

It took a moment for Alessandra's words to sink in, but once it did, Nadia found it easier than she would have thought to let go of some of her worry and return to reporter-mode. At the very least, it was a welcome distraction to keep the shock at bay over what she had just witnessed and survived. Turning around slowly in her seat, Nadia fumbled for the mini-recorder and notepad in her purse while asking as casually as she could, "How did you do that, by the way? Heal him? I haven't come across any reports of Seers being able to do that."

Leaning forward to ensure better sound quality, Nadia noted that though Alessandra's eyes were closed, she also looked better, and the color was returning to her skin. *I should take a picture*, Nadia thought as she reached for her phone, but before she could take the shot, she caught Liam looking at her in his rearview mirror with a deadly glance that made her think twice. She put the phone away before adding meekly, "If you don't mind answering a few questions, of course..."

Alessandra's chuckle was faint as she licked her dry lips. "Don't let Liam frighten you. His looks don't actually kill you."

Nadia let out a nervous laugh but said nothing in response.

"Have you always been able to heal people or did Marcus Akida, Joel's father, teach you that as well?"

"No. It's something new I discovered recently." Though Alessandra knew this interview was necessary, she still didn't trust Nadia with any more information than was absolutely necessary.

"So no one in the Guild knows that you can do this?"

"No," Alessandra replied cautiously.

"What other abilities are you all hiding?"

Even in her exhaustion, Alessandra's temper could still be awakened. "We aren't hiding anything!" she snapped. "They are the ones that force us to live like this! Why would you even say that?"

Not wanting to lose what little goodwill she had gained, Nadia tried to back peddle. "I'm sorry. I don't mean to upset you, it's just from my notes here, it says that you and your... ah, mentor, Marcus, made a practice of hiding your gifts from the Guild. As I understand it, that's how you escaped."

"We did what we had to—to survive," Alessandra explained. "It's not how you make it sound. We weren't free to explore our gifts. Before Marcus, I didn't even know who I was. He gave that back to me. He gave me this life that I have now." It was hard to say his name without tearing up, but Alessandra didn't want to cry, not in front of this woman.

And he wasn't my mentor, she wanted to add. *He was my father. The only father I ever really had.* But she kept silent, because Nadia didn't need to know how deeply his death affected her.

"I see," Nadia added, noting the sudden tightness around Alessandra's eyes before returning to her notes. "He died in Chicago, is that correct? What killed him, by the way? They never recovered a body from the scene."

They don't know, Alessandra realized with surprise before exchanging a glance with Liam.

"We don't know," Alessandra lied smoothly, but Nadia wasn't so sure.

"How could you not know," she began before the roof of the car buckled in on her with a loud crash, bringing sharp metal down to the hairline of her blonde-brown roots and splitting the delicate skin open.

Besides the sound of Nadia's screams, there was no time to speak as Liam instinctively slammed on the brakes, causing the car to skid out and swing sideways in the downpour. Realizing his mistake, Liam eased off the brake as he pushed in the clutch and began turning the wheel in the opposite direction of the skid.

Though he managed to keep the car from going into a complete tailspin, their speed made it impossible to avoid a side collision with the low concrete barrier that separated the incoming lane from the outgoing traffic. The trunk of their car took the brunt of the impact as they crashed then bounced back from the barrier.

When they finally came to a stop, Alessandra and Liam's eyes were wild as they turned their gazes from the torrential rain outside their windows towards each other.

"What was that?" Alessandra whispered.

Other than the sound of Nadia rifling through her purse to find something to stop the bleeding, the car was silent.

"Did I hit something?" he wondered aloud, but even as he said it he knew it didn't make any sense. There was no front impact. *No matter how fast I was going, I would have felt or seen something*, he reasoned.

"Of course, you hit something! I'm *bleeding*!" Nadia cried from the backseat, but Liam and Alessandra ignored her as they continued to try to discern if and how they could be in danger.

Outside their car, the rain came down like a pale silver sheet, making it difficult to see anything farther than ten feet in front of them. With their car stopped and perpendicular to the road, they were in a dangerous position. Except from what they could see, the area was deserted.

"I'm gonna check outside just to be sure," Liam said, as he reached for his door handle. Alessandra's grip on his arm was stronger than anything he expected from her as she halted his movement.

"What is it? Do you see something?"

"I don't... I don't know." Alessandra admitted with growing concern. "I just don't want you to go out there."

"I'll be right back," Liam promised, soothing her hand on his arm until Alessandra loosened her grip.

Stepping out of the car with the hoodie from inside his jacket over his head, Liam checked the roof first. To his surprise, the entire roof was sunken in with scratch marks radiating outward from the center of impact. Running his hand quickly over the imprint, he could feel that it was slightly deeper in the back, where he presumed Nadia had been hit.

But other than the indent, there was no residue on the car or debris in the road to indicate what had caused the damage. Before opening his car door, Liam took a quick glance at the front of the car to confirm what he already suspected — there was no sign of a head-on collision of any kind.

Liam had been out of the car for less than a minute, but by the time he returned to his seat, he was soaked.

"Did you find anything?" Alessandra asked anxiously.

"Nothing," he replied in confusion as he shook his jacket out and put the car in gear. "It doesn't make any sense."

"Well, something hit us," Nadia said angrily, keeping her cashmere scarf pressed firmly to her forehead. Watching the speedometer climb rapidly as Liam pulled off, she was just about to suggest that they slow down when they heard the faint echo of a high-pitched screech that was just loud enough to cut through the heavy downpour of the rain.

Liam stepped on the gas a little harder as he reached for the rearview mirror, adjusting it in an attempt to try to get a clearer view.

"Do you see anything?" Liam asked Alessandra.

"Nothing… nothing, just darkness," she whispered back with her eyes shut tightly. "Darkness coming towards us."

Less than an hour had passed since Nadia had witnessed at least half a dozen things that defied basic laws of physics and human anatomy, so she didn't know what to make of the sound that now had her on her knees and pressed desperately against the back windshield of the car — hoping to find a logical and non-threatening explanation.

"There's nothing out there," she proclaimed in relief. "I don't see anything."

Nadia was just about to turn back around in her seat when she saw it — just a black dot far out in the distance of the rain — a dot that had not been there a second ago but was now growing larger as it came toward them, quickly.

"Maybe it's Ben..." Nadia offered hopefully. "Maybe they turned around to meet us."

Grabbing his phone to call Vincent, Liam wanted to believe it. But his hope was short-lived as he looked down to see the text exchanges between Vincent and Maura which established that Vincent was well on his way to the hospital.

Confirmation came all at once as Liam refocused his attention on the rearview to see that the little black dot had grown and expanded outward as it accelerated towards them.

"That's no motorcycle," Liam realized just as Alessandra emerged from her vision of their entire car being swallowed up in darkness to yell, "Go! Go!"

Liam floored it, grateful for the deserted road that allowed him to drive without restraint. A tense silence surrounded them as they raced forward. Outside, the sound of the rain came in pulses of silence then heavy pounding as they sped through the series of overpasses that were spread out intermittently along the road. At 150 miles per hour, Liam was dangerously close to the limits within which his vehicle could operate safely, but he couldn't stop, not as long as whatever it was behind them was in pursuit.

"Can you see it?!" Liam yelled, facing forward with both hands on the wheel. "What is it?"

"I can't make it out," Nadia shouted back. "It's like a small plane or a helicopter maybe, but it doesn't make any sense. It's flying too low."

Taking another quick glance at his rearview, Liam shook his head. "It's too wide for a helicopter. Besides, what pilot would be stupid enough to fly in this weather?" Nadia didn't have an answer as she tracked the object with growing fear.

From the passenger seat, Alessandra had returned to the Collective as they fought to understand the blind spot in their sight.

Through their vision, they could see Liam's car and the stretch of road they were on clearly, as if they were there, but they could not see the presence that was behind them. Only Maura was able to visualize their pursuer as a dark presence that could be sensed, but not seen. Jared wondered if the Guild could be using some kind of drone or cloaking device as a new weapon against them.

Outside of their Quorum, Lilli worked frantically with Hannah and Kyle to access any satellite imagery that could help them identify what was after them, but they weren't able to pick up anything beyond the same oddly shaped object that Liam saw through his rearview.

In order to keep her senses attuned to her physical surroundings, Alessandra kept her mind slightly apart from the Collective as they focused their energy on overcoming this new limitation in their sight. The separation allowed her the unintended benefit of being able to view the vast amount of information within the Collective with a higher level of objectivity. It was this distance that gave her the insight she needed to see the simple truth that had escaped them.

Opening her eyes, Alessandra's voice shook as she shared her realization.

"It's not a thing that's pursuing us. It's a person."

"That's impossible," Liam countered. "I'm almost at 200 miles an hour. Nothing can move that fast on its own."

Knowing what Liam said was true only brought tears of dread to her eyes as she turned to face him and repeated.

"It's not a thing…"

Liam eased up on the gas as lightly as his panic would allow. They were headed towards the fourth underpass in the road and he needed to slow down and think, if only for a few seconds. In the same moment, he checked his rearview mirror again and saw the black form pursuing them suddenly make a 90 degree turn, straight up into the air and disappear. Despite his better judgment, he allowed himself a moment of relief. *With any luck*, he thought, *whatever it is will simply fly right over us.*

"It's gone. It's gone," Nadia shouted in disbelief as she stared out of the back windshield. "Where did it go?" Before she could reposition herself on the backseat to get a better view of the sky, Liam had pulled beneath the overpass and come to a complete stop.

Liam had no idea where "it" had gone, but he couldn't think about that with the car running at a standstill and temporarily hidden in the dark of the underpass with a blanket of rain hanging over them on either side of the bridge.

Turning towards Alessandra, he asked the only question on his mind.

"They don't know what this is, do they?"

"No," she said, in the same shaky voice as she took his hand.

"Then how do you know it's a person?"

"Because of Maura... if it was some-*thing*, she wouldn't be able to see its light. It wouldn't have an aura. She sees its darkness as all-consuming; there is nothing around it. Just darkness."

Liam wanted to think it through, to reason with Alessandra, but he couldn't. His instincts told him he didn't have time for that. They needed to get moving.

"Ok then." It was all he could manage as he prepared to shift the gears back into drive.

"Aaah, what are we doing here?" Nadia asked in renewed irritation. "Shouldn't we be getting out of here?"

Glancing into his rearview, Liam's gaze was drawn past Nadia's angry face to the long shadow that crept down and expanded out from somewhere on the bridge above them, unseen by Alessandra and Nadia as they waited for his response. Liam pressed his lips together to contain his fear as he shifted the car into reverse and stepped on the gas.

The sound they heard on impact with their pursuer was loud enough to rattle the windows—half-screech, half-roar and wholly terrifying, like no sound they'd ever heard. The next sound was Nadia scream as the back windshield shattered around her and she crashed into the back of Alessandra's chair before falling limply onto the backseat floor.

At first, Liam did nothing, as he felt the car slide into a tailspin, hoping that the momentum would shake off their attacker. But the weight and breadth of whoever was on top of their car had shifted their center of gravity to the point where the wheels of their car were losing traction as they lifted off the pavement. Alessandra stayed pinned down to her seat. Her mouth slowly opened as she looked out of her window to catch a glimpse of their attacker only to find that it was completely covered by something dark brown-black and littered with fine rips and tears, like a thick worn leather tarp.

Meanwhile, Liam was struggling to regain control of the car as it continued to spin. He had just fastened his grip on the wheel when out of the corner of his eye he saw what looked like a charred heel smash through his window and anchor its clawed foot to the doorframe.

The sight of it broke Liam's voice free in a hoarse whisper. "My God… Oh my God…"

The unfamiliar sound of Liam's fear drew Alessandra's attention away from her window to find out what had caused him to gasp in terror. Panic seized her heart as she saw the foot and realized that she was too weak to fight whatever had them in its grip. Helplessly, she turned from the sight of Liam frantically trying to keep them from crashing to the sound of Nadia screaming out again, this time in agony.

By the time Alessandra shifted her attention, Nadia was face-down and slumped over the backseat with two gashes across her back. The rain poured in from the open back windshield, diluting the blood that seeped from Nadia's wounds onto the pale blue pinstripe of her silk blouse.

As if in a daze, Alessandra watched as Nadia clung to the backseat with one hand while the other flailed around on the car floor. Worried that she had gone into shock, Alessandra crawled to her knees and reached for Nadia in the spinning car, only to have Nadia pull away as her hand grasped the object she sought.

Nadia pushed the red button on her mini-recorder as soon as she had it securely in her grasp. With the searing pain in her back, she didn't dare raise her body up. So she let the side of her face hang over the backseat as she prepared to give what she believed to be her final news report.

"This is Nadia Spencer reporting live from somewhere outside of Berlin, Germany. I came here to interview Joel Akida, the man at the top of the UWO's most wanted list, but we were attacked before I could finish and now our car is spinning out of control and I'm bleeding and I can't see anything." Nadia thought her voice sounded rushed, but oddly in control given how terrified she was. In spite of her own hysteria, the evidence of her hardwired training caused Nadia to burst out in a brief spurt of laughter, before she squeezed her eyes closed and continued. "I don't know if this is a set-up or what, but we're under attack and… I'm not *with* these people. I haven't done anything wrong. And… as I said, we're under attack. Something's trying to kill me and I don't think I'm going to make it out alive."

Just above Nadia, Alessandra's outstretched hand was frozen in mid-air as worry gave way to disbelief and disgust as she registered Nadia's words. *I'm not with these people. I haven't done anything wrong.*

"Are you crazy?" Alessandra screamed, leaning farther out of her seat to try to grab the recorder from Nadia. "Are you fucking insane?!"

"Alessandra! Get Down!" Liam shouted as he yanked her back into her seat just before he began swerving the car left and right in a mad attempt to throw their attacker off the roof.

Alessandra's eyes were still seething as they stared back at Nadia, who was now clutching the recorder to her chest with white knuckles. It was only as Nadia spoke that her tears began to soften the whites of her eyes.

"I don't want to die," she whispered through trembling lips. "Please, I don't want to die here."

Pity overwhelmed Alessandra as she looked at Nadia and finally understood that this was just her way of holding on, of handling her fear.

"We'll be all right," Alessandra promised, reaching out to cover Nadia's trembling fingers and the recorder with her own slightly more steady hand. "You have to believe it."

From the driver's seat, the exchange between Nadia and Alessandra was non-existent. Liam's only focus was getting them out of there alive. What he needed to know was how, with the rain coming down and the car twisting and swerving, the attacker on top of their car still managed to keep his hold. Liam could hear his weight across the roof of the car as it bent and buckled the metal. *Anyone would have fallen off by now*, Liam reasoned. *He must be at least 250 pounds.* But as much as Liam needed answers, he knew his first priority was keeping his panic at bay. So he refused to even glance at the strange foot that remained wedged in his doorframe.

It was during one of Liam's particularly sharp turns that their attacker began using that same foot to kick Liam in the face. The first blow was tentative, as if just trying to feel out Liam's position, but the second kick nearly knocked Liam unconscious as his body fell into Alessandra and caused him to momentarily lose his grip on the wheel. The right side of the car began to lift.

The sensation of the car floating off the road was secondary to the feeling of Liam's weight crashing into her while she was still turned towards Nadia. Understanding immediately what was happening, Alessandra sprang into action, crossing behind Liam to grab the wheel and pull it left just in time to bring all four wheels back on the ground.

"Liam!" she screamed, as she struggled to shift her weight more fully into the driver's seat. "Liam, wake up!"

"I'm ok," he said groggily, shaking his head and blinking hard to recover from the blow.

"What should I do?" she asked as they traded hands and positions on the wheel. Liam leaned forward this time, hugging the wheel to just barely avoid another kick.

As if the blow to his head cleared his mind, Liam suddenly looked out into the rain and noticed that they were headed towards another underpass.

He can't see it coming, Liam said, as he realized that the man's head must be faced towards the back of the car. *With his span, he must be at least 7 feet.*

"Can you reach my pocket?" Liam asked Alessandra as he began to speed up.

After a moment of following Liam's intent gaze, he didn't need to say another word.

Crouching down to avoid being kicked, Alessandra slid her slim fingers easily into Liam's side pocket and wiggled out his pocket knife. The next time their attacker's limb was extended, she would be ready.

The next kick saw the collision of the ball of the strange foot with the back of Liam's head, leaving his Achilles heel perfectly displayed. Liam's knife sliced it open, severing the tendon easily. The responding sound was a deafening high-pitched screech of pain. Almost immediately, the attacker dragged his foot from the doorframe and rose up, just in time to meet the steel metal and concrete frame of the underpass as it swept him clean from their car.

Three pairs of ears heard the body hit the pavement, hard. And three pairs of eyes looked back in fear of what creature they would see only to find the hulking figure of a bleeding, naked, but otherwise normal man with an ancient fury in his eyes as he watched them drive away.

CHAPTER 8: FINDING THE NEEDLE

Michael was silent the entire plane ride home. While Nina, Pytor, Aaron, and Tyrol argued about exactly what happened in Berlin, Michael sat apart, half-listening in an attempt to drown out the battle going on in his own mind.

"I'm telling you, the whole thing was a set-up, right from the beginning," Tyrol insisted as he held an ice pack to the right side of his face which was already becoming a tapestry of bruises. "I can't believe you're even thinking of falling for that 'we come in peace' bullshit." The swelling in his lips and the entire left side of his jaw made it hard for him to speak with the conviction he felt.

"How the hell would you know?" Nina challenged. "You were knocked out most of the time."

Tyrol started to give her an angry scowl, but the pain wasn't worth the effort. Plus, Nina wasn't looking at him anyway. She, like her brother three rows away, was staring out the window pensively.

"I don't know," Pytor began slowly, trying to put his English together. "I felt... safe with him. Safer than even with you all, and you are the only Seers I know."

"See, that's the problem here. You're all too young. You don't have enough experience to know when someone is playing you," Tyrol scoffed.

"But he was in our Quorum. He could not lie," Pytor countered.

"He said he was hiding things from us. Maybe he can block our perception of truth, just like he can block our visions," Nina answered, as she turned to look directly at Pytor. "They seem to be able to do a lot of things that we can't."

"They healed that man," Aaron added. "He was dying. I felt it and they... the girl... she *healed* him."

Nina nodded solemnly, trying to distinguish the lies from the truth. Nothing that she had been told by Crane and the Guild's scientists was making any sense. *If we're the ones who are supposed to bring Joel and the other Seers to justice, as they claim, then why were we so obviously outmatched?* Nina knew that their relative lack of experience probably had something to do with it. This was their first confrontation, after all, but she couldn't escape the feeling that there was something else at work here, something she was not being told. She knew that living in a house where she had been whispered about and distrusted for her gift since the time she was seven had made her suspicious of most people. But her instincts were usually right.

Maybe the Guild doesn't know if we can defeat them, she thought. *Maybe this was some sort of a test—a test that could have cost us our lives.* The thought of her team being made the unwitting lab rats in some secret experiment spiked her anger, until she remembered the distinct feeling of safety she had fought against once Joel joined their Quorum. The same feeling Pytor expressed, but she wouldn't dare admit. *He didn't want to take our lives. He didn't even want to fight us,* Nina thought as she recalled the clarity of his thoughts in this regard. The assertion that Joel was somehow out to get them was in complete contradiction to the man she had just encountered. She could see from the concerned looks on their faces that the others felt it, too, or at least everyone but Tyrol. As if to confirm her impression, Tyrol suddenly broke the silence with his own conclusion.

"They're not better than us." Tyrol declared. "They're not better than *me*."

Looking at the bruises that distorted his normally chiseled face, Nina almost laughed until another thought occurred to her.

"What makes you so sure? How do you know?" she asked, unfolding her legs from her chair so that she could lean forward and look directly into his eyes. Even with his swollen lips, Nina could still make out a hint of Tyrol's cocky smirk.

"Because I see things differently. That's how."

And just like that, amidst the nervous laughter of those around her, Nina knew she was being willfully, purposefully lied to, not just by Crane or his scientists, but by the members of her own team.

Feeling truly vulnerable for the first time since she'd joined the Guild, Nina immediately averted her gaze and looked up to find Michael staring back at her from just behind Aaron's seat, with the same knowledge and conviction that she now felt.

Although they were sure that Crane had already been briefed on the events that took place in Berlin, it was of little comfort. The fact that they didn't have to explain their failure would not shield them from his disappointment and the inevitable questions that would follow about the justification for their elevated status within the Guild. Though their interactions with the Guild's Quorums were rare, they were keenly aware of the differences between them. With the exception of the same cataract film over their eyes and their skin's sensitivity to the sun, there were no other comparisons to be made. Quorum Seers, as they were known within The Red Order, were ghosts, both physically and mentally. It often made Michael shudder to think of himself so mentally debilitated.

They had been told by Crane and Andreas that the Seer gene triggered a degeneration of brain functioning in most Seers, causing them to exhibit extreme aggression or profound psychosis. The Luridium, the Guild claimed, was the only way to quiet this disturbance in the brain and allow their extraordinary talents to come forth. Crane and Andreas insisted that before the first of "The Lost Seers," which included Marcus, Alessandra, Kaido, and Lucia, they had never met a Seer for whom the capacity to see the future had not rendered them insane.

To cement their story during the recruitment process, Crane and Andreas had presented them with results from a research project that they had supposedly conducted on The Lost Seers. They claimed that their research was intended to find a cure for the Seers that would enable them to re-enter society. But their research was halted when The Lost Seers deceived them, took their extraordinary gifts and left to use their power to wreak havoc on the orderly world the Guild stood to create and preserve. Crane convinced Pytor, Aaron, Michael and Nina that their power was a threat to The Lost Seers plans, and that Joel would have killed them along with their families if the Guild had not saved them first.

They were also told that the members of The Red Order were carefully sought out in an attempt to continue the research they had begun with Marcus Akida, and that ultimately, The Red Order would play a vital role in freeing others of their kind once the threat of The Lost Seers was eliminated.

Michael, Nina, Aaron, and Pytor each had looked over the documents, and observed Crane's pleading sincerity. They had no idea that the story they had been fed was a complete fabrication designed to deepen their sense of isolation and seduce them into doing the exact opposite of what they believed their purpose to be. In exchange for their cooperation, the members of the Red Order received whatever they desired, which in most cases was simply a nice, safe place to live. Tyrol was the only one of the five members who sought Crane out on his own after seeing him on TV during a rare press conference appearance.

When Christof escorted them into Andreas' office in Geneva after their plane landed, they were surprised to find Crane sitting behind the main desk, leafing through some paperwork, while Andreas sat off to the side like a guest in his own abode. It took several minutes after Christof had left for Crane to acknowledge their presence. When he did finally look up from his paperwork, the displeasure on his face was plain.

"So it did not go well then, in Berlin." His voice was stern as he looked them over one-by-one. "Do you have any explanation as to how you were so easily subdued?"

At the utterance of a direct question, all eyes from the Red Order shifted to the tall girl with the newly darkened hair. As usual, the task of communicating on their behalf fell to Nina. Though it had never come to a vote, Nina had emerged as the de facto leader of their group simply because she was their most dispassionate member and therefore the one most willing to see all sides in a debate. Tyrol's aggression made him both the most feared and least trusted within the group. As the newest, quietest of the Red Order, Pytor and Aaron seemed too passive to ever be considered for a leadership role. Which left Michael, who might have been a better choice (he certainly would have been more liked), except his focus on avenging his parents' death made him too single-minded to offer stability. But this time, Nina's response was anything but even-handed.

"Are you more surprised that we failed or that we're alive?" she asked bluntly.

"Excuse me?" Crane said, meeting her gaze. Nina refused to look away.

"You heard me just fine the first time."

The members of her group were stunned. She had not discussed her suspicions with anyone, not even Michael. Being so closely watched by their security detail, there hadn't been time to discuss anything with him on the plane, so she decided a course of action on her own. If things got ugly, she suspected that no one would back her up, so the mistake, if this proved to be a mistake, would be hers alone.

Crane stared at her for a moment longer before pursing his lips in annoyance and closing the file in his hand.

"I see," he said, rising slowly to his feet. "Does anyone else have a *less emotional* response to my question? Clearly the stress of your confrontation has affected Nina adversely."

"They were more powerful than we expected. We just need more time to practice," Aaron offered in an attempt to diffuse the tension in the room.

"Perhaps, but if this is a matter of time, we—you—will always be at a disadvantage," Crane's voice was low as he made his way from behind the desk, as if speaking aloud to himself. From behind the group, Andreas remained quiet as he observed the increasingly ominous interaction between Crane and Nina.

"Did you know?" Nina interrupted. "Did you know that they were more powerful? How could they be more powerful if what you told us is true? Michael and I tried our hardest, but it was nothing compared to what they could do!"

Crane came to stop right in front of her. "Nina, I can see that you're upset and perhaps a bit unstable, given the energy you have had to exert today, so I will not take your rudeness as insubordination. But you should be very clear about one thing when it comes to our effort here at the Guild. We do not plan to fail—ever. I would never have invested an ounce of thought into you, much less money and time, if I thought you would fail. When I send you to do something, I *expect* you to succeed. Otherwise, I would send someone else. I don't waste time. Everything I do has a purpose."

Bullshit, she thought, but kept it to herself. "That still doesn't answer my–" she said aloud before Tyrol interrupted her.

"We don't mean to antagonize you," Tyrol chimed in as he cut Nina an angry sideways glance. "We're all just a little frustrated. None of us expected this."

"Yes, I know you didn't, Tyrol. I guess we all need to learn a little patience," Crane offered as he turned his attention from Nina to Tyrol. "What happened to your face?"

"I was… distracted by a girl. She appeared in our Quorum out of nowhere. I mean literally out of thin air, but her mind was not connected to us in Quorum. Have you ever heard of anything like that being possible?"

Crane tried his best to suppress the involuntary shiver that went down his spine before asking, "What did the girl look like?"

"I don't really know. She had long bangs, dirty blonde hair, I think, and maybe hazel eyes. I only saw her for a second."

"I see." It was Crane's only response as he began to pace in front of them.

"Do you know how she could do that? Joel said her name was Lilith, but I couldn't tell for sure if she was Lilith Knight. She looked older than the sketches I've seen," Michael added as he looked from Crane's blank expression to Andreas, sitting passively behind them.

After a long moment, Crane spoke. "It's most likely a trick of some kind, obviously designed to get the upper hand."

"I don't think so," Pytor mused aloud. "He was in our Quorum. We would have known if he was lying." After a brief pause, Pytor added, "It seemed like he didn't want to hurt us..."

"Didn't I warn you that they could deceive you... even in Quorum?!" Crane roared. "He used that... apparition to distract you from what your true mission was — to capture them, not to come back here bruised, bloodied, and empty-handed! You're supposed to be a team. How could you let this man attack one of your own this way? How could you let your guard down and allow him to break into your Quorum? What happened to your shield — to your resolve? Have you forgotten what's at stake?"

Nina could see the others around her physically recoil in fear, but while she felt the same, her feet were stuck to the ground where she stood. It was as if he'd slapped her in the face. His anger, his defensiveness, it told her everything his words were designed to hide. When she first woke up to find Crane standing over her, he was the first person she had ever met who was not afraid of her power. At the time, she'd thought it was his sincerity and immense kindness that had drawn her in, but now, standing before the man who was clearly grasping to explain things he knew nothing about, she could see the real hold he had over her. She'd never realized how much acceptance and belonging had meant to her until that moment. Up until then, the simple desire had been potent enough to inoculate her from the truth that they were merely pawns to be played in some larger agenda that had nothing to do with what was best for her or any of them. Nina looked over to Michael, a brother she was only just starting to get to know. What little she knew of him, she liked, and she imagined that in a different world, they might have been friends. But in this life, Nina decided, she was and would always be a loner.

"How would you know how Quorum works?" Nina asked, as she struggled to keep her anger from betraying her as tears ran down her face. "You're not one of us. You can't see the future. You don't know anything more about how this works than we do."

"Nina!" Michael whispered. She could hear the warning in his voice, but she was way past caring at this point. She was back to her old self, not caring about anything.

"She doesn't speak for the rest of us," Tyrol said in a rush, before Crane raised his hand in a placating manner.

"I'm sure of that, Tyrol. I know *you* see me and what I have tried to do here clearly."

Watching Crane's face morph from raw fury to a facsimile of grave concern made Nina sick to her stomach. It was the same expression he'd greeted her with when she woke up from the coma he claimed she'd been in after her parents' car accident. *I wonder if that's even true*, she thought, realizing with increasing conviction that it probably wasn't. *What a fucking idiot I am.* Another tear rolled down her cheek.

"Nina, Nina. What has happened to you? I am so concerned. You have always trusted me. Why do you doubt me now? What has this Joel done to my jewel?" Crane asked as he reached out for her hands.

This time Nina recoiled with such force that she lost her balance, tripping on the edge of the rug behind her.

Aaron reached her first, as the others stood watching her uneasily.

"She was fine earlier," Aaron offered by way of explanation as he gripped her hand to help Nina to her feet. "But now, I..."

Nina yanked her hand out of his as soon as the words left Aaron's mouth. *Really*, she thought, as she took in her peers' looks of genuine fear and concern. From the frown on his face, Nina could tell that even Michael didn't know what to make of her. Only Tyrol was conflict-free, with pure satisfaction written all over his face.

"My dear, I am concerned for your health," Crane began as he motioned for Christof to fetch security. "You're right, of course, I am not like you. I can't see the future, but I am better-versed in the past than you could possibly understand. And I have seen what is happening to you now, time and time again."

"What do you mean?" Michael asked anxiously.

Crane let out a long sigh as the security team came in to hoist Nina up from the floor.

"With the low doses of Luridium that we give you, there was always a risk…" Crane let his words trail off for dramatic effect.

"A risk of what?!" Michael asked impatiently.

"A risk that the dose would not be enough to stave off the psychosis that develops with your gift. We have no choice but to admit your sister to the Guild's medical unit for observation."

The security team whisked Nina away with such haste that no one had time to react. But as she was pulled out of sight, Michael heard the unexpected sound of Nina's voice in his head as she told him, *I'm not crazy, Michael. He's lying.*

They left Nadia Spencer at the train station with fifteen hundred Euros in cash and specific instructions not to contact Ben or anyone else until she reached home.

"You don't want to be intercepted," Liam warned, as he scanned the train station drop-off area from the smashed back windshield of their car for any signs that they had been followed.

Nadia was so shaken up that she barely said a word as Liam treated the wounds on her back and forehead with anti-bacterial ointment and Steri-strips from the first-aid kit he always stashed in his backpack.

"Do you want some Percocet for the pain?" he asked Nadia. She bit down on her lip to suppress a groan as she took the pea coat that he offered her to cover her bloodied jacket and blouse. Nadia shook her head vigorously in refusal. She was confident that the only thing keeping her from passing out was the throbbing pain in her back. She was depending on it to anchor her to reality.

After going over Liam's instructions and pulling Alessandra's hat over her head to disguise her appearance, Nadia was ready to step out of the car and walk away without so much as a backwards glance. She wasn't angry anymore. She'd stopped blaming Joel and the others for her circumstances the moment she saw the strange man lying on the road with his angry eyes fixed on hers. She felt she knew just enough now to want as much distance as possible between herself and the world these people occupied. She sincerely hoped never to see any of them again.

But before closing the car door behind her, she remembered something important.

"What about Ben?" Nadia asked warily as she looked between Alessandra and Liam.

Reading her eagerness to get away from them, Alessandra answered her with all the confidence Nadia would need to leave Germany with no regrets.

"He'll be safer without your presence to draw attention. We will make sure he gets back to his family." It was the last thing Alessandra said before Nadia gave them a final nod and hurried away as fast as her shaky legs would allow. Though their departure bought Nadia a sense of peace, Liam and Alessandra could not shake the feeling of being chased until they heard the heavy metal door to the London warehouse slide shut forcefully behind them.

But the scene greeting them once they returned provided none of the peace they craved. Joel and Vincent had arrived an hour before them, and the lively discussion they were having on the second floor of the warehouse was clear enough to make out from the first floor. Liam and Alessandra's presence in the doorway of the large office area only added new spark to the conversation. Despite their exhaustion from the trip, they were greeted with a barrage of questions.

"What happened?"

"Oh, thank God! What took you so long?"

"Have you figured out what it was?"

"How did you heal him?"

In response, Alessandra could only offer a faint smile in recognition of the deep concern that lay behind the frenzy of questions.

"Give them a minute, everyone," Joel said quietly as he watched Lilli rush to her brother and embrace him.

After a long moment of silence, Liam looked up from his sister's intense gaze to address some of the questions he'd been able to discern.

"We took a longer route to get back. I needed to make sure that we weren't being followed… and no, I still don't know what it was that was chasing us. Lying on the road, it looked like a man, but what I saw clinging to the car by my window was like nothing I've ever seen."

"Well, you saw *something*, right? You said it could fly. I mean, what did it look like?" Vincent asked.

Liam hesitated as he tried to put what he saw into words that wouldn't make him sound crazy.

"It had a foot like an animal, but it was the size of a man's… but distorted," Liam began as he tried to make sense of his memories. "It had to have claws too, because the marks on Nadia's back were definitely not made from broken glass."

Liam paused for a long time before he added just loud enough to be heard, "But, the craziest part, is that I think, somehow, it was able to change from this *thing* to man. The look on his face when we drove away... was pure evil. I'll never forget it."

Looking up into her brother's haunted eyes, she could hear Liam's thoughts as he fought to avoid the conclusion he felt in his heart, but didn't want to accept.

"Do you think it was some kind of... demon?" Lilli asked aloud.

"I don't know, Lilli," he answered honestly. "You know, I don't believe in that kind of stuff, but what I saw — that look in his eyes. I don't know."

Feeling unsteady on his feet from the whole experience, Liam released Lilli with a gentle squeeze and headed towards two empty chairs with Alessandra's hand firmly in his. But when they went to take their seats side by side, Liam surprised Alessandra by pulling her firmly into his lap. Their hands intertwined tightly in her lap as she felt him rest his head on her back and almost immediately fall asleep.

"I don't remember the last time I've seen him so exhausted," Lilli said sadly as her brother began to snore lightly.

"It's not just the drive," Alessandra admitted quietly. "It's what I did. It took a lot out of me to save that man and he watched what it did to me. We haven't talked about it, but I know he's mad at me, as he should be. If you guys hadn't helped me, I don't know if I would have made it."

"I told Liam we wouldn't let you die, but from his thoughts, it was hard to reconcile what I was telling him with what he was seeing," Lilli explained.

There was a brief silence before Vincent spoke up.

"I don't mean to sound callous here, but it seems like we don't know what the hell is happening on several fronts. Ben and I weren't chased by any man-creatures, but I would still like to know what the heck happened in the warehouse. One minute Joel was holding back the hounds, the next minute he was a part of their Quorum. Any ideas on how that happened?"

"I do have an idea… or at least a thought," Joel answered. "As I was trying to catch up with Liam after I left the warehouse, I kept thinking about how it felt to join their Quorum, how *right* it felt, despite my resistance. Now I'm thinking maybe that's because we're not meant to use our power against each other.

"We know from the Collective that we work best together," Joel continued. "Maybe, in a situation where there is conflict, our shields bond together in order to facilitate that union—to neutralize any conflict between us."

"But we're able to block each other. If what you're saying is true, how could that work?" Jared countered.

"Yes, but it costs us every time we block their visions," Lilli answered.

"Maybe against other Seers, our gifts only work defensively. We can block, but we can't attack," Maura added.

Seeking out the one who had been assigned to block him, Joel found Katia sitting in the back corner of their group with her right hand clutching her left forearm tightly. "Katia, did it feel different, blocking me?" he asked, before he saw the blood seeping through her shirt sleeve.

His breath caught in his throat as he shook his head in disbelief. "Katia, you can't keep doing this to yourself."

The tears suddenly welled in her eyes and streamed down her face as she sat in silence.

"This isn't like before, Katia. We're all here. We made it out," Joel tried gently, but Katia just shook her head.

"But you almost didn't. I could have failed... again." Katia's voice was barely a whisper.

"My father's death was not your fault. You could not have saved him. No one wanted to more than me and I couldn't."

"But he said I was the best blocker among us. If I had tried harder, I could have helped more. Maybe..." There was so much pain in her that no sound came out as she cried. Joel fell silent then, truly at a loss for the words that would finally free her from the childhood home where she was always the bad girl, always at fault for anything that went wrong.

From the front of the room, Alessandra gently unwound her hands from Liam's and guided his head down to the large desk to their side before getting up and crossing the room to stand in front of Katia, who still refused to meet anyone's gaze.

"Katia, I am going to tell you something that you don't want to hear, because it's true. Marcus died so that you could live. If he had wanted your help, my help, anybody's help, we would have given it. Any one of us would have been proud to die alongside him and he knew it. He was the only father most of us ever had and we loved him. And he loved us, so he chose to save us. He chose it. Not us. And what you are doing now is destroying what he wanted for us. You hurting yourself is destroying what he died for.

"Look around this room. There isn't one of us who is a better person than he was, but he left us to carry on. And together, we are more powerful than he ever dreamed. He had faith in that. He had faith in us. Now, I don't feel any more worthy than you do to be here instead of him, but I *am* here, and I'm not going to let his sacrifice for me be in vain. You need to decide if this is really how you want to honor the man who loved you enough to give up his life so that you could be greater than he was, because we can't do this without you, Katia. We need you to *be* here."

The response she got wasn't what Alessandra had hoped for, but it felt true enough as Katia fell into her arms and began to sob out loud for the first time since she was a little girl.

As the others came around to embrace Katia, Vincent fell back, uncomfortable with the emotional rawness of the moment. Making his way over to Joel who was at the edge of the crowd, he leaned over to whisper in his ear. "So where do things stand? I mean, do you think the meeting with the reporter was a complete waste of time?"

"No," Joel answered with a small smile on his face. "I can see that we needed this test. And as for Nadia, I don't know. She has her own path to follow, and so do we."

Chapter 9: Ask Nicely

6 months before Berlin

With all the money the Guild had at its disposal, Miguel could not understand why its state-of-the-art medical facility was unable to procure subject beds that didn't rattle and squeak with rusted gears. After two long days of interrogation and torture, Miguel had been called in to clean up the mess and retrieve his charge. The sound of the gurney's wheels screeching and dragging against the floor as he pushed Ming's unconscious body back to her cell annoyed him. Everything annoyed him these days. Miguel was not a man built for petty tasks. He was also not accustomed to sitting idly while someone he considered a true colleague and friend was being abused. The fact that his days and duties within the Guild forced him into doing both warranted, in his opinion, all the contempt he felt.

The first time Miguel was reassigned, shortly after the Alliance's unsuccessful attempt to capture The Lost Seers, he had assumed his demotion was punishment for the colossal failure of the operation. But when the reassignments kept coming, even his pride could not deny the fact that his usefulness within the Guild had diminished, making the creation of The Red Order necessary. Bitter was not a word Miguel would have used to describe himself six months ago. He had always been too busy — too focused on achieving his goals for those kinds of emotions to fester. But with so much time on his hands to ruminate, he knew that was exactly the kind of man he had become.

Miguel managed the weight of Ming's body in his arms easily as he placed his hand on the bio-scanner that made his handprint the second of only two keys to her cell. He pulled the covers over her with care before leaving to collect the food and water she would need to recover from 48 hours of sleep deprivation and dehydration. The sight of the dark circles under her eyes made him suck his teeth in disgust before re-engaging the electro-magnetic bars that kept her confined. *They know she's innocent*, he thought as he walked away. *This is all just for show.*

With his major task for the day accomplished, Miguel slammed the door to his cavernous office and took a seat at his desk. Leaning back into his chair, he closed his eyes and began to replay, for the millionth time, just how he'd gotten to this point. *It started in Salem, with the Knights,* he told himself, remembering the bloody image of Jill Knight in her kitchen. She had left him empty-handed for the first time in his professional career. It was the start of an exponential trend he could now chart with precision, one that continued with Lilli and Liam and was exacerbated by the escape of Marcus and three other Seers. The raids followed shortly after. Within a matter of months, dozens of Seers intended for gathering went missing, never to be recovered or harnessed. Miguel and his team had been all but powerless to stop it.

The attack mounted by The Lost Seers in Chicago had been a pivotal moment, not only for the Guild, but also for Miguel. He would not have even been present for it if he hadn't returned to Chicago from Geneva on an administrative errand. The trip was meant to finalize his transition to the position he'd been serving in for the past month as head of security for the Guild's new prison facility. It was the first time in his tenure that he would not be under Crane's direct supervision and the first time he began to question if the existence of the Guild was truly necessary. While he had seen the videos that featured Marcus and

Alessandra's stories and their miraculous recovery from the Luridium, at that time his belief in the Guild's purpose was not tested. He had witnessed firsthand how the cooperation facilitated by the Seers had prevented wars and brought prosperity to parts of the world that had been neglected for centuries. The Seers' freedom, he rationalized, was a small price to pay for world order.

Before Chicago, it had never occurred to him that the Seers might have a greater purpose or ability beyond serving the interests of the Guild. But that day, Miguel observed the awesome power that Marcus and the others had wielded against the Guild; he saw a young man create certain death with only the air between his fingertips. Miguel had been genuinely surprised to escape with his life as he flew back to Geneva with Andreas and Crane. Though Miguel never spoke of it, the accounts of what happened in Chicago from the few surviving eyewitnesses had become legend within the Guild.

And things had only gotten worse. In the last twelve months alone, the Guild had purified less than half of the Seers they'd intended to gather, forcing the organization into crisis mode. The dwindling supply of Seers made it nearly impossible for the Guild to keep up with the constant demand from countries that wanted what they felt was their fair share of access to the Seers and the power they possessed. Without the ability to satisfy these demands, the very basis for cooperation within the UWO was threatened. In response, the Guild's focus shifted to The Red Order, which was seen as their best hope for solving the problem of the Lost Seers, making Miguel and those in his line of work nearly obsolete.

Fortunately for Miguel, it was also after Chicago that he first met Ming Jhu.

In his position as head of the Guild's prison security, Miguel was essentially confined to a desk from where he supervised men that made his late colleague, Jason Earley, seem like an intellectual. When Ming was brought down to him in handcuffs shortly after Miguel escaped from Chicago, he decided to oversee her confinement personally out of a benign combination of boredom and curiosity. Having had access to the highest levels within the organization, Miguel knew exactly who Ming was when she arrived. He couldn't help but wonder what she had done to fall from grace so quickly. It was, after all, a subject with which he had become intimately acquainted.

Because of the restraints and the sedatives he was ordered to keep her under for the first 48 hours of her incarceration, Miguel had to wait to ask her exactly what she had done to spark the smear campaign regarding her presumed involvement in the Lost Seers' plot to bring down the Guild. Unlike the Lost Seer videos, Miguel knew immediately that the stories on the news were false. *Someone as high-up in the organization as Ming*, he reasoned, *would never have risked betraying the Guild. She knew too much about their instruments of retribution.* Even with his own suspicions and resentment, Miguel never thought of retaliation. He valued his life, even if it was mundane.

Miguel had been a little surprised when Ming opened her eyes on Day 3 and immediately displayed the kind of fear he used to inspire in people on a regular basis.

"I'm not here to kill you," he reassured Ming before offering her a glass of water. When she finally took it after a moment of hesitation, he continued. "How do you know me?"

"Everybody knows you," Ming answered after finishing the water in four large gulps. "When the Guild needs someone gone, from what I hear, you're the last person they see."

Miguel took the glass from her shaky hands and filled it again, considering once more just how far he was from those days. Handing the glass back to her, he let the pity that he felt for both of them show on his face. "I'm not that person anymore. It seems we've both taken a turn for the worse." They watched each other carefully as she drank, both weighing the question that weighed heavily on their minds.

How did you end up here?

As she drank, Miguel pushed a little further. "You're all over the news, you know. They say you've committed treason, that an investigation into your collaboration with the Lost Seers is underway."

Ming took a few unhurried sips before she put her glass down, a little less than half full.

"Is that so?" she mumbled before clearing her throat.

"Your... partner has been very vocal in your defense. She's quite the anarchist, that one."

"Thea?"

Miguel was pleased to see he now had her full attention.

"Yes, over the past 2 days she's managed to cause quite a scene outside the headquarters here."

Ming's face flushed with pride and concern. "Thea's a very persuasive person, but she's... very sick. She should be resting." *What are you doing, Thea?* Ming wondered anxiously. *This isn't safe. You know that.*

Miguel had to smile at the irony. "Well, no one would know she's sick by the camp she's set up across the street. She was sure to be just outside of the UWO's property line, so they can't arrest her. She's started creating a mural symbolizing all the people the Guild has killed in order to exploit the Seers."

Instead of voicing her fears over Thea's safety, Ming kept her focus on the remaining water in her glass as she spoke. "She's a very talented artist."

"And a good promoter," Miguel added. "I saw a reporter interviewing her for the local news just last night."

His words triggered a memory of a fight she and Thea had long ago, at the beginning of their relationship and her work with the Guild. Frustrated that Ming never talked about her job anymore and had stopped taking her to work functions, Thea accused Ming of trying to hide their relationship from her new bosses.

"You just don't want them to know you're a dyke," she'd screamed angrily. "Well, I'm not going to be your dirty little secret. I'm gonna walk in there and tell every single person I see that I'm with you and you're with me!"

In her panic, Ming had roughly grabbed Thea's head between her hands, bringing their faces close together. She'd whispered her warning as if they were being watched.

"You think I'm ashamed? I love you. They already know about you. About us. I can't do anything about that now. I wish I could, but I can't." When Thea tried to pull away, Ming jerked her closer, so that their noses pressed together.

"No. Not because I'm ashamed. I wish they didn't know so that I could protect you, but I can't now. It's too late. But that doesn't mean I want you around them, like a target they can pick off anytime they want. My whole life is a secret, but not you. Not you. Everything I do now, I do to protect you. To protect the part of us they don't already own."

Thea had told her years later that it was that argument that made her realize the gravity and danger of Ming's job. Thea had agreed to keep her distance out of a trust that had spanned over 20 years together. Ming knew that only one thing would cause Thea to cross that line now.

This is her way of protecting me, Ming realized. *So that they can't just dispose of me without a fight.*

Looking over towards Miguel, Ming wondered why he was sharing all this information with her. She couldn't imagine that he thought she could do anything for him in her current state until the one advantage she did still possess occurred to her. *Maybe he just wants answers.* It was a feeling she could relate to and something she'd never had the liberty to give to anyone outside her team of scientists. And she still knew things that she'd never told another living soul, other than Crane. *Maybe now I really will commit treason. If Thea can fight, so can I,* she decided, as she tipped her head to drain her glass.

When Ming was finished, she felt strong enough to get out of the bed and get her own water. Ming waited until her glass was full before she turned towards Miguel and offered him a weak smile.

"So, I know you're wondering what really got me here because I'm thinking the same thing about you. The only question is, do you want to go first, or should I?"

The exchange that would take place over the months that followed would spark the first genuine friendship Miguel had risked since he joined the Guild over a decade before. It would also shatter his understanding of everything he thought his life had been about and crystallize his vague suspicions of the Guild's motives into hardened disbelief.

2 days after Berlin

The Guild had strict regulations to keep all Seers confined to a separate wing of its lead research facility. So when Nina first appeared in the cell beside Ming's, with no warning or instructions, Miguel didn't understand what was going on. Nina was no help, given that her only responses to his questions were silence or "Fuck You!" On her second day, Miguel noticed that Nina's hands had begun to shake.

Great, he thought angrily. *They want her to detox here!* Miguel had never seen a Seer go through Luridium withdrawal before, but he'd read a briefing on it when he first joined the organization. As far as he knew, the Guild had only experimented with detoxification for a month when the drug was first being tested. After the general effects were assessed and quantified, it had never been done again. But from what he remembered, the withdrawal symptoms were severe — full of sweat, bile, and a lot of screaming. Ming had been gone for the last two days for another round of "interrogation." He knew they would be finished with her soon and deeply regretted that Ming would be forced to contend with the wailings of a hysterical girl in her weakened state.

To his surprise, when he picked Ming up, she was conscious and in a wheelchair.

"They're prepping me for the trial, so they need me looking decent for the cameras," Ming said, answering the mixture of confusion and relief on his face.

"Oh," he responded before adding. "Well, I'm not sure you're going to get any rest. They've got a Seer in here who's going through detox. There isn't much I can do for you, but I think I have some ear plugs in my desk if you want them."

A Seer, Ming thought in confusion as Miguel helped her out of her chair and into the bed in her cell. *What's a Seer doing down here... and detoxing?* "Thanks Miguel, I think I'll be alright," she offered honestly. "Who is it?"

"It's Nina. She's from The Red Order that I was telling you about."

Ming couldn't hide the shock on her face as she whipped her head around to face the cement wall that divided the two cells.

"I know," Miguel said in response. "Who the hell knows what's going on anymore?"

"Help me, please. Someone, please help me," Nina whimpered as the sweat poured down her face. She could taste the remnants of vomit in her mouth, but the bowl she had expelled in was gone, replaced by a new one that smelled too strongly of artificial lemon. It made her dry heave.

"Nina, you're going to be alright. It's just the Luridium in your system. You're… almost through the worst. In a few days, you'll feel a bit better."

The voice coming back to her was soothing, but Nina couldn't concentrate enough to recall if she knew who it was as she rocked her body slowly on the ground. Nina imagined that the voice on the other side of the wall meant her words to be comforting, but all she could do was let out a weak sob. *A few days*, Nina thought as she cried. *In a few days, I'll be dead.*

"I know it feels like you're going to die, but I promise you, you won't. You're too valuable to them," the voice assured her.

"How do you know?" Nina managed as she felt her hysteria grow. "How do you know that?"

The long pause that followed made Nina think the phantom voice must have been lying to her just to get her to be quiet, but then she heard the woman clear her throat before answering, "I know because I designed the drug and its effects. I know because I created it."

The power of Ming's words heightened Nina's panic.

"Oh God," she whimpered. "What did you do to me?"

"Shhh," Ming whispered back. "Someone is coming."

Instinctively, both women turned away from the wall, not wanting to expose their communication to anyone. Miguel bypassed Nina, who seemed to have fallen asleep on the floor, to stop in front of Ming's cell.

"Hey, I'm headed out for the night. Do you need anything before I go?" Miguel asked before taking a peek at Nina's motionless form. "She seems to have quieted down."

"No, I'm fine. Thanks," Ming answered, not wanting to frighten Nina by alerting a third party to their conversation before she had gained her trust. "I'll see you in the morning."

When she heard the door close securely behind Miguel, Ming scurried towards the wall again and spoke to Nina in a normal voice.

"Don't worry. That's Miguel. He's one of the few here that isn't unnecessarily cruel, and believe me, in a place like this, that's really saying something. My name is Ming and I'll tell you anything you want to know, but we have to be quiet."

In between spasms and excruciating pain, Nina started with simple questions about Ming's identity and reason for being in the cell next to her, then progressed on to more detailed information about the Luridium and what it was doing to her and the others.

Before Nina, Ming's only knowledge of or exposure to the Red Order came from the details that Miguel had shared and what she could extrapolate on her own. Though she wasn't exactly sure how they developed the drugs used for the Red Order, she suspected that after she was taken, her assistant Mark told them about her research into a less debilitating form of Luridium. Given that Ming had been in her cell for almost eight months and didn't know how much longer her life would be deemed necessary, she decided to be as forthright with Nina as possible, on the off-chance that any information she had might help Nina understand her gift enough to escape.

"The Luridium you have in your system is most likely a modified version of what we give the Guild's regular Seers. I developed it after Marcus Akida escaped to have fewer side effects in terms of mental clarity, time perception, and memory, but the withdrawal symptoms manifest themselves more rapidly and more acutely than what a normal Seer would experience." Ming paused for a moment before adding, "The heightened withdrawal symptoms were engineered to act as kind of an insurance policy… to prevent a Seer from ever getting too far if they decided to run."

Nina rolled onto her stomach, alternately gritting her teeth, grunting and panting through a sudden surge of pain that made it feel like her skull was being pulled right through her scalp. Her whole body was wet from the exertion it took not to scream, but the throbbing in her head was so unrelenting. She didn't dare risk making a sound. In her delirium, she believed her whole body was crying.

The coolness of the concrete floor and the low, muffled sound of Ming's voice were her only comforts, her only link to something outside her own agony. She didn't understand why the pain in her head had gotten worse until she realized she could no longer hear Ming's voice.

"Please… please keep talking," Nina begged.

Ming was pleased that the sound of her voice was now welcome. That had not been the case earlier in the day when Ming's attempts to initiate conversation were met with a vicious tirade. Assuming Nina would want to know more about the other side effects of the Luridium, she eased closer to the wall.

"Umm, well, some of the effects you already know—sensitivity to sunlight, a kind of bleaching of the pigment in the skin, hair, and eyes, cessation of ovulation and menstruation in females, and low sperm production in men, though I was never able to conduct a long-term study to determine if this form of infertility is permanent or temporary.

"Mostly, my research focused on enhancing the Guild's ability to expedite the purification process and extract as much information as possible from each Quorum through the use of various drugs and biotechnology. Crane never cared about the long-term effects of the Luridium or how it damaged your body, as long as it didn't prevent the Guild from using you. I know this must sound so callous, and in truth it is. I have no excuse for what I've—"

"Wait. What about... the study? The study to... cure us?" Nina took advantage of the mitigated pain in her head to push out the words in between quick puffs of air. The low hum of Ming's voice had allowed her nausea to subside enough to lift her body onto all fours and reach for the bottle of water that lay on the floor next to her. The cool water hurt her teeth as she swallowed, but it felt good too, once it made it past her throat.

"What study? I'm sorry, I don't know what you're referring to. Cure you of what?" Ming said confused.

Nina's arms shook so much that she had to lower her head to her forearms. She was exhausted and didn't have the patience or the time for games. She was expending all the energy she had just trying to survive her withdrawal. The information Ming was providing was like a lifeline of distraction, but she didn't have the strength for a cat and mouse exchange. *If this woman wants to help me, she needs to make it straight and simple*, Nina thought in a flash of anger for being forced to have to use her voice again.

"You know… what I'm talking about," she panted. "Crane told us you were working… on a study to make it safe… for us… to make us stable…"

It took a moment for Ming to respond. Having lived with knowledge of the lie for so long, she always forgot that people outside the Guild really believed that the Seers were insane. The Guild's propaganda had been so thorough, so consistent, that not only did the world believe it, but the Seers believed it, too.

"There is nothing wrong with you, any of you. The Seer ability does not make you insane; that's just the lie they tell to justify your captivity. There was never any study to cure you because you don't need to be cured. When you first come into your gift, it can be disorienting, overwhelming even, but if you were ever given the chance, I am sure you would emerge with your visioning and your sanity completely intact."

The implications of Ming's words made Nina's body crumple to the ground.

Despite all indications that Nina did not have the energy, her body was able to produce fresh tears as she shut her eyes. "Crane said he saved us," Nina cried. If there had been anything in her stomach worth purging, Nina was sure she would have thrown up. Behind her closed lids, she felt that she could almost see the thousands of Seers in captivity, like ghosts walking through an underworld they believed was built for their protection.

"I'm sorry," Ming whispered back.

It took a while before Nina could speak again. "All those people, they could be…"

"Free," Ming offered, completing her thought. "Yes, they could be. They deserve to be."

"What kind of people would do this? Why?" Nina's voice was barely louder than a whisper. Between the withdrawal and the truth, everything in her body was beginning to shut down.

"Power. Your gift gives the leaders of this world power over every outcome, every eventuality. You provide a future they can exploit. Your gift allowed them to create a new world order that they defend at the cost of your freedom."

As the initial shock wore off, Nina could almost feel the pieces coming together in her mind: every lie she was told, the Quorums, their elevated position within The Guild, their mission to seek out and kill the one group that knew the truth and could expose it.

"What about Joel Akida and the others? He said he didn't kill our families. He was telling us the truth, wasn't he?" Nina asked as she slumped forward and crawled to her bed.

"I don't know him, but from what Miguel has told me, yes, I believe it is very likely that he is telling you the truth. He didn't kill your family. There would be no reason for him to want to harm you."

As Nina tested the sensation of the pillow on her aching head, she was grateful for the exhaustion that was finally overriding every other sensation in her body. *You need your rest*, she told herself. *You've got to warn Michael, so he can find a way to get out of here.*

After a long moment of silence, Ming called out Nina's name, but the girl on the other side of the wall was already in a deep sleep, dreaming of the conversation she would have with her brother if she could tell him what she knew.

●●··●●

I must be really slipping, Miguel thought as he assessed the hold that was tightening around his neck. *I leave my office for two seconds and come back to this.*

Though Miguel hadn't gotten a look at his assailant's face, he knew a couple important facts already. First, the person straining to keep his hold around Miguel's neck, despite his lack of resistance, was male and stood at just a hair above Miguel's own height. Second, he was not trained by Miguel, which made him an amateur. And third, the moist heat coming off the man behind him was a strong indication that he was far more anxious than Miguel. With so few elements of interest in his day, Miguel decided to play along.

"What do you want?" Miguel asked in a disinterested tone.

"You're going to take me to my sister, right now."

"I don't know who--" Miguel began before Michael cut him off.

"--Yes, you do. I know you have her down here somewhere, and you're going to take me to her now!"

Miguel sighed again. He had been raised in a traditional household where the young never interrupted their elders. He missed those simple rules more and more as he got older. *But then again, I guess I shouldn't look for respect from a youngster who's trying to put me in a chokehold.*

The ease with which Miguel broke Michael's hold and slammed him, face first, into his desk was almost comical, but neither man was laughing.

"You need better training," Miguel said as he twisted Michael's arms higher up on his back.

"I wasn't trying to hurt you," Michael gasped as he tried not to scream. "I just need my sister. Please, I need to talk with her."

Miguel released his hands at once.

"You should have started with "please". You could have saved yourself the anxiety and the embarrassment of trying to coerce me."

"I didn't think you'd help me otherwise," Michael said sourly as he massaged his wrists.

"You don't know what I'd do," Miguel answered coolly. "That's why you should always ask first."

There was no further discussion as Miguel stepped outside his office and waited for Michael to follow.

Michael watched with quiet curiosity as Miguel led him down the dark grey corridor, until he reached a door with a protruding LCD screen where a doorknob should have been. Michael watched as Miguel typed in a 10 digit code before the door popped open. Miguel stepped aside, indicating that Michael should go in first. Across the room that looked part operating room, part prison, he could see his sister, behind the glow of blue-white bars, sleeping peacefully. Beside his sister's cell was a gaunt Asian woman who looked back at him with the barest wisp of a smile.

"Nina," he whispered urgently as he kneeled down and tried not to touch the strange bars that divided them. "Nina, wake up. It's me, Michael!"

At the sound of his name, Nina sat straight up in her bed and turned to see the last image of what she thought was a dream materializing right before her eyes.

"How did you find me? What are you doing here?" she asked, still a little disoriented as she stumbled out of bed.

Distracted by her drawn and thinner frame, Michael could barely register her words. "What are they doing to you?" he asked in shock.

"Nothing," she said. "I haven't had my meds in 2 weeks, and this is what it does to you. You go through withdrawal. They never told us that. How did you find me?"

It took Michael a moment to stop fixating on the protrusion of her collarbones through her t-shirt before he could answer.

"What do you mean?" he asked, finally meeting her sunken eyes. "You've been talking to me in my head, ever since you were dragged away from Andreas' office. I've been hearing you on and off for two weeks."

From the stunned look on his sister's face, he could tell that his experience was news to her.

"You didn't know you were doing that?"

"No... I thought I was dreaming of what I would say to you if I could tell you everything I've learned." Looking around the room, Nina suddenly remembered the point of every imaginary conversation she'd had with her brother, and felt a distinct flash of irritation at his presence. "In my dream, I told you to leave. What are you still doing here?"

Equally annoyed, Michael shot Nina a look of disbelief before answering.

"Did you even think about what you did in Andreas' office? How unnecessary that whole scene was?"

"He was lying and I knew it! I wasn't just going to sit there and let him feed me some load of bullshit!"

"And why not? I had my doubts, too. Do you ever — for a second — think about anybody besides yourself?"

Nina didn't know what to say at first. She had no idea where he was going with this. After a while she added, "Nobody else got hurt. I'm paying for my mistake on my own."

Since he couldn't reach through the bars and shake some sense into her, all Michael could do was shake his head.

"You're the only family that I have left, you know. Did you ever think of that?"

Though Nina recognized the raw emotion she saw on Michael's face as real, she could not understand why it was there. *Why is he taking this so personally,* she wondered.

"Look, I'm sorry, ok? I mean no offense, but we don't even know each other that well."

And then Michael stopped being angry, because he realized that Nina really didn't have a clue.

"We could get to know each other," Michael said gently. "Did you ever consider that? I mean, that is, if you'd like to live that long."

It took a minute for the smile to emerge, but when it did, it was because Nina finally got the reason why he'd risked his life to see her.

"So what's the plan?" she said.

"I don't know, but I've only got about 40 minutes more before the security guard outside my door stops banging the night nurse and notices I'm gone."

"Ok. Ok," Nina said, reaching for the water that would keep her headache from becoming unmanageable. "Ming, are you up? We could use your help."

"What do you need my help for?" Ming asked, pressing her body as close to the bars as she could without getting electrocuted. "What part of 'get the hell out of here' can't you figure out?"

"No, I don't think that's the move," Michael interjected. "From what Nina has been showing me, this is bigger than we can handle on our own. We've got members within our own team that I'm beginning to think we can't trust. We need Joel's help, but we can't reach him from here. We're too heavily monitored. But, Ming, you can. Plus, you can corroborate his story, as an insider.

Michael looked to Nina to confirm her agreement before continuing. "Ming, if we can figure out a way to get you out of here, then maybe you could get a message to Joel for us. Tell him what you know, tell him we need his help to blow this thing wide open from the inside."

"But how?" Ming said wearily. "My trial starts in a week and there are only 2 people who can let me in to or out of this cell, Crane and Miguel."

"Then we're going to have to figure out a way to get help from one of them," Michael said before he jumped at the sound of Miguel's footsteps approaching from where he had been quietly listening in.

"I have a feeling," Miguel said, smirking down at Michael, "that you are about to ask me something, very nicely."

CHAPTER 10: THREE CHOICES

Officially, Nadia was on a two-week vacation from her job. Unofficially, she was hiding out and scared as hell, holed up in a budget hotel room, 10 miles and a world away from her penthouse in New York City.

The train ride from Berlin to Dresden had been a blessing in disguise. While the mode of transportation wasn't quick enough to get her home as fast as she would have liked, the trip had given her the space she needed to leave the feeling of impending death far behind. By the time she'd made her way to Dresden Airport and found the private airstrip that Liam had directed her to, Nadia was calm enough to start jotting down some notes from her trip—questions she needed to answer, follow-up with Ben, a timeline of the exact sequence of everything she had witnessed. She'd learned from years in the field that emotion and stress could easily cloud your memory. For a reporter to deliver an accurate story, one needed to make a record of events as soon as possible. Plus, she wanted to have all this information ready to pitch to her producer the minute she landed. Nadia figured that she deserved at least a two hour news special as payment for everything she'd endured to get this story.

As she bit into the ham and cheese croissant that the pilot presented to her shortly after boarding the small private jet, Nadia added another item to her list of outstanding questions. She needed to make a list of wealthy people who would be most likely to help finance Joel's operations. Nadia's ex-husband had been wealthy enough to leave her their New York penthouse without hesitating, but the kind of wealth that Joel obviously had access to was incomparable. Before she had arrived in Berlin, she'd dug up all she could on Joel Akida. From what Nadia could tell, after dropping out of school at the age of thirteen, he'd had a series of menial jobs that never took him far from London until he turned fifteen. After that, she found no employment record for him and no documented travel on his passport. It was as if he'd simply vanished from the earth before resurfacing in Chicago.

She guessed that his disappearance must have taken place around the same time that he met this mysterious benefactor. *But with limited formal education and immigrant status, where would he have met someone with the means to charter a private plane from Germany to New York at a moment's notice?* Scanning through her slightly damp notebook, she'd checked off his job listings one by one:

Dishwasher

Shoe shiner

Newspaper delivery boy

Coffee/errand boy at a small export company

Shipping day laborer

Bellhop

The last one made her curious. *Maybe he met his benefactor at the hotel where he worked?* Frustrated that her research assistant had failed to write down the name of the hotel, she decided to take the painkillers that Liam had snuck into her bag and get some rest. Sipping hot tea from the metal flask the pilot gave her before taking off, Nadia closed her eyes and remembered she only had 9 more hours until she was home.

"Where are the tapes? All of them! Give them to me now!" Nadia had just walked into her producer Ted Brenner's office to find him blustering, sweaty, and barking at her before she could even open the door fully.

"Ted, what's going on?" she asked. "I walk in the building and the first thing I hear is security telling me you need to see me right way."

"Don't give me that shit! This is serious. I don't know what you're into, but we need those tapes. *I* need those tapes right now." The hand he extended towards her shook with uncontrolled urgency.

"Ted, what are you talking about?!" She yelled back. "I just got off a plane after running for my life! Could someone please explain to me what the hell is going on?"

Ted knew Nadia well enough to know she was stalling, and in that moment of understanding, she saw true panic bloom on her boss's face for the first time. Nadia watched as his gaze shifted briefly from hers to the tall, muscular man who had been trailing her from the moment she stepped from the elevator onto the 48th floor.

"Nadia, listen to me very carefully. The network can't protect you. Do you understand what I'm saying? You need to give me those tapes and anything else you have from Germany—right now."

A chill ran down Nadia's spine as she reflexively gripped the straps of her purse a little tighter. If Nadia suspected it before, she knew it now. She'd never told Ted where she was going.

They got to him.

The realization was like a blow to the head, leaving a high-pitched ring in her ears as the events of the last 36 hours came rushing back in vivid sensations of broken glass, tearing flesh, and the sick trickling of blood down her back. She didn't know if this was the Guild or the UWO or some other shadow organization, but she was sure of one thing—the attack in Berlin and this ambush in Ted's office were absolutely related.

It meant that she was in just as much danger as she had been in the back of Liam's sedan. But unlike before, it would be up to her to steer out of this trap, alone.

Nadia stared Ted straight in the face as she lied. "I don't have the tapes."

Before she could even finish the sentence, she felt her purse being yanked from her shoulder.

"What the hell are you doing?" Nadia asked as she turned towards the man behind her. "That's my private property!" She lunged for her bag, but didn't come close enough to reclaim it as a second man came seemingly out of nowhere, pulling her shoulders back and then down into one of Ted's guest chairs.

A lump formed in her throat as she watched the first man dump the contents of her purse onto the carpeting.

"It's not there," the first man said as he handed the empty bag to the second man while spreading her pens and lipstick cases across the floor with his foot.

The second man was silent as he ripped the cloth lining before turning it completely inside out.

Nadia said nothing, keeping her eyes on the floor so as not to give away her secret.

"It's not here either," the second man announced as he dropped her bag to the floor.

"I thought you said she would be carrying at least an audio-recorder," the first man addressed Ted in an accusing tone.

Ted's eyes darted to Nadia's in time to see the look of betrayal on her face as she looked up from the floor. He had to look away. "Yes, she usually does..." he began before his voice trailed off.

"I told you, I don't have it. And what authority do you have to search my things? Where's your warrant?" In answer to her question, the second man left the room as the first lowered his body so that he squatted down directly in front of her.

"I operate under the full power and authority of the UWO, which is investigating the known terrorist and fugitive Joel Akida and his associates in order to bring them to justice. As such, I have the right to search and seize *anything* that I believe is relevant to that mission. Now, where is the tape?"

"It got destroyed in Berlin. My crew and I were ambushed during my interview with Joel Akida by a group of men who looked just like you and 5 Seers who tried to kill us-- unprovoked. It makes me wonder if you're going after the wrong people," Nadia answered evenly.

"What happened to your cameraman?"

Nadia didn't miss a beat. "He got away from the attack and I haven't heard from or seen him since. I assumed he'd found his way back here."

The first man watched Nadia with his cold blue eyes for a long while before the second man slipped back into the room.

"Downstairs security said she used the bathroom before she got on the elevator."

Immediately, the first man hoisted Nadia up by her arm and began leading her out of Ted's office. Once inside the elevators, Nadia kept her head down, realizing that she needed to put on the best game-face of her life.

When Nadia first arrived in the building, Sid, the afternoon security guard, was more animated than usual for a man who rarely looked up from his newspaper.

"Good Afternoon, Ms. Spencer," the 65- year-old said in a voice so chipper she had to do a double-take to make sure it was him. "Aah, Mr.

Brenner said to tell you he wants to see you in his office right away. He said I should tell you the minute you came in."

That was Nadia's first clue that something was wrong. He should not have been expecting her at all. She hadn't contacted anyone since Berlin and had caught a cab straight to her office from the airport. If it had been any other day, she could have told herself that the sinking feeling in the pit of her stomach was just nerves and jetlag. *Like with all other assignments, he would expect me to head right back to the office once the job was done,* she reasoned. But after everything she'd been through over the past few days, she couldn't dismiss the twisting in her gut.

What if someone tipped him off — someone who had the power to monitor airport security passport scans?

Nadia stood at the front desk, paralyzed by even the thought of what she might face when she walked into her boss's office until Sid spoke up.

"Maybe you should go to the restroom. Freshen up a bit, before you face the music," he offered kindly. Relief washed over Nadia as she took the bathroom key from Sid and smiled broadly. He had just given her a plan.

"That sounds like a great idea, Sid. I'll just be a minute. Call and tell him I'm on my way."

Sid didn't know that she knew that the key was the same for both the men's and women's bathrooms. After checking over her shoulder to make sure Sid's attention was back on his paper, Nadia slipped unnoticed into the men's restroom. With nothing to secure the audio and camera memory card to a dry surface, Nadia opened the decrepit metal paper towel dispenser and hid her notepad and equipment inside.

By the time she'd handed the key back to Sid, she'd already begun second-guessing her instincts. Before she reached the 48th floor, Nadia was convinced that she had been overzealous, until she stepped out of the gliding metal doors to find a large man she'd never met waiting to escort her to Ted's office.

● ● · · ● ●

The ride back down to the lobby barely gave Nadia time to compose herself under the gaze of the two men that appraised her every twitch openly. *It's okay to look tense,* she assured herself. Nadia tried not to let her shoulders fall in relief as they led her straight from the elevator into the ladies bathroom.

"Now exactly what were you doing here?" the first man asked suspiciously.

Nadia took the opportunity to let her contempt show.

"Ah, you know… the usual, pee, poop. It was a long flight."

"Just search the whole place," the first man said to the second.

For what felt like an eternity, Nadia watched in silence as the second man combed through the 3-stall bathroom and vanity sinks with care. The first man never relinquished his grip on her arm.

"It's clean," the second man declared finally. "There's nothing here."

"Well, I did flush. If I had known you guys wanted to see it, I would have left it here for you."

The second man's smirk lasted only a second before he pulled Nadia from the first man's grip and slammed her face-first into the wall.

Nadia screamed as she felt the cut on her forehead open up. A million horrifying thoughts filled her mind as the second man held her head to the cold tile with one hand while kicking her legs apart with his feet.

"Get the hell off me," she growled to no effect. Both men were just out of her range of sight.

She began to hear a high pitched whining sound right before the first man told her to hold still. A moment later she could see a bright thin blue line of light reflect on the wall as it made its way down her body. The second man released her as soon as the high-pitched whining stopped. Quickly, she turned around to see both men focusing their attention on a small hand-held tablet.

"What is that? What did you do to me?" she asked, as she pressed the sleeve of her jacket to the cut on her head. She thought briefly about heading over to the paper towel dispenser, but decided quickly against it. She didn't want to give them any ideas.

"Nothing. She doesn't have it on her. Let's see if they had any luck with the cab," the first man said.

"What is that?" she insisted again.

"It's a portable x-ray machine. You ought to be glad. Back in the day, I would have performed a full body cavity search," the second man said with a wink.

Nadia's hand flew up to slap him across the face, but he caught her arm at the wrist just before it could make impact. He met her scowl with a look of mild amusement as he leaned down to say, "Good afternoon, Ms. Spencer," before dropping her hand and leaving her behind.

Though her whole body felt weak, Nadia forced herself to focus. She waited until the two men were out of sight before she crept into the men's bathroom and slipped the notepad, recorder and memory chip into her pants pocket.

When Nadia finally walked outside the building, she was surprised to see the cab driver that had driven her from the airport sitting on the pavement with his head in his hands. On the curb directly in front of him were the remains of the interior of his vehicle, which had been cut-up and stripped down to the metal frame. Four other men who looked just like the ones she'd met in Ted's office hovered over the large trunk, apparently about to destroy that too.

She was too ashamed to even apologize as she slipped away from the scene as quickly as possible. The next day, Nadia told Human Resources that she was taking a vacation, effective immediately. Certain her apartment was both bugged and monitored, she took a duffle bag, $700 in cash, and a commuter rail to Newark, NJ, where she checked into the first economy hotel she saw. Anyone that knew her would never expect to find her there.

She left her cell phone and laptop in New York, along with anything else that had the potential to be traced or hacked. Her only plan was to have time to think and figure out what exactly she had walked into. With no access to her computer, Nadia scoured the news for coverage of the Seers, desperate for anything that would give her a clue as to the whereabouts of Joel and the others and the Guild's efforts to find them.

It was in watching these reports that Nadia began to focus her attention on the Guild protests in Geneva. When Ming Jhu had been arrested 8 months before, Thea Case's public vigil had been an endearing human interest story about one woman's determination to see her lifelong partner treated fairly. At the time, Nadia didn't think the story would survive a week in the frenzied media cycle. But in the months that passed, what began as a one-woman plea turned into a public hearing against the Guild and its mission. Sympathizers with the Lost Seers and those suspicious of the Guild in general began to rally around what had become the "Free Ming Jhu" campaign. As a popular local artist, Thea proved surprisingly adept at making the connections and partnerships that would keep her cause in the news.

Watching one of Thea's weekly press conferences, Nadia finally found what she needed — a way to prove some of the claims Joel Akida had made in his interview with her. A reporter in the crowd asked Thea what she ultimately hoped to gain from the continuation of her protests, given that Ming's trial was a little over a week away.

"You know, Ming never talked about her work. She was forbidden, which should tell you something. How can a benign topic like rehabilitation be a top secret endeavor if something ugly isn't going on beneath the surface? Ultimately, what I want from this—what all of us want here—is the truth. Ming was extremely knowledgeable about The Guild's operations as well as the state of the Seers themselves. If what Joel and the other Seers are claiming about the Guild's motives of exploitation are true, we all deserve to know it. Ming has those answers and I'm sure she has many more. Securing her freedom to find those answers should be our top priority."

"But she's facing the death penalty," the reporter countered, "and from what I hear, the Guild's case is pretty air tight. Do you honestly see her ever being released?"

"Well, first of all, it's easy for them to say their case is 'air-tight' given that the trial will be closed to the public and none of us can examine the evidence they claim to have against her. But I am a believer in truth and we here, are seeking that truth. When you seek the truth, it will find you. The world needs to hear what Ming has to say."

When you seek the truth, it will find you.

The phrase made Nadia hit the mute button on the TV remote. *Didn't Joel say almost the exact same words to me before we were attacked?*

Nadia started packing her bags immediately. She wasn't sure exactly how she would make it happen, but she needed to meet with Thea as soon as possible. A couple hours of library research and emailing Thea, half a day of begging her sister for money, and two days of traveling on her doctored-up and recently deceased mother's passport, had gotten

Nadia to Geneva in less than 72 hours. Three years before, Nadia had done an exposé on human trafficking. Never did she think she would use those same resources to smuggle herself out of the US and into sovereign UWO territory.

Thea rushed into the decidedly untrendy coffee shop where she and Nadia had agreed to meet ten minutes late, with no time to spare. When she plopped down in the booth across from Nadia, she got right to business.

"Ok. Let's hear your interview tape," Thea said without introduction.

"Not here," Nadia whispered as she looked around. "Are you sure you weren't followed?"

Thea stared at Nadia for a moment, taking in her tense disposition before she decided to slow down and set her purse on the table. "Yeah, I'm pretty sure I'm not being followed."

"How do you know that? They could be anywhere," Nadia asked.

"I don't know. Someone could storm in here any minute, but I've been at this for 8 months now. I pretty much eat, sleep, and shit on camera, so I think by now they assume that if I'm going to do something interesting, I'll probably have a camera crew with me."

Nadia stared at the freckles on Thea's pretty, round face. She could usually tell when someone was bluffing, but the fact that she was herself a fugitive of sorts made her anxious and unsettled. Nothing was as it should be.

"Ok," Nadia offered finally. "You said you had something to share that could verify what Joel Akida told me in our interview. What is it? Do you have her files or some documents? We can take them to my car and I'll–"

"I don't have the verification with me," Thea interrupted

"Why not?" Nadia hissed. "I told you I was coming. I don't have time–"

"I said I would have it by tomorrow, but I wanted to hear the interview with Joel Akida myself first and make sure I could trust you before I hand it over."

Exasperated, Nadia leaned back in her seat. "Alright, so if I let you listen to Joel's interview, what do you have that can make this stick?"

"Ming. I should have her back by tomorrow night."

For a long moment, Nadia's mouth hung open as her eyebrows shot up in surprise. But when her shock wore off, she immediately began gathering up her things. "I don't have time for this. I risked too much just to come here. I don't have time for fairytales…"

"Sit down," Thea ordered. "I'm serious. I was contacted a few days ago by the man who is holding her prisoner. He's going to help her escape. I don't know how, or even why. All I know is that she is supposed to be charged tomorrow at the UWO Internal Affairs Court. They will make the escape when they transfer her from the Guild's prison to the court."

Nadia scrutinized the details before she sat back down. "Exactly when is all of this supposed to happen?"

"Two pm tomorrow. If you think your place is secure, I can bring her to you immediately after. You can do your interview, ask your questions. You'll have 1 hour and then we're out of here."

"Where will you go?" Nadia asked out of curiosity.

"That's none of your business. You will have an hour to ask your questions and get the proof you need. That's all I can offer."

Listening to Thea, Nadia couldn't help but feel that the risks were beginning to outweigh the potential gains on every front. The memory of how it felt to be moments away from death were not so far away that she couldn't recall them—vividly.

"But how do I know if she can corroborate Joel's story? What you're talking about is a lot of risk for something that may or may not pan out. I'm not ready to get back in the middle of a fight between the Guild and its fugitives for merely the hope of some new information. I've been through that already and I don't plan to risk my life for this story again. When I talked to you, I thought you had some documentation, something tangible…" Nadia replied as she looked back at Thea unapologetically.

Thea held Nadia's gaze for a moment before finally reaching for her purse.

"If you're not willing to risk your life, I don't know why you came here. You contacted me, remember? I thought you wanted answers. I have something better than documentation; she was their head of Research and Development. If you think she doesn't know every detail of what the Guild has been doing, then you are kidding yourself. Whether or not what she knows is worth risking your life for is a decision only you can make. I've got nothing to do with that. But if you want the truth, Ming can give that to you."

"But there's no guarantee your plan will be successful. She could die tomorrow and then what?"

We all could die tomorrow. I was supposed to die 8 months ago, but I found something worth holding on for, Thea thought, but kept that to herself. She didn't know what Nadia's problem was or why she'd come so far to find the answers she now seemed so scared to get. *Maybe she's afraid of the responsibility she'll have once she knows the truth.* Either way, Thea couldn't dedicate any more time to figuring Nadia out. Pulling a napkin from the metal dispenser, Thea scribbled the number to the new cell phone the man from the Guild had provided for her. He told her it was the only communication device she was allowed to use starting tomorrow.

Shoving the napkin in Nadia's direction, Thea rose to her feet.

"Look, I hate to use a male metaphor here, but I don't have time to think of a more poetic way to say this, so here goes. I can't help you find your dick, ok? You have to do that on your own. If you find it before tomorrow and decide you want to use it, give me a call. Ming will have the answers you need."

By the time Nadia looked up from the 10-digit number on the napkin, Thea was already out the door.

Chapter 11: Redemption

It felt like it had taken Miguel a lifetime to figure out just what his true purpose was. To have lived that long and been a part of so much destruction would have been a tragedy without an opportunity for redemption. And when it finally came, he grabbed it with both hands.

The decision to help Ming had come without conflict. It was as simple as walking across a darkened room and offering Michael and Nina a hand up and a way out. Miguel, Ming, Nina and Michael each agreed to play their roles, keep the secret between them, and sacrifice their minds, their bodies, or both, for the chance to throw one more rock in the water—to stand against the ocean that must be stopped, that could be stopped if they only had the courage to resist the tide.

Nina would agree to rejoin The Red Order, shut her mouth and bide her time. When the inevitable came and Crane arrived to re-assess her willingness to comply with his agenda after the passive torture of her withdrawal, she would repent and succumb to the reintroduction of Luridium into her system. She agreed to do this even after Ming had warned her that her dependency on the drug would likely be greater than before, and the pain of withdrawal when she did finally detox would feel truly unbearable.

Michael's job was to convince Crane that Nina had seen the light and was truly his disciple once more. It only took Michael two days and a promise to be Crane's ally in "watching over her" for Crane to come down personally and escort Nina back to her room. The resolve in Nina's eyes, as her lips trembled when Crane took her hand, was the first truly inspiring thing Miguel had seen in years. Michael followed behind her with only a hint of tension on his face as Nina left her cell, looking every bit the dutiful brother, rescuing his sister from herself.

The rest of the plan was up to Miguel. When he'd said he might know a way to reach Joel and some of the other Seers, he wasn't sure if his idea would work. Miguel had never forgotten the determination with which Mrs. Chang had fought Jason off that day, so many years ago in Chinatown. At the time, he immediately recognized that the kind of devotion to protect that she displayed for Liam and Lilli came out of love — mutual love. Though Liam and Lilli ultimately eluded them, Miguel always suspected that the fact that he and Jason had left Mrs. Chang alive would make it likely that Liam and Lilli would contact her again. It was a theory he'd never gotten the chance to test, until yesterday.

With only four days left until Ming's trial, Miguel had to act quickly. Having no idea if Mrs. Chang actually kept in touch with Lilli or Liam and if so, how long the process of communication took, he needed to make sure he conveyed the urgency the situation required. For that, he needed to pay a personal visit. Miguel arranged for a flight from Geneva to San Francisco under the guise that he was visiting a brother with whom he had long since stopped communicating. When he arrived at Mrs. Chang's shop the next morning, Miguel waited until she had at least two customers in her store so that she would not try to run the minute she saw him.

Peering through the window of her store, Miguel was pleased to see that Mrs. Chang had aged well. Though her hair had surrendered the last of its black strands to grey, her stride was sure. And when the cool air rushing past announced his presence at the door, her eyes shone with immediate recognition. Miguel watched Mrs. Chang take a barely noticeable step back as she scanned the room in fear for her customers before glancing toward her countertop. At that moment, he imagined that she had a gun somewhere near the register, perhaps just in case they ever met again. The thought made him smile kindly at her.

Her beeline towards the register counter confirmed his suspicions. Though she was closer to the register, he knew he could beat her there with ease. He laid his left hand on top of her right, just as she reached under the counter. The skin on her hand was paper thin but vitally warm to the touch, in complete contrast to the cold defiance that greeted him when their eyes finally met. He held her hand firmly when she tried to yank it away.

"Please 阿姨 *auntie*. I need to get a message to Lilli and Liam. I need your help," Miguel whispered as close to her face as she would allow.

The endearment caused Mrs. Chang to shudder with fear. *What does he want?* She wondered as she snatched her hand away as quickly as she could without drawing attention.

Positive that she wouldn't be able to ready her gun in time, she used the only weapon she had against Miguel. "I would never help you — with anything. Leave here before I call the police," she hissed back.

"You can shoot me if you want," Miguel replied, flashing a glance to her left hand, which was still under the counter. "I won't leave and I won't fight back. I'm not here for that, not anymore."

Miguel slowly pulled a folded piece of paper from inside the front pocket of his trousers. Mrs. Chang eyed him suspiciously, but he continued. "This message is from two Seers *inside* the Guild. They know about the lies that have been used to capture them and they need Joel's help — Lilli and Liam's help — to expose them. They need the kind of help only the Lost Seers can provide."

Against her will, Mrs. Chang's eyes were drawn to the paper. She hadn't heard from Lilli in over six months, not since she received a letter with a picture of herself and a tall black man embracing against the background of a small church. Lilli was beaming with happiness in a purple dress while the young man wore a loose fitting shirt and pants in white and embroidered gold. Mrs. Chang knew roughly where Lilli was and exactly how to contact her. But she couldn't imagine sharing that information with the man that stood in front of her, under any circumstances. *What will he do when I refuse,* she wondered, before looking out at the two remaining customers in her shop. *I can't risk their lives,* she thought before returning her attention to Miguel.

"I have customers. I help them first, then *maybe* I help you," she said finally before making her way out from behind the counter.

"Of course," Miguel responded eagerly, stepping aside and pretending to browse as he watched Mrs. Chang rush through her sales. When the last customer left, she locked the door behind them and began pulling down the blinds to the small grocery store as she spoke to Miguel.

"I have been waiting for you for three years now. Every morning for three years, I take my gun out of its lockbox, and every night I lock it back up. I promised myself that I would shoot you on sight if you and your friend ever showed your faces here again." When she pulled the last blind down, Mrs. Chang turned around. Miguel noticed immediately that all the tension on her face from earlier was gone. She looked peaceful as she stood across the room, with her hands folded gracefully over her belly.

"But today, Mr. Peel came early for his order and I was in such a rush to fill it that I forgot to unlock the box." Her gaze was steady as she met Miguel's; she was a woman with no fear and nothing to lose.

"You're not going to help me, are you?" Miguel asked.

"I told you that already," she said matter-of-factly as she pointed a withered finger to her ear. "Your hearing maybe is not so good since the last time I saw you."

It had been a long time since Miguel felt genuinely nervous about anything, but staring back at Mrs. Chang, he knew he didn't have anything he could threaten her with, nothing that could possibly sway her.

"But I'm telling you the truth. I'm… not in the position I was before. I don't have that power anymore. I'm just trying to do this one thing right, to be on the right side for once."

Mrs. Chang shook her head in disbelief as she crossed the room to sit on a step stool she often used to reach the tea leaves she sold in bulk.

"I watched the news this morning, you know," she said once she was settled in. "Saw them reporting on how you people were close to finding Lilli and Joel and I thought it was a lie. I *prayed*. But seeing you standing here—now I know it was a lie because the Guild must really be desperate to send you here to ask me for help."

Watching her ease with grace into what he knew she presumed to be the last moments of her life was chilling. Absently, Miguel wondered if, when he met the moment of his own death, he would be so composed. Miguel could feel the sweat on his back as he realized that Mrs. Chang was more willing to give up her life than trust him with the information he needed.

No, he thought with renewed determination. *The plan won't work without her help. You have to make her believe you.* Miguel could see her body tense as he began to walk towards her, but he didn't stop until he reached the foot of her stool. He kneeled down in front of her.

"No one sent me. No one knows I'm here," he began. "And you're right. The news is lying. They have no idea where Lilli is or how to find her. Everything they've tried, including men like me, has failed. That's why I need your help. I finally understand who it is I've been working for and what I've been protecting all these years." The shame was so overwhelming that Miguel could no longer look Mrs. Chang in the eye.

"I thought I was noble, strong enough to make the hard choices, to sacrifice the few for the good of the many. Most people don't have the stomach for what it truly takes to lead, but I do. I always have. I told myself the life of the Seers and their families was a fair price for peace and a better world. But now I know that all I've really done is sacrifice the many for the power of a few. I've been like a shield for cowards. Now I know that what they have—what the Seers have—is in all of us. It is our legacy. And the Guild wants to keep that from us, so that the whole world is blind to the power that may lie in our hands."

Miguel paused then to look at Mrs. Chang and gauge her reaction. Hidden behind the hard lines of her mouth and the scrutiny in her stare, Miguel found a slight quiver at the edges of her eyes that told him she was struggling to hold on to her disbelief. Encouraged, he continued.

"This is not some kind of trick," he urged, leaning his chest into her knees as he placed the note in her hand. "We need your help to make this right. The woman who they have in custody now, Ming Jhu, she told me the truth. She can prove everything I'm saying, and she will. In three days, I'm going to help her escape. I am one of only two people who can open her cell, so they will know immediately that it was me who helped her. They will kill me and most likely claim that I was working with Ming all along."

When Mrs. Chang began to shake her head in disbelief, Miguel pressed closer, gripping her hand which held the note more tightly.

"When you see it on the news, you'll know everything I am telling you is true. Pass on this message. Let Lilli and Liam know that I didn't work alone—that there are other Seers who know the truth and need their help to expose it."

Mrs. Chang's hands shook with the effort it took to resist the sincerity in his eyes. Reflexively, she squeezed the note he gave her tighter. When Miguel had walked into her shop, she noticed right away that he didn't have the air of invincibility that he once carried with him, but she didn't expect humility and regret. She didn't expect him to come seeking her help. In confusion, her mouth opened slightly before she realized she honestly didn't know what to say.

"You don't have to do anything now," he assured her. "Just wait three days; then you'll know everything I am saying is true." Miguel didn't wait for any indication of her agreement as he rose to his feet and headed towards the front door. He knew there was nothing more that he could offer than the truth. Before turning the latch to unlock the door, Miguel looked back at Mrs. Chang. He wanted to tell her in that moment that she was his last chance to try to undo everything he had done for the Guild, but he'd already reached the limit of his vulnerability. From her stool, Mrs. Chang could still see the desperate need in his eyes for her to give him the trust that they both knew he didn't deserve.

That is why you pay with your life, she thought sadly before she uttered aloud, "Good luck."

The kindness of her gesture surprised Miguel. In response, he gave her a small smile as he nodded his thanks and headed out the door.

Ming had never been a superstitious person, but every detail about today seemed worth stressing over. Her palms were so sweaty that she didn't dare touch the fabric of the cheap suit the Guild provided for her as a "courtesy." Not only would the sweat be obvious, but she was pretty sure it would most likely leave a mark, which, in her paranoid mind, would somehow be viewed as an obvious sign that she was planning to escape.

Get a grip, she told herself, as she wiped her hands on the bed sheets and tried unsuccessfully to stop pacing.

She had been waiting for this moment for seven days. She'd been there that night when Michael first came to visit Nina. She'd heard the words and the promises—the plan that would free her from this place, this life, these people, but in her heart she'd tried to resist the hope. She agreed, if successful, to do her part, to try and find a way to expose the Guild. And now she had a plan. From Miguel, she learned that she would get an opportunity sooner than she thought. Thea had managed to arrange an interview with a reporter that very day—if, of course, Miguel showed up and they didn't both get killed first.

Miguel had seemed shocked enough, almost wounded, when she'd told him the truth about the genetic potential that all humans shared with the Seers. When she first discovered it, she was stunned herself.

Ten years before, Ming had been secretly running her own research on the Seers as her way to exercise her love for the open-ended possibilities of science once it became clear that Crane was only interested in exploitation. She'd been working on a theoretical model for genetic cloning and modification of the Seers when the computer produced an outcome that was identical to the DNA of a normal human. The only difference was the synthesis of genetic material that had been previously disregarded as junk DNA. The new model suggested delineation in Seers' capacities that corresponded with variations that occur naturally in the general population. After running the model several times, she realized it wasn't a mistake.

For Ming, it was a watershed moment—the most exciting discovery of her career and possibly of modern science.

She gathered up her notes and ran to Crane's office unannounced. Immediately, she began babbling and waving data sheets in his face. She excitedly described her discovery and the need to gather a large sample of DNA from the Seers and the general population in order to begin research on developing a catalyst to reintegrate the "junk" DNA into the chromosomal sequence.

She had been extolling the virtues of her findings for ten minutes before she even noticed that Crane hadn't said a word. By the time she noticed the silence, Ming turned around to find him gathering up her notes from his desk. Without a word, he rose from his chair and threw them on the open flames of his fireplace.

"What are you doing!?! That's my work! Didn't you hear anything I said?"

"Who else knows about this?" The question was his only response.

The way Crane stalked toward her made her entire body flush with fear, causing her to stumble in bewilderment. When he finally stopped, her back was up against the wall.

"Who else knows?"

"No one," she stammered. "I came to you first. I don't understand…"

"Your findings are irrelevant to the work we do here—the work *you* are supposed to be doing here. If you share this—tell a single living soul, continue your research in any way—Thea and anyone else you care about even remotely will suffer in ways that will make you wish I had only just taken their lives. I will make you choke on their blood. Do we understand each other?"

It was the first time he had ever threatened Thea directly, though Ming had dreaded the coming of that moment for years. Uncontrollable tears ran down her face as she nodded quickly. Ming left the minute Crane stepped aside. That night she destroyed all the evidence of her discovery and never told another person of her findings until Miguel.

Ming looked at her watch. *"Where is he?"* she mumbled aloud. It was 1:21pm and Miguel was scheduled to transport her to the courthouse at 1:15. But when the door finally opened, the well-groomed man that emerged holding the handcuffs that were meant for her was no one she recognized.

He's not going to make it, Ming thought, as the hope she'd tried not to feel burned away like acid in her stomach.

"Hello, Dr. Jhu. Mr. Le Dieu has asked me to prepare you for transport to court. He'll be down shortly to escort you to the trial personally." The stranger before her spoke in an all-business tone. He appeared ready to speak again before a dull popping sound coincided with his mouth closing again in an odd way. His eyes hovered on her for a moment before he collapsed dead on the floor.

Ming was frozen in place as she watched Miguel step unceremoniously over the man's body to place his right hand over the scanner that unlocked her cell. His left hand held his gun.

"Come on." It was all he had time to say as he grabbed Ming by the arm and rushed her out of the room and down two flights of stairs. Ming could barely keep up as they reached the underground garage and stopped abruptly at the last vehicle in what appeared to be a six-car motorcade.

Seeing Miguel through his side view mirror, the car's driver exited the armored luxury sedan at once, opening the back door for Miguel and Ming. Miguel met his hospitality with a knife to the stomach. As the man doubled over, Miguel used his momentum to shove him into the backseat.

Quickly, Miguel turned his attention to Ming. "Get in," he ordered as she stared back at Miguel in horror.

"He's dead," she said incredulously.

In response, Miguel pushed her in on top of the dead man and slammed the door shut before getting into the driver's seat.

"Echo 1 is ready. Motorcade proceed," Miguel said calmly into his earpiece as he put the car in gear. As the sedan moved forward and they cleared the garage, Ming rolled onto the floor of the vehicle. Fearful of the dead man falling on top of her, she scrambled to her knees and began banging on the privacy screen that separated the front from the back seat.

"Miguel! Please!" she yelled. "I need to get out of here. Let me climb up."

Confused, Miguel lowered the glass.

"Look, I'm sorry I was late. When I heard Crane decided to see you before the trial, I had to make some quick arrangements."

"It doesn't matter," Ming said, as she squeezed her body through the narrow opening. "I mean, thank you for coming. I just can't stand the sight of blood." As soon as Ming settled into the front seat, she felt instantly calmer. As she reached over to buckle her seat belt she caught Miguel looking at her with the same look of disbelief she always got when she told someone about her phobia. Once her seatbelt was fastened, she gave Miguel the same answer she gave everyone else. "That's why I'm a *researcher*."

"I see," Miguel said as he kept his eyes on the road.

They drove for 30 hopeful seconds before she felt brave enough to ask, "How long before they find out?"

It was then that Miguel heard the thin, menacing tone in his earpiece that he had been waiting for.

"This is Crane Le Dieu. Miguel Far has helped Dr. Jhu escape. Find them! I repeat, the prisoner has escaped!" Crane shouted.

Miguel's initial plan had been to simply escort Ming through the motorcade and let her out discreetly somewhere on the street where she would meet up with Thea and Nadia before leaving the country that night. But when Crane reassigned Miguel from Ming's detail at the last minute, Miguel had to improvise. By the time Crane was finished shouting, each of the brake lights on the 5 sedans in front of Miguel were lit up. Immediately, Miguel swerved to the left and began speeding down the one-way street of Rue Jacques Balmat. At the end of the block, Miguel made a sharp left into the oncoming traffic of Georges-Favon Boulevard.

Miguel ignored the sound of cars colliding behind him as he navigated through the panic of the drivers around him. He made it three blocks without incident before one of the motorcade cars rammed him in the back, forcing him to make a sharp left in order to miss the garbage truck directly ahead. The man pursuing them was not as fortunate.

"Here!" Miguel said, as he threw a cell phone in Ming's direction. "Text Thea. Tell her to meet you at Parc Saint Jean. There's an art festival there—tons of people where you can get lost in the crowd. I'm going to let you out as close to the festival as I can, then you need to run. Tell her you'll be there in 10 minutes."

Ming nodded frantically as she typed, sending the text to the only number that was plugged into the phone. "What about you?" she asked when she was finished.

"I'm going to lead them away," Miguel answered in a voice that was solemn and final.

"Miguel, I don't know what to say--" Ming began before Miguel cut her off.

"There's a duffle bag on the floor with some clothes. You need to change now."

There was so much Ming wanted to say to Miguel, so many words of gratitude that couldn't penetrate the intensity of the moment. Even if she somehow found the clarity, they were engulfed by the sound of sirens, reminding her that if she didn't focus, she wouldn't survive. And so she dressed as quickly as her seatbelt would allow as Miguel drove through the streets like a madman.

By the time she pulled a black wig that was the exact shade and length of her own hair and a tan oversized cap from the bottom of the duffle bag, Miguel had managed to get them over the Pont de la Coulouvrenière bridge in one piece. The car was banged and battered from every end, but not a shard of glass had shattered nor had a single bullet penetrated the exterior. Miguel had just turned the car around from a stint of reverse driving when he noticed Ming's confused expression.

"The wig is for him," Miguel explained as he jerked his head towards the backseat. "Listen… When I go under the overpass, you need to jump out. You'll have to roll because I can't stop. Otherwise, they'll know." Unlike when he had asked her to get into the backseat of the car with a dead man, Ming now understood that Miguel was absolutely serious.

"Ok," Ming croaked as she stuffed her hair into the cap and pulled it tightly over her head, hoping that it would act as some protection for her skull. When Miguel added that he would 'slow down as much as he could,' Ming took it as a measure of kindness even though she hadn't seen Miguel go less than 60 miles per hour ever since they pulled out of the garage. Eventually, he slowed down to 15 miles per hour before leaning over to push the door open and motioning for her to get out. She only had time to plant a quick kiss on his cheek before she jumped. By the time she recovered from the pain of impact to open her eyes, his car was already gone. With renewed energy, Ming forced herself to her feet and hid in the shadow of a small doorway as Miguel had instructed until all the cars pursuing him had passed. Then she waited another sixty seconds before she ran toward the woman she knew was nearby, waiting for her.

After dropping Ming off, Miguel waited until he heard the helicopters to make his final move. There was no point in setting up a decoy if no one was around to see it, he reasoned before pulling over. The inevitable shots fired overhead gave him time to set up the ruse. *Don't they know this is a level 10 armored vehicle*, Miguel thought with more than a little professional annoyance. He hated dealing with amateurs. *Nothing's going to get through here,* he thought, as he climbed through the backseat divider and put the wig on the driver. He knew once he opened the doors, the helicopter would be forced to cease fire because for this level of betrayal, Crane would most certainly want them brought back alive to fully experience his punishment. When Miguel kicked open the door and found his theory correct, he pulled the driver's arm over his shoulder and ran out the car.

Miguel was sure someone would eventually figure out that the person he was dragging toward the alley was the wrong height and build to be Ming, but he also knew that this would be discovered and discussed after the heat of pursuit, when it was too late to matter. Miguel dragged the driver's body down the darkened alley for a few blocks before discarding it on the side of a dumpster. He could hear the sound of the dogs barking in the distance and knew it wouldn't be long before he was captured. He'd dropped Ming off over thirty minutes ago. If all went as planned, she should be well out of their reach by now. But he kept running through the streets anyway, because anyone who took his life from him would have to earn it.

He didn't hear the sound of wind and something impossibly fast rushing past his right side until it was too late. It knocked him back from a well-lit street into the alley from which he had just stepped. He was sure there had been nothing in front or behind him until the second before he was knocked down. He guessed that whatever attacked him had been at least five feet in height, but when he got back to his feet he couldn't see anything but shadows in the alley. As he stepped forward to make his way back into the street, he heard a low growl that seemed to ricochet off the brick walls. Miguel took a step back until the growl rose to a sharp snarl followed by a voice that seemed half-animal, half-man, and vaguely familiar in its menace.

"Where is she?" the voice snapped, but in that moment Miguel was incapable of speech. His body was frozen in the realization that something he was utterly unprepared for was about to take place. Resisting the urge to scream, Miguel drew his gun with no more faith that it would save him than if his eyes could see through the pitch-black around him. He fired three shots that echoed so loudly off the brick walls that it hurt his ears. He got nothing but rough laughter in response.

"Where is she?" the strange voice said again. It was closer to him now, though he still couldn't see.

"She's gone," Miguel finally managed.

After he spoke, there was a moment so quiet that Miguel could almost imagine that whatever had addressed him was gone, until he saw the shadow on the wall three feet above his head span out into the shape of a claw. Before he could even gasp, the claw was over his nose and mouth, with talons that dug into his scalp and punctured his flesh as his body was lifted into the air. All around him was the smell of disease and roasted flesh. Yet still, Miguel could not see his assailant until a pair of bloodshot eyes within a grotesque head emerged from the dark, inches from his face. Paralyzed with fear, the sight reminded Miguel of the horrifying depictions of the damned that he'd endured as a frighten boy in Sunday school. Only this time, his nightmare was real.

"I trusted you Miguel. More than almost any human, I trusted you. But rest assured, whatever you have planned will fail. I will stop them," the beast before him promised as it slammed Miguel into the wall and near unconsciousness. "I will take everything from them that should be mine. But first, you will pay me for your betrayal."

Miguel was granted one last breath as the beast that held him removed its claw from his face. And in that second, Miguel thought of Mrs. Chang's hands resting peacefully over her torso and knew he would not face his death with any approximation of her grace. Instead, he let out a scream worthy of the last sound he would make as his head was pulled back by his hair just before his throat was ripped out by a set of mangled, jagged teeth.

CHAPTER 12: PRIME TIME

In the weeks since Joel completed his interview with Nadia, he'd had almost no time to wonder when or how she would use the information that he shared with her. The exchange between Katia and Alessandra had forced their entire team to come to terms with exactly why they were each a part of the Restoration Project. Though the discussions that followed were sometimes difficult, it resulted in a team that was more committed and focused than even before.

This renewed energy helped to keep their various operations working together, as they were all pulled in different directions. The Guild's campaign against them brought with it an unintended surge in new Seers who sought out Joel and the others. Some came in hopes of finding refuge from The Guild, while others simply sought a place to find some answers about who and what they truly were. The effort it took to coordinate the necessary resources to secure their safety had Joel, Alessandra, Liam, and Vincent traveling most of the time.

Back in London, the first human trials for the Restoration Project were well underway and starting to show results, even within the first week of administering the drug. Hannah and Marshall were the first to begin having dreams so vivid that they were difficult to distinguish from reality—even hours after they had awakened. But there were other signs as well. Almost all of the 19 candidates experienced some bouts of blurred vision, disorientation, and what they described as periods of "hyper-alertness," when everything from colors and sounds to the feel of water on their skin seemed more intense. Understanding the side effects and progression of the treatment proved all consuming for everyone involved in the process.

So they were genuinely surprised when Ngozi burst into a training Lilli and Tess were conducting on meditation to announce that Nadia Spencer had broadcast a report on the Seers late last night from a student-run college TV station in Geneva that had gone viral in less than 12 hours.

"They're about to play the video in its entirety. They claim Joel is on it," Ngozi said anxiously. There were always reports of Seer sightings and "exclusive footage" on the news that, more often than not, turned out to be complete fabrications. Since Chicago, Neva, Hasaam, and Ngozi had learned to let all the hype fade into the background noise of their lab. But the newscaster's mention of Nadia Spencer's name caught her attention. Since her meeting with Joel, Nadia had been MIA from the news network. When Ngozi heard Nadia's name in conjunction with a small student-run TV station, she knew that it was worth checking out.

By the time Lilli and Tess made it to the 2nd floor break room with the Restoration Project recruits, Eli, Neva, and Hasaam where already crowded around the large computer monitor that was streaming the program live. They waited in silence as the camera feed switched from the newscaster's grave face to a static-filled screen that slowly cleared into the image of an exhausted Nadia sitting on a folding chair across from the Guild's 2nd most-wanted fugitive, Ming Jhu.

"Good evening, ladies and gentleman. This is Nadia Spencer, live and reporting to you this evening as a fugitive to bring you a story of unimaginable proportions—a story you won't find on any other network because, frankly, the UWO does not want you to know what I am about to tell you. In bringing you this story, I have been through some of the most horrifying and awe-inspiring experiences of my life. I have been shot at, attacked, threatened and almost killed in my efforts to uncover the truth about the Seers. But I am not the only one who has made sacrifices for the truth. I was informed by a colleague I cannot name to protect his safety, and the safety of his family, that my former boss and mentor Ted Brenner was found dead in his home yesterday, most likely tortured and killed for his inability to track me down and retrieve the tapes that I am about to share with you. Learning of his death finally gave me the courage I needed to bring you this story.

"My special guest tonight has had a similar experience. As I speak, she is being accused and hunted for a crime she didn't commit. I bring her to you exclusively and very likely for the last time. After this interview, she will attempt to go into hiding from a power so great that it could fool and control the world with its lies — lies I intend to expose.

"I was not able to broadcast this report through my employer, World News Today, because they have been under severe pressure from the UWO to suppress this story, threatening my integrity as a journalist and the freedom of the press everywhere. I would not be able to bring this story to you if it were not for the fearless media students at the University of Geneva who allowed me to commandeer their studio in the pursuit of truth. After tonight, the world will owe you a debt of gratitude for your courage."

"My head hurts too much for this shit," Eric mumbled as he turned to leave the room. He was suffering from a severe headache as a result of the Restoration treatment and had little patience with what he felt was Nadia's overly dramatic build-up. Eric had almost crossed through the doorway into the hall before he finally heard something that was worthy of his attention.

"My special guest tonight," Nadia continued, "is one of the most wanted women in the world—Dr. Ming Jhu. As the former head of Research and Development with the Guild, Dr. Jhu had intimate knowledge of the Guild's work with Seers and what turns out to be the Guild's nefarious campaign, spanning over two decades, to exploit their gifts for the sole purpose of gathering wealth and power around the world. She is prepared to tell you her story tonight. But before you hear from her, I would like to air another exclusive interview with none other than Joel Akida, the Seer you know as the man responsible for the bloody terrorist attack in Chicago eight months ago. He and the other "Lost Seers," including Lilith Knight, Alessandra Pino and a group of an estimated 30 other unverified Seers and collaborators, have been vilified in the media as cold blooded-killers ready to unleash the madness of the Seers on an innocent world. But I can attest to the fact that Joel and his group saved my life from the very group that claims to be protecting us from them. I invite everyone viewing this broadcast to watch the interview with Joel Akida, then hear what Dr. Jhu has to say and decide for yourself."

The next two hours were filled with Nadia's unedited interview with Joel, followed by Ming's detailed and scathing account of the Guild's global effort to catalog, gather and control every Seer in any country, implicating not only the Guild, but also the UWO and every world leader within its ranks. That information alone was enough to push the broadcast forward and incite an international outcry demanding change and accountability. But what elevated the broadcast beyond anything Nadia, Ming, or even Joel had anticipated was Ming's admission that Joel was right—that the genetic marker the Guild stated was unique to Seers was in fact dormant—but present— in every human being. Up until Ming watched Joel's interview with

Nadia, she had no idea that anyone else had discovered the link, much less found a way to reactivate these abilities.

"If Joel has managed to find a catalyst for the reintegration of this genetic material," Ming stated during the interview. "I don't think it's possible to overstate the significance of that. It would change the world, the way we think, the way we communicate. It would be the next stage of human evolution."

Fully alert, everyone in the break room watched the news in uncertain silence.

"This," Lilli whispered, "changes everything." Before she could continue her thought, Lilli was interrupted by the sound of her cell phone ringing in a tone she had reserved for only one person. Without a second glance, she quickly answered her phone.

阿姨，你還好嗎？發生了什麼 ? *Auntie, are you ok? What's happened?*

聽著親愛的。我有一個消息要告訴你，有些人需要你的幫助。

Listen, dear. I have a message for you from some people who need your help.

Once the complete interview aired on network television, the response was swift, with protests breaking out all over the world. Most centered around state buildings and UWO facilities, with local leaders taking to the airways and the steps of their capitals in an attempt to appease and deny, but the fire had already been lit. By the time the Guild released its official statement, shock had given way to rage. One by one, peaceful protests turned violent.

Twelve hours before, the Guild's extensive internet and communications monitoring unit discovered the initial broadcast from the University within 15 minutes of it first airing. Nine minutes after it aired, the Guild's security team had stormed the small TV station only to find it empty and broadcasting remotely, despite Nadia's claim that it was a live taping. The team's heat signature detector, which could measure remnants of body heat on stationary objects, determined that the room had not been occupied in over an hour. Before they could determine the location of the remote broadcast signal, it was too late. Segments of the video had already begun appearing on the internet.

Once the interview was reported back to the Guild, internal fighting erupted among the Guild Council and top UWO officials as they scrambled to prepare for the inevitable spread of Nadia's video while trying to decipher how much of Joel and Ming's statements in the interview were actually true.

As the central figure in most of Ming's account, Crane was summoned from pursuing Miguel to answer to the Council. Annoyed and slightly disheveled, Crane walked into the meeting without an ounce of fear or remorse.

"Why have I been called back here?" Crane demanded.

"You're here because your incompetence has brought us to the brink yet again!" the Council Chair shouted back. "While you've been running around mindlessly, Ming has been busy. I assume you have seen Ming's interview. Did you even try to find her or is it your plan to ruin us?"

"My plan was to retrieve her... and Miguel," Crane answered coolly.

"Well, it's obvious you failed on one account. Do you at least have Miguel?"

Crane's eyes narrowed at the Chairman as he responded. "No. Your summons interrupted me before I could finish the job."

"Who cares about any of this? None of it matters now." Deidra Pile began. "In a few hours, that video is going to hit the networks. They'll be forced to air it because it'll be everywhere else." Shifting her gaze from the Chairman to Crane, she continued. "What I want to know is if it's true. Did you know the truth about the genetic marker?"

Crane let out a contemptuous scoff as he surveyed the Council in front of him. Even Andreas eyed him with open suspicion from across the room.

"You're like children," he responded finally. "Do you believe every bedtime story that's read to you? Of course it's not true! If it were, don't you think I would have tried to access that power in myself? Wouldn't that be something we would all want?" When no one responded, Crane continued. "Don't you see their plan? They are offering false hopes to the masses in return for allegiance, for loyalty. How can you not see how obvious this is?"

As Crane spoke, Andreas studied his every move. He knew his colleague well — well enough to know when he was lying. Andreas had counted two lies so far. But confronting Crane in this forum would not be to his advantage, so he watched the man he had once considered a confidante and friend and wondered about the depths of other things that Crane had kept from him.

Weighing Crane's words, Deidra found that his explanation still didn't make sense. "Why would Ming make this up? I've never known her to be prone to that sort of thing before."

"Because she was *in league* with them, all along, as I told you. Good God, wake up, people! You can't be persuaded this easily."

Leaning forward, Yusef ignored Crane's condescension. He was far more interested in how the UWO could survive the backlash from Nadia's video. "You're very confident given the severity of the situation we face. Since you seem to know so much, how do you propose we move forward? We surely don't have long before the video reaches mass distribution."

"We wait." Crane responded simply. "It makes no sense to try to stop what has already been let loose. We need to use this to our advantage. People will be angry, and we should let them be. Their anger will be our opportunity to strike."

"Strike?" Deidra asked with alarm. "People already don't trust us. Without trust, you can't govern, so I fail to see how you think mounting a war against our own people will solve anything?"

"They may not trust us, but in 24 hours, when the anger boils over into the streets, they will need us to do what we do best, to restore order. Each country will declare a state of martial law, giving us not only the authority to contain the protests, but also the freedom we have lacked to find and dispose of Joel and his associates once and for all. With martial law in place, all the legal constraints that have sabotaged our progress will be removed."

"So until then, we do what? Just sit here and take your word for it?" Deidra scoffed.

"*You* should be coordinating our resources," Crane snapped. "So that we are ready when things get out of hand. Deny Ming and Joel's claims, maintain an appearance of innocence, but be ready."

To Deidra's complete dismay, the Council seemed in almost unanimous agreement with Crane. Knowing it was useless to try to be the lone voice of reason, (especially since she didn't have a better idea), Deidra settled back in her chair.

"Is there anything else you think *we* should be doing to clean up your mess, Crane?" she asked.

"As a matter of fact, there is. Nadia Spencer mentioned during her interview with Ming the extremely well-financed operation she witnessed while with Joel. Find out who is providing those resources and cut them off."

As Deidra watched Crane turn and leave the room, she had to admit that Crane finally had an idea that she could get behind.

As the meeting broke apart upon Crane's departure, Andreas leaned over to his assistant, Christof who was dutifully at his side, finishing his notes from the meeting.

"Christof, I need you to find out some information for me as discreetly as possible," Andreas whispered.

Christof pretended to continue typing as he focused his attention on his boss. "Of course, sir. What do you need?"

"I want you to find Miguel Far's body."

Christof did a poor job of masking his confusion. "But… how do you know he's dead, sir? Crane said he wasn't able to find him."

"Crane is lying." Andreas insisted, as he kept his gaze on the departing Council members. "He found him and he killed him, I'm sure of it. What I need to know is why he's hiding that fact. I also need you to arrange a secret meeting with the members of the Red Order. I need to understand their reaction to all of this."

"I'm afraid that isn't possible," Christof stammered, uncomfortable that he knew more information than his boss. Alarmed, Andreas turned to face Christof directly.

"Why? What's happened?"

"Crane ordered most of the members into solitary containment an hour ago. He said that he suspected there was a traitor among them."

Andreas was silent as he tried to figure out why Crane failed to mention this information to him and the Council, until he remembered an important detail in Christof's statement.

"You said that most of the members were put in solitary containment. Which members aren't under suspicion?" Andreas asked.

"Only Tyrol, sir."

Andreas could almost feel the answers he was looking for just outside his grasp. He knew he had some of the pieces, but a clear picture of exactly what was going on eluded him.

"Find Miguel," Andreas finally said in frustration.

Without so much as a glance in his boss's direction, Christof put his tablet and phone in his satchel and rose from his chair. "Right away, sir," he whispered before heading out.

CHAPTER 13: CALLING

Looking up at the star-lit sky against the strange "mogotes" hills that surrounded the soft earth of the Viñales Valley in Cuba, Joel was a world away from internet access and sound bites of breaking news, but he knew the minute that Nadia's video made the network news from listening to the stream of Lilli's thoughts in his head. He'd had to leave London soon after he got back from Berlin to conduct a few raids, assist Alma with the set-up of their latest Rescue Center in Cuba, and guide the latest Seers safely to that location. Normally, Lilli would have been with him, but the start of the Restoration Project trials made that impossible. He'd been travelling a lot over the past three weeks, and though they were mentally and spiritually inseparable, the physical distance was beginning to wear on them both. He needed to go home.

But the spiraling events of the last few hours would make travel even more difficult than it usually was. After Nadia's video was released, the lack of a timely response from the UWO did exactly what Lilli had foreseen it would: spur the anger of people around the world. There were riots in almost every major city. But worse than that, there were already people claiming to be Seers who were taking advantage of people's desire to access this new ability. In the four hours since the interview was aired, some were already claiming followings and god-like status among mortals. It was one of the moments that Joel had dreaded most in his life — the senseless grab for power over something that no one could control.

He knew what he had to do, but he was not quite ready to come out of the shadows and lead the world into a new understanding of itself — an understanding that went against everything that was conventional and safe. But he'd set things in motion nonetheless. With Alma's help, he finished and posted a short video discouraging violence and urging people to use caution if they met someone who professed to be a Seer. Heeding Jared's warnings of the Guild's plans, Joel also alerted viewers to the impending martial law decree and urged people to remain calm.

After taping the message, Joel had stepped outside to get some fresh air and make a needed phone call. Xavier Renoit, his friend and financial backer since Joel was 16 years old, needed to be warned. Joel dialed his private number with a sense of foreboding in his heart. They had been through so much together in the last seven years. Joel had just begun working as a bellhop at the Excelsior Hotel in London when he first met Xavier. Xavier's wife had died years ago of a rare complication while giving birth, leaving him and his three-year-old daughter Adaline alone to deal with the whirlwind of publicity and attention that resulted from being one of the richest and most eligible men in the world. That day, Joel watched with fascination as Xavier exited his private limousine with Adaline wrapped inside his arms to shield her from the throngs of photographers that were there to welcome him home. He had just come from the lucrative New York Stock Exchange launch of a company he'd started only two years ago that was quickly valued at over fifty billion dollars. The press wanted a statement on his meteoric success. It was a typical scene for some of the hotel's more high-profile penthouse residents, but Xavier treated the entire spectacle with disdain. He brushed past the cameras and reporters with nothing more than a gruff "no comment" as Joel quickly opened the door to let them inside. Joel was staring down the last remnants of paparazzi when the front desk manager came out of the hotel to make a request.

"Mr. Renoit's daughter is throwing a fit upstairs. He asked if we've seen some kind of yellow flower down here. I told him we hadn't, but he keeps calling, so I figured I'd ask you. Have you seen it?"

When Joel scanned the pavement and didn't see anything, he turned back to his supervisor and shrugged.

"Don't worry about it. Something's wrong with that girl, anyway. She's three years old and doesn't speak a word. He needs to put her somewhere, or something," the manager mumbled before heading back into the hotel. Having grown up in an orphanage, his manager's suggestion offended Joel, but he said nothing. Joel was just about to leave for the night when he noticed a small yellow flower crushed between the hotel driveway and the curb. Joel carried the flower carefully to the front desk manager's office, only to find him rubbing his forehead in frustration as he clung to the phone.

"I'm sorry, Mr. Renoit, but we've looked everywhere. It's not here, sir. I'm not sure what you want us to do. We could send you up a bouquet of flowers if you like."

Joel cleared his throat and held up the flower that rested in the palm of his hand.

"Thank God," the manager mouthed silently before cutting off Xavier's pleading. "Oh, good news, sir! Our bellman just found it. I'm sending him right up… yes, sir. He's on his way."

In the elevator, Joel could hear the sound of Adaline's screams from several floors away. When the ornate silver and copper doors opened, he was met with a completely frazzled version of the man he'd seen exiting his limousine an hour before.

"Thank you," he said in a voice thick with emotion as Joel handed him the flower. "Please come in."

As soon as Xavier sat down on the floor and handed Adeline the flower, she closed it between her chubby hands and smiled.

"Papa fleur," she said with surprising clarity.

"Oui, papa fleur," he whispered back as a tear fell down his cheek. Smiling higher, Adaline kissed her father's cheek then rose to head down the hall.

"She saves every flower I give her," Xavier explained as he turned to Joel and began wiping the tears from his face. "I'm sorry. She doesn't speak often, but when she does... I always cry. I'm tired, I guess. She's been at it for almost an hour now. I don't know what I would have done if you hadn't found it."

"It's no problem," Joel began, as the sight of Adaline walking back down the hall with her pajamas caught his attention.

"Excuse me," Xavier said, as he turned towards his daughter. "I need to put her to bed. Please stay. I'd like to repay you. She's tired; it shouldn't take me long."

"It's ok. I was headed home anyway," Joel mumbled as he turned toward the elevator before Adaline caught him by his pants leg. Joel looked down at her curiously as she hugged his calf and waved goodbye before returning to her father.

The look of utter shock on Xavier's face caused Joel to worry for a moment.

"Please, don't leave. I need to speak with you," Xavier said finally before lifting his daughter into his arms.

It was that night that Joel learned that Adaline had been diagnosed with autism and that she had never spoken to or displayed affection to anyone other than her father, until Joel. That night they also learned how much they had in common, from losing their fathers at young ages and growing up poor. But unlike Joel, Xavier had been raised along with his four siblings by a hard-working mother who died before she ever saw her youngest son make his first million as a sophomore in college. Though Joel never shared the details of his parents' deaths or why he had dropped out of school, after that night, he and Xavier struck up a casual friendship. It was Joel's first since leaving Ngozi in secondary school.

But the turning point in their relationship came later, when Adaline suddenly became ill. With all the money in the world at his disposal, Xavier tried every doctor, treatment, and specialist. But no one was able to accurately determine why his daughter lay listlessly at his side. Seeing his friend in so much pain, it was the first time Joel was motivated to use his gift for anything other than trying to find his father. Joel was so surprised by how quickly the vision came to him that he didn't question if he should risk revealing the answer to Adaline's sickness to her father. He was certain that this was the reason why they had met. To his surprise, Xavier displayed only the slightest hesitation when Joel, with no medical or scientific background, told him that his daughter had a rare but curable genetic mutation called Wilson's disease. In truth, Xavier would have tried anything to save his daughter.

Watching Adaline's recovery finally convinced Joel that his gift was more than just a cruel paradox. He realized that he had been given his visions for a reason, and if he chose to find that purpose, it could be used to save people's lives. For Xavier, the decision to help was even simpler. After Adaline's diagnosis was confirmed, Xavier knew Joel was a Seer, though Joel never admitted it to him and refused to discuss how he came to the diagnosis. Xavier was not offended by his friend's silence. He understood that the Seers were feared and hated within society, but he didn't care. Joel had saved his daughter's life, and from that moment on, Xavier pledged his support and resources to help Joel with whatever he needed, whenever he needed it. No questions asked.

Despite the millions of dollars spent and the many struggles over the year, Joel knew their friendship was as strong as ever when his friend picked up his call on the first ring.

"Are you alright?" Xavier whispered as he moved quickly out of the bedroom where his daughter was sleeping and into the hall. "We've been watching the news. Ada is very upset. She's worried about you."

"I'm ok. We're all ok for now. Tell her not to worry. Listen, you need to be careful, Xavier. The Guild will be searching for you now. They are trying to figure out how all of this is financed. I don't want you to be caught in the middle."

Xavier was silent as he listened to Joel on the phone. He was still reeling from his friend's interview with Nadia Spencer in which he revealed for the first time exactly what he had been working on for all these years. Though he was worried about Joel, he was also intensely proud of the man he had become.

"It is a privilege to play a small part in what you are doing." It was Xavier's only response.

"Xavier... There are no words for what you have done for me."

"Then let's not use any," Xavier chuckled. "I'll be careful, ok? I've already taken care of most of this anyway. There is no paper trail for them to find."

"Just be sure. I don't want you..."

"I will. Now go. You know you have to make an appearance. It needs to be soon; there are too many questions now. People need to see your face."

"I know," Joel sighed reluctantly, "But they won't understand. It's not about me--"

"They won't understand it until you tell them. Remember, you were born for this. This is your gift."

"I know," Joel sighed again as his friend wished him good luck and hung up the phone. "I know."

The opportunity came before Joel even had a chance to hesitate. On the way to José Martí International Airport, Alma informed him that they would need to stop in Havana for gas. Although the petrol station on San Lazaro was the most reliable in Havana, Alma warned Joel that the wait to fill up would be at least 30 minutes. After a few minutes of inching towards the pump at a snail's pace, Alma saw Joel's tense expression and suggested that he take a short walk across the street along the Malecón, the broad esplanade that hugged the Cuban coast line with weathered walls. Grateful for the suggestion, Joel jumped out of the van. As the waves from the gulf spilled over the concrete barrier to spray his body with cool water, Joel felt refreshed and glad he'd taken the moment to stretch his legs and clear his thoughts. He hadn't gone more than 150 feet before the first person noticed him and whispered her suspicions to the group she was with. By the time, Joel heard the commotion there were half a dozen people walking behind him.

"¿Es usted?" *Is it you?* The young woman who first noticed him shouted. "¿Usted es Joel Akida? El hombre de las noticias?" *Are you Joel Akida? The man from the news?*

Startled to recognize his name in the unfamiliar language, Joel turned around to see six pairs of eyes staring at him in awe. His stomach turned and he felt a lump form in his throat as they waited for his response. But before his panic could set in, he forced himself to breathe through it. His ambivalence about taking his leadership of the Restoration Project into the public arena had clouded his visions of this moment for years. Looking now into the eager woman's face, he finally accepted that this was exactly how it was supposed to be.

"Si," he answered tentatively, keeping his eyes on the small group that was now standing before him.

"Es él! El Vidente!" *"It's him! The Seer!"* the young woman shouted before rushing towards Joel and taking his hand.

"¿Puede decirme mi futuro? ¿Puede verlo ahora?" *Can you tell me my future? Can you see it now?*

Joel looked around to find the streets that had seemed nearly empty a few minutes ago quickly filling with onlookers. He also saw Alma jump out of her van and run towards him with the rest of the crowd.

"No, I can't see your future now. That's not why I'm here," he told her, slowly and solemnly.

"Tell us what's going to happen!" another person shouted.

"Why? Quiero saber." *"I want to know,"* the young woman pleaded as she held Joel's hand more firmly. As Joel felt the insistence in her grip and the crowd pressing in around him, he closed his eyes to try to decipher the things that were being shouted at him.

"¿Qué pasara?" *What's going to happen?*

"Quiero ser un vidente!" *I want to be a Seer!*

"Quiero ser uno de ustedes." *I want to be one of you!*

"Creemos en usted, Joel! Creemos en usted!" *We believe you, Joel! We believe in you!*

"¿Qué pasara'?" *What's going to happen?*

Though his visioning was not perfect given the escalating chaos around him, through Prime, he was able to understand enough to know that they were all asking the wrong questions. He opened his eyes as he felt Alma's energy drawing near enough for her small hand to reach his shoulder.

I'll translate for you, she offered, as Joel stood to the height of his father and addressed the crowd.

"I can't tell you what happens next in your own lives. That is up to you. You don't need to believe in me. You need to believe in yourselves because you *are* one of us, just as I am one of you. You have the same abilities that I have. The only difference between us is that my mind was given back the connection that we as a people have lost—our connection to each other and to the life that binds us all together. We are the first, but it is you, through your actions and your decisions now, that will determine what happens next; you who will restore this legacy. Look amongst yourselves; you are the future Seers of this world, not me."

Undeterred by the crowd's silence and the sound of sirens approaching, Joel continued.

"But before you seek to have that connection restored, before you take the treatment that you've all heard about, that we hope will give you back the sight that you have lost, ask yourselves first—Are you ready to serve the future you wish to see? Are you ready to be responsible for your part in it? Because the future you see will not always turn out the way you want. It will require you to… sacrifice things that are precious to you, but it is what is meant to be. The only gift, the only peace, is in knowing your role and accepting it. If you are ready, if you surrender, then you will have sight. With that sight comes power, but you cannot have power without surrender."

Waiting for Alma to finish translating his words, he looked out into the crowd to find their blind faith replaced with the thoughtfulness and doubt he'd hoped to see. It was a good start.

By the time she'd translated his last phrase, they were surrounded by blue and red flashing lights as the Cuban authorities pressed through the crowd towards Joel and Alma. What both the authorities and Joel did not expect was for the crowd to begin pushing back.

"Déjalos en paz! *Leave them alone!"* the crowd shouted at the police as they formed a human barrier between the authorities and Joel and Alma.

The young woman who never let go of Joel's hand led them through the crush of people who moved willingly out of their way. As Joel and Alma passed through the crowd, onlookers brushed hands over their backs like well wishes.

When Joel finally rose up, he was amazed to find them near the open door of Alma's truck.

"Salud," the woman whispered before disappearing back into the throng.

Joel kept his energy focused on the crowd as Alma inched the truck towards the nearest alley and watched with rare pleasure as the police fired tear gas canisters that somehow never released their gases into the crowd before finally giving up and retreating in frustration.

CHAPTER 14: PAPA FLEURS

*D*on't stop kissing me, Joel urged, as he felt Lilli pull away to unbutton her shirt. *Stay with me.*

In response she moved closer, so that their hands brushed up against each other and got in the way as they tried to undress. The awkward, extra effort made them laugh but their lips never parted.

It took Joel nearly three weeks to make it home from Cuba. By the time he and Alma made it to the airport, the network news stations were already reporting on his speech in Havana thanks to an anonymous post on YouTube the moment he left the crowd. Though martial law had yet to be declared, the UWO used its authority to ground all outgoing flights from Cuba and enforce a search of all passengers and incoming vehicles, effectively cutting off that route of escape. It took a few more hours for Alma to charter a boat that would smuggle Joel to Jamaica where, for a small fortune, they could find another pilot ready to fly him out.

From there he travelled by car and on foot through Central America and into the US using a network of Seers with whom he had formed relationships over the past 7 years. But it was his old friend, the Escort, who finally got him a ride on an oil tanker in Texas that was bound for England. The journey had been arduous, but Joel found it strangely cleansing to be out in the world again. In the small towns and dirt roads that he had stayed on to avoid capture in Central America,

Joel reconnected with the basic kindness and compassion of everyday people. Some knew who he was and asked him questions about his experience as a Seer, what the Restoration Project hoped to accomplish, and what he thought the world would be like if everyone could do what he could. To his surprise, these discussions were filled with curiosity and caution more than desire for power. Most people he met were not sure if they would want the power to see the future if it could be given to them. What they wanted most was peace, happiness for their loved ones, and an opportunity for a better life.

While having these conversations and listening to the stories people shared, Joel realized how his isolation over the past 7 years had warped his view of the world. He'd been so focused on protecting himself and working against the Guild that he'd grown to distrust almost everything and everyone around him. While he knew this was essential to his survival, it had also made him forget the difference between the Guild and the rest of the world. If he was going to lead, he needed to remember who he was really trying to reach. His trip back had given him the chance he didn't know he needed to reconnect with the heart of what really mattered.

And that included Lilli. When Joel finally walked through the door of their warehouse, he was surprised to find it completely silent. From the open floor plan of the building, he could see that most of the lights from the first and second floor were off. There was a warm glow emanating from the windows and the open door to their third-floor loft, but it was quiet. Too quiet.

Slightly confused, he began to climb the steps. Lilli had told him earlier that she was working on a surprise for him when he got home and that she wanted to disconnect their minds for the day to make arrangements. At the time, he'd wanted to protest, but feeling her excitement, he couldn't say no. The moment she released her consciousness from his, the sensation of being cut off from her felt like a part of him had suddenly gone deaf and blind. In the weeks that he travelled, his connection with Lilli had been constant. From her, he learned that Alessandra, Tenzen, and a few other Seers had begun reaching out to people through video and random appearances to show their support and make sure that the Guild's lies didn't go unchallenged.

Through their connection, he also discovered that shortly after Ming's escape, Nina and Michael's involvement was discovered during a Quorum in which they were unable to block Aaron's vision of an older woman calling Lilli to inform her of Nina and Michael's request for help. In response, Crane kept Nina and Michael under heavy sedation to prevent them from attempting to make contact with any of the Lost Seers. Though Pytor and Aaron were initially questioned, they no longer drew Crane's suspicion.

But what Joel cherished most was their ability to share every conversation, every impression he'd had on his journey back to London. Their own discussions on what he experienced made them both excited about their role in whatever the future held. Having come to rely on seeing and understanding the world through their joint perception, he found it more difficult than he would have thought to go through the day focusing only on what he could perceive.

Reaching the landing to the third floor, Joel felt a rush of disappointment as he faced the open door to their loft and found it empty.

Maybe she went out for some food, Joel consoled himself as he made his way to the door with his head down. *I could search for her…*

Two steps before he made it through the doorway, he suddenly smelled her perfume and felt the dewiness of her skin as her consciousness came rushing back to him.

The rest of Joel's body was frozen as his head snapped up to find her standing just inside the door. He blinked several times at the sensations that inundated his mind.

His stunned expression at seeing her face;

Her excitement over the sudden racing of his heartbeat;

The coolness of their wood floor under her bare soles;

And her concern over the raw soreness of his own feet.

And the blossoming joy of just being in each other's presence again.

Joel could tell by the dampness of her hair that Lilli had just showered… and dressed, though he had no idea why she'd bothered with the latter task.

At hearing his thoughts, she giggled.

"Hi," she said shyly, but he could only shake his head as he finally closed the distance and kissed her.

The depth of their ability made touching an exquisite thing — multi-layered and profound, as their minds and bodies slowed to experience each caress as it was both given and received. In the beginning of their relationship, they had moved quickly out of anxiousness and need, but as their connection grew, it often became too overwhelming for their minds to process their dual sensations and the emotions those sensations inspired. So they took their time, coming together slowly as they savored each touch in a way no other couple could.

But there were times like tonight when their lovemaking was both overwhelming and not enough, calling them to something that could not be experienced in their human forms. Times when the desire to merge into one inseparable being was nearly all-consuming. It was something they discovered shortly after they were married, when their communication became almost solely thought-based. During a particularly long visioning session where Joel and Lilli quorumed for hours, seeing things and events unbound by time or space, they began to experience a feeling of weightlessness, as if they were floating just above the floor. For a moment, the separate boundaries of their skin seemed to melt away into one mass. The feeling was one of both utter euphoria and boundless peace, until they registered the sensation of surrendering their bodies—not as spirits drifting away, but as something powerful expanding outward from within. Shared fear forced their eyes open as they stared at each other with a strange glow emanating from underneath their skin. It was the first time they'd stretched the limits of their gifts and transcended their bodies to the place where consciousness ends and death begins.

This incident was the first of several they had experienced together and talked about in secret. Knowing that death was something they could choose together removed the fear from the eventuality. But the implications for their work and their families were enough to keep them grounded on this side of reality. Sometimes, though, in between the bliss and fatigue of their love-making, they would talk softly about what it would be like to truly exist together as one, letting the theories and ideas they would come up with lull them into the most tranquil slumber.

It was after three o'clock in the morning when Joel woke suddenly. Unsure of what had jolted him out of his sleep, he looked down to find Lilli draped across his body, holding him possessively, the way he liked. Even in their sleep, their minds connected, and his lips curled up into a slow smile as her dream filtered in, giving him an explicit understanding of what woke him up. From the ache in her muscles and the depth of her sleep, he knew she was too tired to try what she was dreaming about, but as he rolled her body off of his gently, he resolved to wake her up with an equally satisfying compromise in the morning.

As Joel got up to head towards the bathroom, a vivid flash of Xavier being shot and falling down into a black hole nearly knocked him back onto the bed. Working to keep from panicking over the sudden image, Joel made his way to a chair at the far side of their bedroom in hopes of keeping Lilli undisturbed. He sat down and tried to focus, but his heart pounded faster and his palms grew sweaty with every reoccurring image of his friend tumbling into darkness. By the time he realized that his visioning wasn't going to work, Lilli was kneeling at his side.

"What are we going to do?" she whispered anxiously, knowing all too well what Xavier's friendship meant to him.

"We have to warn him," Joel said sadly. "We have to tell him to get ready."

⬤ ◦ · · ◦ ⬤

Xavier had been up most of the night. While packing the car with two suitcases full of Adaline's clothes and her favorite things and gathering up the small cash supply he had stashed around the château, he had little time to think about what he knew was likely to happen soon. He needed to be out of the house within the hour.

The call from his attorney's office had been a shock. Given the multiple layers of precaution he took to guard his financial dealings, he had never expected the Guild to discover his identity. His attorneys were among the very best in the world, equally respected and feared by their peers and adversaries. But as he found out tonight, even they were not able to completely thwart the unlimited power of the Guild.

The mistake had been small, but unavoidable. Even with time running out on his own life, he couldn't bring himself to regret the decision he'd made. The names of people listed on a succession of guardianship document were required to be filed with the French probate office. The process allowed the state to verify the identity of the person who would be granted custody of a minor in the event that both parents were deceased. While Xavier's attorneys had managed to have the documents sealed from the public, the probate office still kept a record on file.

Locked in some administrator's office, this would never have been a problem. Anyone wishing to verify guardianship had to provide court authorization and show ID. His attorneys had also paid handsomely to be forewarned if any such request was made, giving them the opportunity to circumvent any requests and protect their client's privacy. But the list of billionaires around the world was short, and under martial law, suspicion was enough to gain access to anything. His attorneys had already been fighting a battle with the UWO over the review of his financial statements. When this yielded nothing unusual, the UWO demanded all of Xavier's personal documents. When the few strands of due process held up in court to protect Xavier's rights, his attorney advised him that they would still collect the guardianship document from the Probate office as a precaution.

Xavier's attorney had promised to meet him with the document at his residence in Marseille by 10pm. He'd waited anxiously by the phone until one of the law firm's most senior partners called Xavier at 11:15pm to inform him that his attorney, along with four men on the firm's personal security team, had been shot and killed by a group of men they believed were sent by the UWO to steal the file. The document identifying Joel Ismael Akida as the sole guardian of Adaline Marion Renoit was gone.

So by the time Xavier received Joel's call a few hours later, he already knew what he was going to say.

"I'm sorry—so sorry—that I couldn't protect you from this. I'm sorry I ever got you involved," Joel said.

"Don't be, Joel. I'm not. I know Ada will be safe with you. I'm grateful you agreed to take care of her for me. Are you sure Lilli won't mind? You agreed to this a long time ago..."

"Of course not!" Joel insisted, pulling Lilli's body closer to him. "Lilli and I would be honored to have her."

Both men struggled to keep their emotions at bay as they laid out the particulars of where they would meet to transfer Adaline safely into Joel's care. The will, the money, Adaline's needs, all of it they had discussed years ago, before Joel began searching for other Seers like himself. In the event of Xavier's death, Joel was the executor of the entire Renoit estate until Adaline reached the age of 21, at which time Joel would manage the estate on Adaline's behalf. Xavier had already instructed his attorney's to give Joel any and all help he needed to secure his and Adaline's safety and well-being.

Deciding that a public location would provide the greatest deterrent for an outright attack, they agreed to meet at 4pm the next day at Jardin Albert I Park near the Fontaine des Tritons in Nice. A popular jazz festival was taking place there and would provide some measure of anonymity within the crowd.

Lilli and Joel didn't sleep the rest of the night. By 7am, Katia, Jared, Maura, Alessandra, and Liam were gathered at the warehouse with grave concerns over the blind spots in their collective visions of Joel's meeting with Xavier. Like Joel, they could see Xavier being shot, but the timing and exact location that Alessandra could usually pinpoint without effort eluded her and the rest of the group. Jared and Katia's assurances that they were not being blocked by the Guild's Quorums gave them little comfort as they contemplated who else would have an interest in hiding the outcome of their meeting. As a precaution, Katia, Maura, Lilli, Alessandra, and Liam decided to accompany Joel to the meeting.

Walking into the park, it was almost easy to forget the real reason they were there standing amongst the crowd. The mood was jovial and relaxed as people swayed to the live jazz music being performed in the park's amphitheatre and piped through several speakers.

Katia smiled in fascination as she looked out into the stream of people, just enjoying themselves in the late afternoon sun. Though Katia was 24 and secretly harbored a great interest in music, she had never been to a live concert in her life. Despite the severity of the situation that brought them here, Katia was also excited about the addition of a child into their lives. She'd missed the children at the commune terribly since they'd had to leave Iowa, and she looked forward to being surrounded by the purity of a child once again. Sensing Maura's gaze on her, Katia looked back to where her friend was standing a distance away with Joel, Alessandra, and Liam. Maura smiled back briefly before returning her attention to seeking out any source that might be a danger to them.

Maura spotted the little girl from Joel's description first, noting that she must have grown almost a foot since the last time Joel had seen her. To her surprise, the little girl smiled and waved in Maura's direction, as if she knew her. Maura watched curiously as Joel bent forward with his arms open to receive her. Adaline moved quickly towards Joel with an even broader smile, but she didn't let go of her father's hand.

"My god, you're huge!" Joel whispered as he hugged Adaline tightly. She giggled softly, but said nothing in reply as she looked over his shoulder to the other members of his group shyly.

Still hugging her, Joel was surprised to feel Adaline's hand wiggle into his jacket pocket and leave something light inside. He moved immediately to retrieve it before Adaline held him closer and whispered into his ear, "It's for later. Don't look at it now."

"Ok," he said with a chuckle, assuming that she might have been embarrassed to share what ever she'd given him amongst so many new people.

Pulling back slightly to reach for Lilli's hand, Joel changed the subject. "This is my wife, Lilli. Do you remember her from the pictures I sent you?"

"Yes," Adaline said aloud in a slightly raspy tone. "I remember."

"Hi," Lilli said without extending her hand. "It's nice to finally meet you. Joel has told me so many wonderful things about you."

Adaline nodded her head in response, then slowly extended her hand. "It's nice to meet you, too."

Lilli was stunned by the gesture. Joel had warned Lilli that, with the exception of himself and her father, Adaline did not like to be touched. Lilli looked between Joel and Xavier for approval before taking the girl's hand.

"It's ok," her father mouthed as he looked down at the exchange proudly.

When she finally touched the girl's palm to her own, Lilli felt an immediate exchange of energy followed by a flash of the same image of Xavier's death that she first saw in Joel's mind, but the image was clearer than even she or Joel had seen. Lilli realized with alarm that the new scene she saw took place in almost exactly the same spot in which they were standing.

"Be careful," Adaline leaned in and whispered before she withdrew her hand from Lilli's grasp.

Both Joel and Lilli's bodies straightened anxiously as they began searching the area around them.

Xavier noticed the change in their posture immediately, but didn't want to say anything about it in front of Adaline, who seemed peaceful and happy as she leaned against him.

"Thank you again for this," Xavier began as he watched Joel intently, trying to discern what had caused the sudden change in his mood.

When Joel turned back to Xavier, his eyes were filled with pain and sorrow. "I'm sorry, Xavier, but I don't think there is any time. We have to go now… for Ada."

Xavier thought he had cried himself out the night before, on the drive here, but tears sprang to his eyes readily as he tried to face the moment he dreaded most with courage. His legs buckled as he knelt down to speak to his daughter one last time.

"Ok Ada, it's time to go. You remember what I told you?" he said in a shaky voice.

"Yes, Papa."

"Ok then, go with Joel. He's going to take good care of you."

There was no sadness in her face as she wiped her father's tears away. "Yes, Papa."

"I love you, baby. I love you always. Always. Don't forget that."

The tears were coming so fast that she had to use her palms to clear them from his cheeks.

"Don't cry, Papa. Don't cry."

"Ok, I won't," he lied as the tears continued. "Now, go on."

Adaline didn't seem to be paying his farewell any mind as she continued to clean his face with her hands, but he couldn't manage to tear himself away from her. He only just heard the vague sound of a woman's distress that drew the others' attention.

"Katia!" Maura shouted as she watched her friend being pulled into the crowd by a man whose color did not go beyond a grey black emptiness that she had witnessed only once before.

Maura's scream tore Joel and Lilli's attention from the crowd and the exchange between Xavier and his daughter. Alessandra and Liam immediately took off after Katia as Joel and Lilli continued to scan the area.

"One last hug, Papa," Adaline said as she smiled brightly at her father. "Pick me up for one last hug."

Pulling the old cigar box of dried flowers that she'd insisted he carry from underneath his arm, Xavier lifted his daughter easily, savoring the feel of her warmth against his chest.

He didn't hear any sound to make sense of the burning sensation that pricked his back, he just knew that his heart had stopped and he was falling helplessly backwards into darkness with his daughter's arms still clasped around his neck. He thought he'd seen Joel's body flinch backwards away from them, but he didn't know why and couldn't find the focus to care. With his last breathe he watched in wonder as every flower he'd ever given Adaline seemed to float in the air around him, bathing them both in petals.

"Papa Fleurs," he heard Adaline say in a voice that quivered and faded.

He couldn't think of a better way to die.

CHAPTER 15: TO WRESTLE WITH DEMONS

Every feeling of excitement, warmth, and hope she'd had was drained from her the moment he uttered three simple words.

Where is Marcus?

Shame and guilt rushed in like a tidal wave to fill the void and drag her under. She barely noticed the strange man and his terrible grip as he led her away from the crowd.

It had all started so well as they waited for Joel's friend Xavier and his daughter Adaline to arrive. Staying close enough to see her friends, Katia had taken a few deliberate steps away from the others, allowing herself to feel a part of the crowd and to adopt their carefree energy. Though she knew she couldn't wander off, she wanted to simply indulge in the revelry around her, if only for a second. But a second proved too long.

He approached from behind with a voice as smooth and seductive as velvet, wrapping around her mind with no give or room to back away.

"Excusez-moi, mademoiselle. Puis-je vous poser une question? "

Excuse me, miss. Can I ask you a question?

The voice spoke in the language she knew best. She turned towards it willingly.

When their eyes met, Katia was surprised to find that the man stood at least a foot above her with a face that was more weathered and older than the voice betrayed. From his features, Katia imagined that he might have been handsome at some point in his life, but that time had long since passed. Despite his marred features, she felt transfixed as his deep-set gray eyes appraised her openly. Without hesitation, he reached for Katia's hand, enveloping her in a familiar warmth that radiated throughout her body. He stepped forward. Before she had time to wonder whether or not she should allow him to come so close, he whispered the three words that broke her.

"Où est Marcus?" *Where is Marcus?*

She wasn't sure if it was the sudden pain of his grip around her hand or his words that caused the tears to prick her eyes; they were both secondary and far off compared to the shame that overcame her. Despite all the progress she had made over the past few weeks and all the ways she knew it wasn't true, she couldn't stop herself from answering his question, if only to herself. *He's dead,* she thought. *He's dead because of me.*

Whether it was the tears running down her face or the way her body seemed to buckle with grief, she didn't know, but the man before her seemed satisfied with her response. He nodded as he grabbed her around the waist and drew the side of her body to his. The surge of guilt that followed caused her to gasp in actual physical pain, without a thought of trying to escape the hands that held her. From what already seemed like too far away, Katia heard Maura scream her name. She looked up in time to see Joel turning his attention towards her a fraction of a second before he was shot in the shoulder. The scene pulled Katia back into the world around her as she saw Joel and Xavier torn away from each other like two halves of a fallen tree.

Katia's eyes shifted to the little girl she'd hoped to meet, Katia watched in horror as the tiny red dot on the back of Adaline's cream sweater spread out undisturbed by the still body beneath.

It was only then that she registered Liam and Alessandra's voices, clearly and loudly bellowing her name. But by then, the man who held her had moved them both farther into the crowd so that she could no longer see Joel or even make out Liam's tall shape above the rest. Frantic to make sure that Joel was alright, Katia struggled against the hands that held her, but his grip was unmovable.

"You killed him, too," the man hissed into her ear. "They are all going to die because of you."

"No!" Katia screamed as she shut her eyes against the memory of Joel being shot and stumbling back, just like his father had. She'd been powerless to stop either. In that moment, her hate for her own existence coursed through her veins like a jagged knife. With a sick satisfaction, Katia opened her eyes to find her arms and legs sliced open and bleeding, inflicted by a singular desire that she'd never felt so strongly before to destroy herself once and for all.

In her despair, Katia hadn't realized how much she had distanced her mind from the Collective until she felt Maura's thoughts clinging to the edges of her consciousness.

Katia! Come back to us! This isn't you! Maura spoke to her. *I can see his color infecting you. You have to fight him, Katia! This isn't you anymore.*

But he's dead. They're both dead, because of me, Katia sobbed.

Katia, I'm here! Joel's thoughts were clear and strong as he spoke to her. *We're coming to get you.*

Relief cracked through the darkness in her mind. *You're alive,* she gasped, before Joel continued.

It's just a graze. Why would you think I was dead? Joel began before he heard the answer in her thoughts.

Don't believe anything he says to you, Joel warned. *Stay with us. We're coming.*

Renewed, Katia began kicking her bloody legs in the first real attempt to fight back since the man had taken hold of her. It was then that his touch began to burn.

Looking down at the large hand that wrapped around her wrist, she could see her own skin begin to blister and peel underneath the edges of his grip. The pain was excruciating, but not beyond what she could manage. Katia had burned herself before – many times. But the more she tried to jerk and jostle her body to disturb his gait, the more steadfast his movement seemed to be. Desperate to find anything that would help her break his hold, Katia focused on the environment around her. The first thing she noticed were the trees and the street lights passing by her at an abnormal speed. And though it felt like they were walking, her feet were completely off the ground.

Slowly, her mind came into focus. *No one should be able to do this,* she realized as she looked around to see that they were at least a mile from where she had been standing less than 3 minutes ago. The grip on her body felt like it would crush her bones, but she resisted the panic inside her so that she could stay connected with the others.

Something is wrong, she thought with growing clarity. *We're moving too fast and his touch- he's burning me with his hands. Something's not right.*

Is he a Seer? Alessandra asked warily.

No, I don't sense that connection, Katia answered. Testing her theory, she tried to reach out to his mind in Prime, but her thoughts didn't seem to register with his at all.

Determined to try to find answers, Katia twisted her body from its backward position so that she could see his face. "Who are you?" she yelled into the side of his neck. "Where are you taking me?" In response, his grip grew impossibly tighter, and with it she could feel a new wave of sorrow taking over. Memories of her family kicking her out into the street and the bitter loneliness of her childhood flooded her mind, causing her body to go momentarily limp under the weight of her sadness.

He's using you! Maura yelled back. *He's using your grief, your shame, to control you. Don't let him,* Maura begged. *Please.*

The idea shook Katia's mind fully awake. Ever since Berlin, Katia had been slowly trying to honor the sacrifice that Marcus had made for her. In the weeks that followed, she'd finally accepted her right to heal from the pain of her past. Up until today, she had been proud of the progress she had made, claiming a little bit more of herself with each day — right up until the moment he touched her.

Through the Collective she could see Joel, Lilli, Liam, and Alessandra all running towards her — risking their lives for her. Beyond them, she sensed Jared, Tess, and so many others rooting for her survival, willing to do whatever it took to fight for her life. And in their love and conviction, she finally understood that her own guilt and shame had not only held her back, it had held everyone who cared about her back as well. The same guilt that made her vulnerable was now making all of them vulnerable. And she would not allow that to happen — not anymore.

The minute her body registered her decision, the blood stopped flowing from her cuts. Katia closed her eyes and focused the hate and loathing this man was somehow able to inspire in her outward, shifting their purpose from a means of self-punishment to a weapon of protection. Katia had never heard the guttural sound that escaped from the man beside her, but she recognized the sound of pain immediately. Encouraged, Katia opened her eyes and looked down to see the first deep gash appeared on his forearm.

"Who are you?" Katia roared again as she cut him across the face with her thoughts.

The man tried to move faster, but stumbled as Katia began tearing the flesh on his legs. At the same time, Katia flooded the Collective with every detail of her interaction with him, from the change in the temperature of this touch to his inhuman speed and strength to their exact location where he seemed to slow down a few feet from the Gare Centrale Thiers train station. The blood pouring from his arms made them slippery enough for Katia to finally free one of her arms, but before she could use it to any advantage, he whipped her body around like a rag doll and threw her down against a concrete wall near the entrance to the station. Unable to stand from the broken bones in her ankle and right arm, Katia watched as the man stalked towards her.

"Enough!" he shouted. "You've served your purpose."

As he reached out to strike her dead, Katia used the last threads of her consciousness to sever the hand aimed at her. The screech he let out before stumbling away was deafening, and unlike any sound a man was capable of making.

With her last thought before slipping into unconsciousness, Katia made sure that the others understood that what they were chasing was not human.

Running at full speed, it took Maura, Joel, Lilli, Alessandra, and Liam another 2 minutes to make their way to Katia. Alessandra knelt down immediately to assess her wounds, as the others scanned the area for any sign of being followed.

"She's alive," Alessandra said in a gust of relief. "And not too badly off, given what he did to her. I think I can heal her enough to move her," Alessandra began before catching Liam's wary expression. They had already had a fight about how and when Alessandra should use her healing abilities. She wanted absolute freedom. Liam wished they could forget she'd ever discovered the gift. They decided on a compromise — she would do whatever she could without putting her own life in peril.

"It's not like before, Liam. I promise. She's in much better condition than Ben was." When Liam didn't respond right away, Alessandra added, "We can't leave her here."

"I know," Liam finally admitted. "Alright, but don't push it. Someone's already called the ambulance," he said, hearing the sirens drawing nearer. "They should be here soon."

As Alessandra began her work, Joel and the others tried to ignore the open stares of those around them as they sought out Katia's assailant.

"Maura, can you sense him? I can't see anything clearly," Joel asked, but before Maura could answer, they heard muffled gunshots followed by the screams of passengers from the underground train platform. Seconds later, people came pouring out of the train station as they tried to escape the gunmen below.

"You, wait here!" Joel shouted to Liam as he, Lilli and Maura went for the steps.

Before Liam could think of a reason to protest, they were gone, swallowed up in the crowd as he watched his sister run towards the place everyone else was trying to escape. Standing guard as his wife went into the deep meditative state needed to heal Katia, Liam anchored his focus to the things he could control rather than the familiar feeling of helplessness that gnawed at his confidence. Keeping the crowd of growing spectators at a safe distance was easy enough. He was an angry man with guns openly displayed. One shake of his head towards an over-eager man and his camera was enough to let everyone know that they could look but couldn't touch.

But when the tone of the whispers around him shifted from curiosity to fear, Liam caught the frozen gaze of two young men as they stared at something on the ground. Gasps and screams of fear followed as the crowd around him began to back away and run.

It only took Liam a second to discover what had caused everyone to flee. Less than 20 yards away from where he stood lay a severed hand with burnt dark brown-black flesh and large fingers that curled up in the shape of a claw with sharp talons at the end of each tip. Liam recognized the hand immediately.

His throat went dry as he knelt down to stroke Alessandra's back. He kept his eyes fixed on the strange shape as he spoke.

"Baby, you need to hurry up. We've got to get the others. I think something's coming for us."

From behind him, he heard Katia emit a small gasp as she regained consciousness. Risking a backwards glance, he felt a pang of relief as he saw that Alessandra, though perspiring slightly from her efforts, was vital and unharmed.

"Who's coming?" she asked anxiously as she helped Katia sit up.

"Them…" Liam replied as he pointed to the severed hand on the ground.

Amidst the swarm of people trying to escape, Lilli, Joel, and Maura fought their way down the steps. Following the sound of frightened whimpers and gunfire, they made their way to the main platform to find four soldiers lording guns over a group of 20 passengers cowering on the ground.

In front of the hostages stood Tyrol, Pytor, and Aaron. Pytor and Aaron wore somber expressions as they stared back at Maura, Lilli and Joel, while Tyrol stood apart with a devious grin.

"We're happy you could join us," Tyrol said triumphantly. "It's been a while since our last reunion."

Fighting back the flash of regret he felt for not letting Vincent kill Tyrol in Berlin, Joel spoke first, "What do you want?"

Seeming even more pleased by Joel's brevity, Tyrol's grin spread impossibly wider. "We've come to do a little exchange. You for them. If you agree, no one needs to die here, but if you resist, well, let's just say it won't end well for these people here, or you, I'm afraid."

Lilli tried to mask her concern as her eyes darted around the room in hopes of seeing Michael and Nina.

"Looking for someone?" Tyrol asked Lilli knowingly.

Lilli narrowed her eyes in disgust, but did not answer.

"As I'm sure you can imagine, the events of the last couple of weeks caused quite a stir in our little group. We've had to keep a close eye to make sure no one was consorting with our enemies. Unfortunately, we discovered we had a few traitors among us. Nina and Michael aren't quite as adept as you would have liked at blocking their thoughts during Quorum. We know they've tried to contact you."

"We already know what you've done," Joel answered back. "And you should also know that we're not going to let you just walk away. One of you murdered a man and his child today. You will pay for that."

"A child," Tyrol muttered curiously. "Hmm. I didn't see that, but then again, I'm guessing by the look on your face that you didn't either." Tyrol paused, hoping to get a rise out of any of the Seers in front of him. When they remained silent, he shrugged and continued. "Makes you wonder who could have blocked both our visions of the outcome of this meeting. I've got to be honest with you; I didn't think that we would be able to get you here, but Crane said that he would handle it, so we came. And here you are."

Standing in front of him, Maura, Lilli, and Joel had some of the same questions that Tyrol expressed. But instead of engaging in a back and forth with him, they used the time that he spent gloating to figure out a way to free the hostages.

By the time Tyrol finished, they'd worked out the first part of a tentative plan.

"What you have planned," Maura began, "isn't going to work out the way you think. All the people behind you fear you more than they do us. They, for the most part, are decent people. They want to stay alive more than they want to kill us. You are the worst person here."

Tyrol stared at Maura for a long moment, wondering if they shared the same talent.

"How do you know that?" he asked finally.

"Because I see who you are, who all of these people are. I don't need to quorum with you to know you think only of yourself," Maura answered

Tyrol lost his smile as he listened to Maura's truthful assessment of him before he finally spoke. "I've also never met another person who can see things the way I do. It's… curious."

Maura hesitated for a moment. Though she'd never met another Seer with her ability either, she didn't particularly want to trade stories with the man in front of her. But she needed to keep him talking, in order to give Joel and Lilli time to finish connecting with the other people in the room. So far, all the hostages and hired security were on board and had agreed to stay down no matter what. The only people who remained undecided were Pytor and Aaron, and neither of them wanted a fight if they could help it. Reluctantly, Maura kept talking.

"I see color, mostly, or the absence of color sometimes. But unlike you, I seek out the good in people. You, on the other hand, are drawn to evil things."

"That's because I like to win," Tyrol sneered. "And the bad guys always seem to have the upper hand, don't you find?" Tyrol waved his hand around the room to prove his point.

"No," Maura answered, "Not today."

"That's because you think I'm the worst thing in the room."

His choice of words sent a shiver up her spine. *He knows what tried to kill Katia,* she told Lilli and Joel. *He knows, and it excites him. He doesn't fear it.*

"I said you were the worst *person* in the room, not the worst thing. I sense its presence, too, though I can't see it. But you're wrong if you think you can benefit from whatever it is. It doesn't need you and when it's finished with whatever you think you're doing for it, it will destroy you. That is its only power."

"We'll see," Tyrol said nonchalantly, but Maura could see that his confidence had been shaken by her words. "In the meantime, let's see how good you are. Bring up one of the hostages."

When no one moved, Tyrol looked to the back of the room.

"Did you hear what I said?" He roared. "Now!" When his demands went unanswered, Tyrol turned around, intent on retrieving one of the hostages himself before Aaron's voice broke his stride.

"This is wrong, Tyrol," Aaron said in a soft, but determined tone. "These people haven't done anything wrong. There has to be another way."

Tyrol opened his mouth to argue, but then shut it quickly as he finally registered the changing mood of the room. Among the security team that had entered the tunnel under his authority, not a single man was willing to look him in the eye. The evidence of his command had somehow evaporated in the short time he wasted talking with Maura. In a quiet rage, Tyrol extended his fingers so that no one behind him could perceive the movement, and with a slight twitch, he snapped the necks of each guard who betrayed him. The sound of bones cracking echoed off the walls as the soldiers' bodies collapsed in unison. The underground platform erupted with loud gasps and screams of terror.

Pytor took a step towards Tyrol in a frightened attempt to stop him from hurting anyone else, but Tyrol proved too quick. Tyrol extended his hand towards Pytor with the intention of grinding the bone of Pytor's sternum into his heart, but he couldn't complete the task as Joel barreled towards him, knocking him to the floor.

The next few seconds happened in a blur as Pytor clutched his chest and fell to the ground. Simultaneously, Lilli and Maura went into action, yanking the hostages to their feet and guiding them towards the staircase that exited the tunnel. But it didn't take long for the physical struggle between Joel and Tyrol to escalate into the full use of their powers. As Tyrol lay trapped underneath Joel's body, watching the hostages he had planned to use as leverage get away, his anger bubbled out into a force that propelled Joel's body off of him and into the ceiling before he came crashing down to the floor. Watching the first of the ceramic tiles break off and pepper a stunned Joel with rubble gave Tyrol a renewed sense of purpose as he got to his feet and began shaping the force of his energy towards the first of two pillars that held up the archway to the stairway exit of the platform. The sound of metal and concrete folding in on itself was deafening as the first pillar exploded, sending shards of ceramic, concrete and steel throughout the room. Moments later, the archway began to crumble. But before the heavy debris could make its full decent to crush the hostages below,

Lilli used her energy to create a barrier between the fallen debris and those around her as Maura continued to usher the hostages through. Recovering from his fall, Joel used his energy to throw Tyrol across the room before tackling him again in an attempt to stop him from destroying the second pillar.

But the damage to the structure was done. Maura was only able to get the first group of hostages safely through before the second pillar began to give way. If she continued through, Lilli could easily keep the tunnel open for the others, but when it fell it would cut her off from Joel, leaving him alone to deal with Tyrol and whatever presence Maura sensed.

"Go! Go!" Lilli shouted to the hostages behind her. When they scurried past, Lilli turned to Maura. "Take them the rest of the way. We'll find another way out!" Maura only had time to look back at Lilli for a moment as she pushed the hostages forward and out of the stairway that was quickly disintegrating around them, but the risk of what they were both prepared to do hung in the air between them.

Be careful, Maura answered back before the last person ran by and the remaining ceiling began to crumble, erasing Lilli from her view.

The force with which the concrete and steel pummeled the steps behind her shook the ground as Lilli raced back down the stairs to escape its path. Suddenly, she felt a gust of fresh air behind her as dirt began to mix with the dust. She realized that the collapse of the ceiling had created a sinkhole in the street above, sending chunks of debris from the street and sidewalk into the stairwell. Leaping from the last step of the staircase onto the platform, Lilli crashed down and rolled inches away from where the avalanche finally stopped.

Disoriented and covered in dust, Lilli sought Joel out only to find him gritting his teeth under the weight of Tyrol on top of him. In her peripheral vision, she could see Aaron holding Pytor's limp body and begging Tyrol to stop, but she didn't understand what was taking place until she noticed the bones in Joel's face seemed to pulse in and out as if being broken and rebuilt in a painful repetitive pattern. It was then that she saw Tyrol's fists clenching in and out. She remembered the similar gesture from Alessandra's thoughts in Berlin.

He's trying to crush him, Lilli realized.

Lilli knew that with their bodies so close together, there was no way for Joel to shield himself from Tyrol's attack. With a blinding rage, she was on her feet in an instant, barely noticing the sudden burn in her right calf. Her only thought was to get Tyrol off of the man she loved. But as she lifted her foot to run towards Joel, something caught her by the tail of her jacket and yanked her face-first back onto the floor. Furious at whatever had delayed her progress, Lilli was about to roll over and face her attacker, but was stopped by the wide-eyed terror in Joel's expression as he looked at some point behind her and then back to meet her eyes. The look of pure fear on his face was something she had never witnessed in her life.

Before she could begin to try to understand what was causing him to be so terrified, she was jolted to her feet, then grabbed around the waist by an arm that held her in an iron grip. It was only then that she saw through Joel's mind the image of herself being held captive by a monster. The beast stood 9 feet tall with filthy, ruined skin that stretched across its immense body like worn, cracked leather, covered with fresh and healed over scars. The protruding forehead, cheeks, and jaw of his face were exaggerated and grotesque along with a twisted black mouth that when opened to speak revealed a blackened collection of twisted teeth.

"You are the one I came for," he rasped as he held Lilli high above the floor with one enormous arm. His other arm quivered oddly at his side as it dangled without a hand.

"Yes!" Tyrol hissed excitedly above Joel as he held him down. "Now you see what I'm talking about. Just give in. It's useless. God only knows what he's going to do once he gets his hands on her."

It was exactly what Joel needed to hear to override the unfathomable pain of feeling his bones being crushed and rebuilt while he was completely conscious. He felt his purpose, the total of all the energy he had summoned. In that moment, any pain he had ever endured meant nothing compared to the need to get on his feet and fight.

Joel could no longer feel the pain as he focused his attention on Tyrol's pulsing fists. In his determination to save Lilli, the effort it took to break Tyrol's wrists was as easy as blinking an eye. Tyrol's screams of pain seemed distant as Joel felt his energy surge and ripple throughout his body, repairing what was broken and restoring him to his full strength.

The beast watched in growing concern as Joel rose up from the ground.

Undecided about exactly what to do with Tyrol, Joel's energy left him hovering in mid-air, until he heard Tyrol ask the beast for help.

"Please," Tyrol begged, as the beast backed away from Joel. "I helped you find her." It was all Tyrol had time to say before Joel made his decision and Tyrol's body burst spontaneously into flames. In that instant, the beast unfolded an enormous pair of torn, weathered wings and took to the air as Joel ran towards them. But, hopelessness filled his eyes as he realized he couldn't run fast enough and Lilli's outstretched hand slipped through his fingers.

Unable to keep her body from being dragged into the air by the thing that held her, Lilli projected her mind toward Joel as he clawed up the rubble after her. But her image only haunted him as he screamed her name until it faded with the light of the street as she fell into unconsciousness.

CHAPTER 16: TAKEN

The image of a young girl laughing faded in and out of Lilli's mind like a crumbling photograph.

"Be careful," the girl whispered before bursting into a cascade of dried flowers. "Be careful." Her voice echoed into the bottomless dark of Lilli's mind.

What does it mean? Who is the little girl?

Lilli couldn't remember anything. All that was true was the feeling of weightlessness, as if her body was spread out and suspended in mid-air. She passed out again before she could ask herself exactly how that could be.

Hours later, a bright light shined behind the thin cover of her eyelids. She flinched, squeezing her eyes tighter in a vain attempt to block out the glare. But the light grew brighter. Someone with rough hands grabbed her face and held it tightly. Resigned to her inability to escape, Lilli tried to open her eyes. The light was blinding as it burned and caused her eyes to tear, but she didn't feel enough or know enough to even be afraid. The feeling of being detached from her body, her own mind was wrong, uncomfortable, but she couldn't form a single thought as to why she felt the way she did.

"How much of the sedative did you give her? It's been nearly 12 hours. I thought she would have recovered a bit more by now."

"I filled the dart as you instructed, Master. I did everything exactly as you instructed."

"Yes, I'm sure you did. I'm not angry," the other voice replied with a sigh. "You did well. This one has haunted me for quite a while now. I almost can't believe she's here."

"How is this girl able to haunt *you*, Master? She is only a Seer."

There was a long pause before the Master answered.

"No, she is no ordinary Seer. She is... special in a way that I do not understand. She made me feel fear for the first time in... centuries. You have brought my nemesis to me."

There were no more words spoken as the hand that held her released its hold and the light in front of her went out. Temporarily blinded by the sudden change in lighting, Lilli sat motionless with her head hanging down as she heard a few muffled noises fade into silence. Lilli was aware that she was sitting upright, but she couldn't feel the chair beneath her. In the midst of the darkness that surrounded her, uneasiness grew in the pit of Lilli's stomach as she sensed the absence of something even more essential than her body. Her lips moved in the shape of a word her mind did not recognize.

A menacing laugh came from behind her moments before the chair she was sitting on was kicked out from under her. With a gasp, Lilli dropped to the floor on her knees, then fell forward. It was only as she raised her hands to brace herself that she felt the drag of chains around her wrists. The rusted metal cut her cheek as she collapsed on top of her hands.

"Joel?" The voice scoffed. "He will not come for you. You can't even organize your thoughts enough to contact him. I've made sure of that. Mixed in with the sedative I gave you is one of the oldest versions of Luridium. Its suppression of higher cognitive functioning is so effective that it prevented visioning in nearly every Seer in our trials. Some couldn't even remember their own names, which, I think, is what you are experiencing right now."

Lilli's pupils finally adjusted enough to the dark to look up into the face of the man who was now squatting down before her. Her stomach tensed in a way that suggested she knew him, but like the image of the little girl before, his face had no context or meaning.

A smile spread across the man's face as he raised a finger to brush away a lock of hair from her cheek.

"You don't even know who I am, do you?" he cooed. "Don't worry, love, you won't feel a thing until I want you to, and by then, you'll remember exactly who I am."

Madness. Every part of Joel that was not focused on finding her was in a state of madness. His skin was at once chilled and sweaty. His body was rigid though his heart threatened to beat right out of his chest. The sob that stuck in his throat hollowed his voice whenever he spoke, while his eyes burned, wide and dry. But most of all, Joel could not be touched, not by anyone. He could still feel the wisp of Lilli's fingertips as they slipped through his hands.

Liam was only slightly better. He had been right above the sinkhole as it began to cave in, with no time to do anything but hoist Katia up into his arms as he and Alessandra moved just in time to avoid being sucked under. By the time they recovered their footing, a new wave of people poured from the station, running as fast as they could from the danger they had barely escaped. Maura emerged last, seeking out Liam with controlled fear spreading across her face.

She didn't make it to them. As Liam stared at Maura, tracking her approach, he watched her eyes suddenly shift from his to someplace above his head. He watched as her steps came to a halt and her hands flew up to cover her mouth. From behind him he could hear Alessandra gasp, "Oh my God."

Liam turned around to see his sister, dangling in the air, trapped in the arms of a creature that should not exist. Except Liam had seen this demon before; he just didn't know what it was until now.

As if Lilli's distance drew the sound nearer, the next thing Liam heard was Joel screaming her name as he climbed his way up from the sinkhole. His hands were bloody by the time he reached Liam and their eyes met, sharing the same lost expression.

After escaping to one of the homes Xavier owned in the area, Liam, Alessandra, Katia, and Joel spent the next two hours searching — every Quorum, every Seer in the Collective that could tell them anything about her whereabouts. Though there were plenty of suspicions about who the creature was and what it all meant, their discussions stayed focused on the very narrow path of things that might be related to their first priority — bringing Lilli home. Through Quorum, they went over every detail in Katia, Maura and Joel's memory from the past several hours, hoping to discern the clue that would lead them to her location. But there was no information to be had. As each door they opened proved fruitless, it became clearer that whoever had orchestrated this plan was operating outside the Quorums and the Guild. It also became apparent that whenever the creature they witnessed in Berlin and Nice was involved, their sight became clouded. Beyond Maura's ability, they were unable to perceive the actions or even presence of these creatures among them.

Once the Guild was eliminated as the source of the attack, the question remained whether or not this creature acted alone or in concert with someone outside the Guild, and, if so, who would have cause to single Lilli out among Seers. From inside the Quorum, Joel thought back to the day of his father's death. It was the first day he and Lilli had ever physically met and the first time she had projected her mind outward to threaten a tyrant who cowered at the very sight of her. As the Quorum observed Lilli's memories in his mind, they knew that somehow Crane was behind Lilli's abduction. The only question now was how to get to him.

As the Seers quorumed, Liam worked with Ngozi and Eli over the phone to scour every satellite image Xavier's communications company could give them. Using this information, they were able to track the creature's flight north into Italy, but from there the weather patterns obscured his image, making it almost impossible to project his final destination. Unable to sit still while his sister was in danger, Liam decided to try to track the creature's travel from the ground. Armed with an exact GPS location of his last sighting just west of Turin, Liam was ready to go within 15 minutes, heading into Italy by car.

"It's obviously found a way to hide its existence this long. I doubt if this... *thing* is just going to keep flying around to wherever it was planning to go," Liam spoke over speakerphone to Eli as he loaded extra clips into his backpack.

"Are you going alone?" Eli asked warily.

"Yeah," Liam answered without bothering to look behind him. "They're still in Quorum and I just can't..."

Liam jumped a little at the sound of Alessandra's voice coming from behind him.

"Of course he's not going alone," Alessandra said tersely as she stepped to his side and grabbed her own backpack.

"I thought..."Liam began as he immediately registered her displeasure with his plans. "I thought you needed to stay here and do your thing. I don't want to stop that. You guys probably have a better chance of finding her than I do, but she's my sister and I... I just can't sit here. I have to do something."

"I can do my *thing*, with you," Alessandra said with more understanding. "We'll find her, Liam. Together, we will find her."

Walking towards them, Joel spoke up. "What you said before, Liam, I think you're right. Maura cut off his hand. It could have slowed him down."

Though it was the best lead they had, the thread of hope between them was barely strong enough to withstand the weight of their despair.

"We'll let you know the minute--" Joel whispered as he stopped next to them.

"I know," Liam answered, raising a hand to place on Joel's shoulder before he remembered and let it fall to his side.

"I'll stay connected," Alessandra added before taking Liam's hand to leave.

After Liam and Alessandra left, Joel broke away from the others to focus all his energy on finding her. He'd felt it the moment Lilli lost consciousness, just before she disappeared. Part of the reason for this he knew could have been the altitude, but he'd also found a tranquilizer dart among the debris at the station which suggested the use of some sedative—Luridium or worse—was involved. As the hours ticked on, Joel knew there could only be two explanations for why he could no longer sense her presence—she was dead or the drugs they'd given her had stolen her ability to connect. Everything within him implored her to hold on, to reach out to him for even just a flicker of a moment, but the undertow of silence stretched on in his mind leaving him to all his own worst thoughts and fears.

Joel stared out the window of Xavier's apartment for a long time, wondering how far Lilli was from where he stood. Anxiously, Joel jammed his hands into his jacket pockets to ward off the chill of Lilli's absence only to find the letter that Adaline had given him right before she died. Remembering his friend and the little girl who had been gunned down in front of him, Joel's heart broke a little more as he took the rolled up envelope from his pocket and spread it open. The small inscription he read on the front of the letter was like a jolt of electricity to his entire body, casting everything that happened in a whole new light.

Read this after Lilli is taken

Adaline was a Seer. Though the truth was as plain as the ink on the envelope, Joel couldn't reconcile it with the little girl he had known almost all her life. *But Ada was only ten,* he reasoned. He'd never heard of a Seer besides Lilli for whom the gift had manifested so young. While Joel usually could sense a Seer as soon as their ability began to emerge, looking back at all their interactions, he realized, the clues were subtle, but clear. *But why didn't I sense it,* he wondered.

Replaying the events of the day and how difficult it had been to discern any details about Xavier's death before they reached the park, Joel realized their vision got clearer the moment Adaline touched Lilli. As he looked down at the envelope again, he could feel the tremor growing in his hands.

Why would she block us from seeing her father's death, he wondered. But the question he feared most was what else she might have known that she waited until now to tell him. Joel tore the letter open, letting the envelop fall to the floor as he unfolded the handmade parchment inside.

Joel,

Please don't be mad. I am sorry I couldn't let you and your friends see Papa's death. I knew it would have hurt you both too much to know in advance. Don't worry about me. I am with Papa, which is all I've ever wanted anyway. From what I can tell, getting shot doesn't even really hurt that much.

I know you know this, but I can tell you're going to feel bad, so I'll say it here. There is nothing you could have done. The Guild tested me when I was born. If I hadn't died with Papa, they would have still killed him and I would have died with them after they used me, the same way they use others like us. So I'm glad I got to go this way.

I know you will find Lilli. I just don't know how you will find her. In my mind, I see her floating or suspended, but it doesn't really make sense. After that, she kind of fades, but I don't see her die. The vision feels more like she changes somehow, but I don't understand. It's like she's still here, but she's not. Sometimes, I wished I could have told you what I am. I know you would have taught me how to use my gift better. But I guess I saw the things that were most important to me. I hope Lilli is ok. I like her. You guys make a really nice couple. Anyway, I have to go. Papa will be in soon to tuck me in and I don't want him to catch me writing this. I love you, Joel, even when I'm gone.

Ada

His tears fell freely as he clutched the letter tightly and pressed his forehead against the glass. Adaline's words gave him few answers and no comfort as he stared out of the window, feeling more lost than he ever had in his life.

Seven hours after Lilli was taken, they had a breakthrough. While monitoring the Guild Council, Jared had noticed the shift in Andreas and Crane's relationship over the past year. Crane had all but shut Andreas out of the process of overseeing the Red Order, especially after finding Tyrol, leaving Andreas more time to grow suspicious of Crane's agenda within the Guild. As Jared began to focus on Andreas as a means of getting to Crane, he saw how they would be able to use Andreas' secret investigation into Crane to turn him into a reluctant ally.

When Alessandra saw Jared's vision, she immediately began reprogramming their GPS device.

"Wait, we need that-- " Liam began before Alessandra cut him off.

"We need to go to Geneva," Alessandra said with cautious excitement. "Jared's found someone—someone who can help us find Lilli."

Before Alessandra had even finished her sentence, Liam was already making a U-turn towards the highway.

"How long?" he asked, trying to keep his anxiousness in check.

"The GPS says 2 hours and 39 minutes, but we're going to make it in just 2."

It looked like Andreas' impromptu meeting with the Guild Council chairman was finally winding down, as the man rose from Andreas' living room couch unsteadily. Andreas stood up from his chair and tried not to appear too excited about the departure. For an hour and fifteen minutes, Andreas nursed his club soda while the Chairman drank glass after glass of his best scotch as he droned on about the need for the Guild to get a handle on the press and control the damage caused by Ming's tape.

Andreas had always suspected that the Chairman was more of a glad-handing bureaucrat than a leader. He'd brought his concerns to several people's attention before, but while the Guild's operations were unquestioned, no one cared about the difference. Now everything was cause for scrutiny. Under different circumstances, the open display of weakness might have truly irritated Andreas, but he had other, more important things on his mind. Thirty-two floors below his penthouse, Christof sat in the parking lot waiting to report on what he had discovered from the Coroner's office. Andreas had already sent home the security detail that usually followed him everywhere, so that there would be no prying eyes to challenge the secrecy of his meeting with Christof.

The strategy session with the Chairman was supposed to have been an hour-long affair over dinner. His request for a night cap had been unexpected.

"I would never say this to his face, of course—Crane's so full of himself, you know—but I thank God for him," the Chairman said, pausing at the front door. "He may just hold us together."

Reaching the end of his patience, Andreas put a firm hand on the Chairman's back as he all but pushed him through the door and bid him goodnight. As if the cool air from the hall sharpened his senses, the Chairman turned and squinted towards Andreas, as if seeing him for the first time this evening. "You're not trying to get rid of me, are you?" He asked sincerely with a slightly hurt expression.

"Of course not," Andreas responded before shutting the door in the Chairman's face. Ten minutes later, Christof was making his way into the living room.

Andreas didn't notice Christof's startled expression until he sat down.

"Are you alright?" Andreas asked impatiently. "I'm sorry for the wait. The Chairman went on and on and I couldn't get him to stop before–"

"I'm sorry, sir, but may I have a drink?" Christof clenched his hands together as he spoke and rocked back and forth on the couch.

"Water?" Andreas asked. From everything he knew, Christof didn't drink.

"Aah, if that's all you have. Otherwise, I think I would prefer something stronger – sir."

"The last of the scotch is in the bar, over there," Andreas pointed out as he leaned against the floor-to-ceiling windows that overlooked Geneva. Watching Christof carefully, he waited until the young man had poured himself a glass and took the first sip.

"What's happened? What did the coroner tell you?"

The alcohol burned as Christof took it in, but he finished the glass quickly before making his way back across the room to retrieve his bag.

"He's dead, just as you suspected," Christof began as he reached for the file. "They just don't know how or what killed him."

"What do you mean, 'what killed him'? They're only so many ways..." Andreas began as he came around to the couch. But when Christof opened the folder on the coffee table, he lost his train of thought. Miguel was barely recognizable. Half of his face looked like it had been ripped off, while his neck and shoulder were severed and ground into hanging chunks of flesh – by what, he couldn't imagine.

"What happened to him?" Andreas asked quietly as he turned away from the photo. "Was he attacked by an animal after his death?"

"The coroner said he was alive when this happened. A stranger in the street found him, barely an hour after he died. He was still warm when they collected him. There were no signs of any animals that could have done this in the area."

"Well, something happened to him. Was he dragged... maybe from a car?" Andreas asked.

"They found saliva." It was Christof's only response as he kept his focus on the corner of Andreas' coffee table.

"What are you saying? That *someone* did this to him? You can't possibly believe that!"

"There was a match," Christof whispered, all but ignoring Andreas's questions.

"A match for what?" Andreas asked. He was seriously beginning to question Christof's mental state.

"A DNA match with the saliva. As you know, the Guild screens all its employees to see if they test positive for the Seer marker, so we have all of our employees' DNA on file. When the coroner said he found saliva, I had him run a DNA search because I couldn't think of anyone else outside the Guild who would want Miguel dead—who would have the means to do... what was done to him. I didn't really expect for anything to come back, but it did."

Andreas felt perspiration break out over his body, but he kept his voice steady as he asked Christof his next question.

"And what did you find? Who is it?"

CHAPTER 17: VISUS

It was then that Christof met Andreas' gaze, with all the anger and distrust he felt.

"You already know, don't you? You sent that *thing* to kill Miguel, a man who did nothing but serve the Guild, and serve you! Is this the price of disloyalty? Is this what you'll do to me if I step out of line!"

Though the timing was unexpected, Andreas always knew this day would come. Since Andreas first hired Christof, he regarded him as a very smart and capable young man. But over the years, Andreas had been puzzled by his ability to maintain a surprising naivety about the nature of the Guild's work and his involvement in it. He'd never realized that Christof had been a true believer in the Guild's mission, right up until tonight.

Though Christof's assumption was incorrect, Andreas couldn't summon the gall to be offended. Under different circumstances, Christof might have been right—he just wasn't tonight.

"I didn't do what you're accusing me of, not this time. I don't know who or what attacked Miguel… that's why I sent you, to find out."

A knock on the front door startled them both.

"Were you followed?" Andreas whispered in a panic before he tiptoed to the door to check the peephole.

Christof shook his head, too frightened to speak as he rose from the couch and retreated further into the room.

Christof held his breath as Andreas leaned in and watched as whatever Andreas saw made his head jerk back just before the door was kicked in, knocking him to the ground. The man and woman standing at the door stepped inside quickly and locked the door behind them.

Holding the side of his face as he staggered to his feet, Andreas glared at Liam and Alessandra with a healthy mix of fear and indignation.

"How dare you!" Andreas began before the sight of Liam raising a gun to his head cut him off.

"Shut up and move over there with your boy," Liam instructed. "I have no problems killing you, so don't give me a reason."

Andreas looked away, moving quickly and silently next to Christof.

In contrast to Andreas, Christof stared openly and in awe of the two people standing before him.

"How did you find us?" Christof asked in a daze.

Alessandra raised an incredulous eyebrow at him, but said nothing.

Already impatient, Liam cut to the chase. "Where's Lilli?" He looked directly at Andreas.

Genuinely surprised, Andreas stared back at Liam, dumbfounded. "I don't know what you're talking about," he began. "I don't have her. I haven't done anything."

All expression drained from Liam's face as he pulled a cloth and duct tape from his back pocket. Without a word, he strode towards Andreas, striking him once with a powerful blow to the head. As soon as Andreas fell to the ground groaning in pain, Liam knelt down and stuffed the cloth into the man's mouth before yanking him upright and sealing his mouth with duct tape. Beside them, Christof leapt away, trying to create as much distance between him and Andreas as possible.

"Now, you're going to have to write it down," Liam said in an icy whisper as he dragged Andreas to the coffee table. "Because if you don't, I will beat you to death and no one who gives a damn is going to hear you scream." When Liam dropped a pen on the table, Andreas grabbed it at once.

"I don't know. I don't know," he wrote furiously on the manila folder that Christof left there. And then he saw the photos of Miguel's mauled body and realized—maybe he did know the person who might be responsible. Before Liam's hand dealt another blow, Andreas grabbed the closest photo to him and shook it furiously at Liam and Alessandra.

Straining to make out his words, Alessandra stilled Liam's hand as she snatched the photo from Andreas. Shock rippled through her body as she saw Miguel's injuries and realized that he looked like he had been mauled by a large animal. Handing the picture to Liam, she turned to Christof.

"What happened to the man in the photo? Do you know how he died?" Alessandra asked him.

When Liam turned to face him, Christof realized that this was his one and only opportunity to avoid ending up like Andreas. He didn't hesitate to answer.

"The coroner said it was most likely some kind of large animal, but the DNA sample says it's human."

Staring at the photo, Liam realized that he recognized Miguel from the news as well as from a confrontation in Chinatown that seemed a lifetime away.

"This is the man they say helped Ming escape. They claim he was a traitor, but he was one of the men hunting Lilli and I before we made it to the Commune," Liam explained to Alessandra before turning his attention back to Christof. "Have you seen this… animal? Do you know where we can find it?"

"No, I've never seen it. I didn't know anything about it before today, but I don't think it's just an animal. I know you probably won't believe me, but like I said, the DNA says that it's human—that it's a man."

"What man? Do you know who did this?" Alessandra asked.

"Yes. You know him, too. His name is Crane Le Dieu."

"Do you know where we can find him? We think he took my sister yesterday."

Confused, Christof looked between Liam and Alessandra doubtfully. "When?" He asked. "I saw Crane less than twelve hours ago in his office here. He said he was leaving early for the day, but that wasn't before five o'clock. Are you sure?"

Liam and Alessandra exchanged an alarmed look, but kept their thoughts to themselves as they turned back to Christof.

"We're not sure of anything right now," Liam confessed, "But we know whatever took my sister wasn't human, at least not all human."

"Can you help us find Crane? We need to know where he is," Alessandra explained anxiously.

"He has a place in the Morges. I've been there once on an errand. It's about an hour away from here. I don't remember the address off-hand, but I can show you the way," Christof offered meekly as he withstood Liam's scrutiny.

At the sound of a loud knock on the door, Alessandra nodded to Liam to open the door before turning back to Christof.

"Ok, let's go," she said, sidestepping Andreas as she went. "Joel is here."

Lilli could hear slow, steady breathing from somewhere nearby, but she didn't open her eyes as she tried to feign sleep for as long as possible. She needed time to gather as much strength as she could muster before she faced him. Though her mind was still too clouded to vision, she was grateful that she had enough awareness to understand that she was drugged. She knew her name, she knew Joel and the little girl who had warned her that this would happen. Adaline, the little girl who everyone thought was autistic turned out to have visioning capabilities beyond any of them.

Lilli still couldn't tell how long she had been out, but she knew from the brief glimpse she stole when the man who watched over her briefly left the room that it was dark outside. She also knew that the chains around her wrists and legs extended from the ceiling down to the floor where she slept on a bare but clean mattress, made dirty by the dust and grime from the clothes she still wore. The walls and floors of the large circular room were made of ancient, smooth stone with only one window that she could see without turning her head.

Despite her best efforts to remain still, she jumped at the sound of a heavy door crashing against the wall.

"Finally! She is awake," the man exclaimed. Lilli didn't move.

"Leave us, Saubos," she heard him say before the sound of steady breathing receded behind the locked door.

"Now, let's get you up, shall we?"

Knowing that her brain was still sluggish, Lilli didn't waste time wondering what he meant by that. Instead, she pictured Joel's face along with Liam's and Alessandra's, and everyone she cared about to remind herself why, no matter what happened next, she would not give up. She would hold on as long as she could because she knew they were coming for her and when they arrived, she needed to have some piece of herself left for them to find.

With her eyes shut, she was not prepared for the stinging, stretching pain in her shoulders and legs as the chains pulled her up and out of the bed by her limbs. With determination, she used her hands to grip the chains and keep the metal cuffs from digging into her wrists, but there was nothing she could do to mitigate the pain in her ankles. As she got closer to the ceiling, her arms began to shake from the strain. When the pulling finally stopped, her entire body was suspended in mid-air, face-forward, but bent back in an awkward crescent shape.

As Crane stepped in front of her, he wasn't sure if he was delighted or disappointed by the lack of response on her face in seeing him.

"You don't seem surprised at all to see me again. I find it hard to believe you saw this moment. I know my kind are difficult for you to see."

Lilli stared at him defiantly. Though she hadn't seen this moment, in her heart she knew it was him somehow. But she wouldn't give him anything to make her defeat sweeter than it already was.

"Oh… not talking today? You had so much to say the last time I saw you." Crane teased. "Well, that's alright. We'll have plenty of time to get to know each other. I plan to kill you very, very slowly."

Lilli couldn't help the shudder that went throughout her body. Crane's smile widened.

"Well, at least you're more responsive than you were a few hours ago. I was worried you wouldn't be any fun. I do like a good fight, and I can tell you're going to try your best to give me one."

As if to prove his point, Crane ran a hand down her arm. When Lilli tried to pull away, he grabbed her by the shoulder.

"I'm going to have so much fun with you," he cooed before Lilli spat in his face.

"So much fun," he sang, as he used two fingers to wipe the saliva off his cheek before sucking them dry.

Lilli closed her eyes to suppress her scream.

"Oh, do open your eyes," he said playfully as he walked away and removed his shirt. When Lilli didn't comply, Crane's anger spiked.

Stomping over to grab her face with the same rough hands he'd used earlier, he squeezed Lilli's cheekbones together painfully until she was forced to look at him, if only to stop him from breaking her bones .

"You *will* do as I say," he hissed. "Or I'll bite each of your fingers off... one by one. Do you understand me?"

Lilli didn't say anything in response, but she kept her eyes open and on him, realizing that if she was going to survive, she needed to start talking.

"Why are you doing this?" she asked quietly.

"Because I can. Because you have everything I want, everything I used to have and is now denied me. Because if I can't have sight, then I will steal yours. Because you're weak enough to let me do it. Because you are cursed with death and I am cursed with eternal life. Because I hate you."

Lilli hadn't expected a real answer and while she couldn't keep track of everything he said, she knew he was not joking about any of it.

"Who are you?" she asked, hoping to put some of his words in context.

"You can't see me now. There was only one person in all my eons here who ever saw me as I truly am and you killed him yesterday. His name was Tyrol. But don't worry, you'll find out who I am just before you die. You'll see. But, let's not get ahead of ourselves."

Crane walked over to a small table covered with a dingy towel, then carried it back to where Lilli could see it more clearly. Looking up to ensure she was watching, he pulled back the towel to reveal two rows of what looked to Lilli like rusted tools.

Reading her expression, Crane frowned. "Well, I guess they don't look like much to you, but they are exquisite at what they do. These are all my favorite toys. I hand-picked them just for you."

Lilli's eyes widened in fear as she looked over the table and began to recognize the instruments for what they were.

"There it is—the fear. Now you're beginning to understand," he winked before picking up a small bowl. "We don't have plumbing on this level. I'll just be a moment." Crane said, as he left the room.

Watching him disappear through the doorway, Lilli finally let the full understanding of what was about to take place explode in her mind. Her chest felt unable to take in air as she looked at the sharp, jagged edges of the things he planned to use on her. In vain, she tried to extend her mind out, to call for help or see a vision of what was to come, but between the panic and the drugs, she couldn't focus her thoughts, much less her breathing to achieve any semblance of a meditative state.

You need to transcend your body, she heard herself say. *But how?*

Transcend, she heard in the little girl's voice.

Transcend.

She knew exactly what that meant, but could she do it? She and Joel had done it before, but only after hours of visioning together. Transcendence meant death, crossing the line between the limits of her mortality and the infinite space where only spiritual beings reside. Could she do it alone? Would her physical death be gradual, or all at once? Would Liam forgive her? Would Joel?

Although she wasn't sure if Liam would forgive her, she was certain that if Liam found her in the state Crane planned, it would destroy the part of him that he was just beginning to find, the part of him that wanted life more than death. The answer to the second question, she knew was yes. Joel would follow her as soon as he was able. And with that realization, she decided to try. Death was imminent either way. If she could, she would have a choice in it. Lilli noticed that even in the few seconds that she had been thinking about it, her breathing had become calm and deep, even with the burning in her arms and legs.

Up until that moment, Lilli had always believed that it was her mind that had controlled her ability to vision. But for the first time, she wondered if she had been wrong. Her body had known Crane was dangerous even before her mind could comprehend the thought. She had uttered Joel's name when she couldn't remember it. It occurred to her then that maybe the source of her power might reside in a place deeper than her perception.

Closing her eyes, she turned her body over to itself, relaxing into and beyond the ache in her limbs. Keeping her mind as quiet as possible, she hoped to find a place beyond where the drugs and her consciousness could reach, a place where truth could be accessed and held beyond the constraints of knowledge.

Lilli didn't hear Crane when he returned to the room and dropped the bowl, shattering ancient ceramic and boiling water all over the stone floor. Furiously, he stormed towards Lilli, who was beginning to show the faintest shimmer of golden light despite the absence of the sun in the early dawn.

In disbelief that her fear of him could have dissipated enough for her to fall asleep, Crane stopped in front of Lilli and slapped her hard across the face. When she did not respond, he raised his hand to strike her again before she slowly opened her eyes. Her skin appeared incandescent.

"Stop," she said in a voice that was stronger and more mature than the girl he'd left a few moments ago. He raised his hand again, ready to slap her once more, but he found his hand could not move.

"What have you done?!" He yelled angrily as he clasped his frozen hand and tried to pull it down, but the answer she gave was nothing he expected.

"I see who you are," Lilli said, as she let her eyes roam the façade that Crane wore to hide himself. "I see you."

Crane backed away.

"Show yourself. Be who you are," she ordered as the bolts unwound themselves from the metal cuffs at her hands and feet. When the shackles released, her body floated to the ground in a gentle graceful movement.

Though Lilli did not repeat her words, they echoed in Crane's mind. In a mix of horror and relief, he found himself needing to comply, wanting to meet her request.

Having already taken off his shoes, Crane stepped back again and unbuckled the belt of his trousers, so that when his pants fell to the ground he stood naked before her.

He leaned forward slightly as the transformation took place, crying out in pain as his bones broke and extended in a disjointed and unnatural pattern of stops and starts. As his bones grew, his skin stretched, turning from a deep red to bruised purple to finally a hard and weathered black-brown. His new skin was covered with the evidence of a ruined life with scars, boils and open wounds that festered and stunk. With Crane's body arched over, Lilli could see the skin on his back tear as his spinal column split in half. His cries became an animal-like screech as tentacles grew out of his spine to form two massive wings that spanned the entire width of the room. When they were fully formed, Crane stood to his full height of 20 feet. Though Lilli was dwarfed in comparison to his height, she felt no fear standing before him.

"Now," he said growling down at her. "What would you have me do?"

"Die." She said simply.

The bitterness in his laugh vibrated and bounced throughout the room. "Do you see the pain it causes me to reveal myself to you? I have dealt with it for millennia. If I could die, don't you think I would have by now? This is my punishment—my hell—to watch such a feeble race as you bear the gifts that I used to have, to see the things I used to see. Now my vision is dark. I see nothing but the stupidity of your pitiful existence. Cut off from your own purpose by petty, meaningless pursuits. You don't want—you don't deserve—the power you have, the power God gives you. That's why you sell your soul to me for nothing."

"You stole life from those Seers." Lilli answered calmly. "You took their lives, ruined them for your own gain."

"Ruined them," Crane growled. "*I* am ruined. My entire existence is suffering. You don't know anything about what it means to be ruined! You aren't even capable of experiencing the pain I suffer daily. It is not possible for your kind, though I have tried."

"You chose the existence you have now; no one did this to you."

"I wanted more. I *wanted* everything," Crane said, without remorse.

As she was about to respond, she heard Liam banging on the door, shouting her name before Joel told him to stand back. A second later the door fell from its hinges and crashed to the floor.

The relief on their faces from seeing Lilli was quickly replaced with horror as they saw Crane towering above her with his appearance completely unmasked.

Crane faced them with a smirk on his twisted mouth, but before he could move, Lilli spoke.

"You will not harm them."

Again, her words resonated and controlled his resolve with a strange power he had never experienced before. Bewildered, he stared at Lilli for a long moment.

"Why do your words control me?"

"I speak to you with a voice that you have long forgotten. I speak to you in truth."

"You have no authority over me! My kind has ruled yours for thousands of years!" Crane roared as he raised his hand to strike her. When she made no attempt to move, Liam and Joel lunged forward, but the blast of the heat sent them flying back into the wall as Lilli uttered one simple word.

"Burn."

Immediately Crane was engulfed in flames that singed but did not disintegrate his skin. "Killing me will be the end of all of you! I command legions!" He roared in agony before Lilli spoke again.

"I released you. You will not exist to hurt anyone or anything again."

When it was clear that Lilli didn't need their help, Liam and Alessandra watched from behind the doorway as the hardened, leather layer of Crane's skin began to fall away, leaving tender flesh that quickly reddened and blistered in the flames. With each second that passed, he became more human, as if the flames themselves were peeling away his immortality.

Joel stood just inside the room, watching the evidence of the choice he knew Lilli had made. He had sensed her mind the minute she reconnected as they raced down the Lake Geneva countryside to the remote castle that Christof said was Crane's. At the time, he knew her consciousness was different, clearer, faster, but he didn't know why until he stepped inside the door to see the familiar glow of her skin. Though it shocked him, he felt grateful that she'd been able to find a pathway out of the torture Crane had planned for her. As soon as this was over, he knew he would follow her on that path.

By the time the flames died down, Crane's twenty-foot frame had been reduced to the charred figure of a slender eight-foot man. Lilli stared at his body for a long moment with an uneasy feeling in her heart before turning to leave. The first face she saw was Joel's smiling back at her as he extended his arm to take her hand. Though her skin felt slightly more pliable, he held it tightly. Liam was speechless as he reached Lilli and crushed her to his body, finally letting the tears that he had been holding for almost a full day break free. Pulling back slightly to look at her, Liam was surprised to see how well she looked after having gone through so much.

"You look pretty good for someone who was just kidnapped by a twenty-foot demon," he joked with tears still rolling down his face. Lilli chuckled lightly but didn't respond as she folded back into her brothers' arms. She knew she would have to tell Liam soon, but not today.

With Alessandra leading the way down the stairs from the tower to the castle's lower levels, they stopped briefly at a room that lead to a large terrace where they could see the sun rising over the shimmering waters of Lake Geneva. Taking in the stark beauty of the scene, Lilli crossed the room and opened the French doors that led outside. Following her onto the terrace, they stood in silence for a moment, letting the beauty around them wash away the nightmare they had endured as they welcomed the coming of a new day.

But they didn't linger long. Christof was waiting in their car along the road and they were all anxious to return home. They were about to turn from the terrace when they heard the sound that stopped them in their tracks. From somewhere below, a loud, screeching sound cut through the cool morning air, followed by an answering cry of the same tone. Before they could make out exactly where the sound was coming from, they saw it – two pairs of black-brown battered wings extending above the town and into the sky, screaming as they raced into the sun.

Cerece Rennie Murphy lives and writes just outside of her hometown of Washington, DC. In addition to completing the *Order of the Seers* trilogy, Ms. Murphy is also developing a children's book series titled *Enchanted: 5 Tales of Magic in the Everyday* and a book on understanding marriage/relationship advice for single women entitled *More than the Ring*. To learn more about the author and her upcoming projects, visit her website at www.crmurphybooks.com.

CPSIA information can be obtained at www.ICGtesting.com
Printed in the USA
BVOW07s1623230914

367913BV00001B/5/P